PRAISE FOR LAURA WRIGHT
AND THE MARK OF THE VAMPIRE SERIES

Eternal Beast

"Absorbing and edgy, darkly seductive—everything vampire romance should be! *Eternal Beast* is an enthralling read. . . . Laura Wright turns up the heat and takes you on a wild ride. I can't wait to see what's next!"
—Lara Adrian, *New York Times* bestselling author of *Darker After Midnight*

"Grabs you by the heartstrings from the first page and pulls you along until the cliff-hanger of an ending. . . . [The] complexity of emotion is what makes Laura Wright's books so engrossing. . . . One of the best new series and authors around, I highly recommend *Eternal Beast* to all lovers of paranormal romance."
—Sizzling Hot Book Reviews

"This has been a series I love to read and seem to fall more and more in love with." —Paranormal Reads

"An incredible installment to the series. . . . If you haven't experienced this series yet, you are totally missing out." —Literal Addiction

"Laura Wright has done it again and totally blew me away. . . . Laura Wright has created an original and extraordinary world, and I am her fan girl for life."
—Book Monster Reviews

Eternal Captive

"Riveting. . . . There are plenty more stories to be told in this fascinating universe." —*Romantic Times*

continued . . .

"An action-packed read . . . enough twists that leave one anxious for the next in the series."
—Night Owl Reviews

"Very sexy. . . . The emotional strength of the story elevated this above other paranormals I've read of late."
—Dear Author

Eternal Kiss

"The perfect book for anyone who likes sexy, dangerous vampires with dark secrets."   —Fresh Fiction

"Complex and riveting."   —*Romantic Times*

"A super urban romantic fantasy due to the powerful Wright mythos."
—The Merry Genre Go Round Reviews

"A great ride where a sweep-off-your-feet romance ignites within a high-risk plot. Laura Wright has found her niche in the paranormal romance genre with her larger-than-life Roman brothers!"
—Leontine's Book Realm

Eternal Hunger

"Just when it seems every possible vampire twist has been turned, Wright launches a powerful series with a rich mythology, page-turning tension, and blistering sensuality."   —*Publishers Weekly* (starred review)

"Dark, delicious, and sinfully good, *Eternal Hunger* is a stunning start to what promises to be an addictive new series. I can't wait for more from Laura Wright."
—Nalini Singh, *New York Times* bestselling author of *Tangle of Need*

Also by Laura Wright

Mark of the Vampire Series
Eternal Hunger
Eternal Kiss
Eternal Blood
(A Penguin Special)
Eternal Captive
Eternal Beast
Eternal Beauty
(A Penguin Special)
Eternal Demon

ETERNAL SIN

MARK OF THE VAMPIRE

LAURA WRIGHT

A SIGNET ECLIPSE BOOK

SIGNET ECLIPSE
Published by the Penguin Group
Penguin Group (USA) LLC, 375 Hudson Street,
New York, New York 10014

USA | Canada | UK | Ireland | Australia | New Zealand | India | South Africa | China
penguin.com
A Penguin Random House Company

First published by Signet Eclipse, an imprint of New American Library,
a division of Penguin Group (USA) LLC

First Printing, November 2013

Copyright © Laura Wright, 2013

SIGNET ECLIPSE and logo are trademarks of Penguin Group (USA) LLC.

ISBN 978-0-451-24016-3

Printed in the United States of America
10 9 8 7 6 5 4 3 2 1

To my family, who I love so much.

GLOSSARY

Balas—Vampire child.

Beast—Another, and far less derogatory, name for *mutore*.

Bloodletter—A Pureblood vampire with the ability to remove memory, emotion, and sickness from the mind of a Pureblood. According to their laws and beliefs, they will not touch an Impure for fear of tainting their gift.

The Breeding Male—A *paven* of purest blood whose genetic code and structure has been altered by the Eternal Order. He has the ability to impregnate at will and to decide the sex of the *balas*. He is brought in by Pureblood families to repopulate one sex or the other in times of dire necessity. He is uncontrollable, near to an animal, and must be caged.

Credenti—A vampire community, ruled and protected by the Eternal Order. Both Purebloods and Impures live here. There are many such communities all over the world, masked by the Order so that humans barely notice their existence.

Duro—Tender word for "brother."

Eternal Order—The ten Pureblood vampires who have passed on to the middle world, yet make the laws, punish the lawbreakers, and govern every vampire *credenti* on Earth.

Eyes—The New York City street rats who run the sales of drugs, blood, and bodies to both human and vampire.

Factions—Areas within the Rain Forest community that shelter different types of shifters. The Rain Forest Factions are Avians, Mountain Beasts, Land Dwellers, and Water Lords.

Gemino—Twin.

Gravo—Poisoned vampire blood.

Imiti—An imitation vampire, one who can take on the characteristics of a vampire if he or she drinks blood regularly.

Impurebloods—Any combination of human and vampire. They have no powers, no heartbeat, and can live in the sun. They have fangs only when blood is consumed. Males are blood castrated, their sex drive removed through the blood by the Order. Females are blood sterilized and branded with an *I* on the inside of their thighs.

Impure Resistance—The rise of the Impures who wish for equality within the Eternal Breed.

Meta—The transition every Pureblood female makes into adulthood. Happens at fifty years of age. Though the female can still remain in sunlight, she needs and craves the blood and body of her true mate.

Mondrar—Vampire prison.

Morpho—The transition every Pureblood *paven* makes into adulthood. Happens at three hundred years of age. This state of being is as powerful as a *paven* can get. He is sunlight intolerant, and the need to find his true mate becomes impossible to deny.

Mutore—A Pureblood vampire shape-shifter. A Beast. A child of the Breeding Male gone wrong. Is considered less than trash, and a bad omen for the breed. Is usually killed right after birth when he or she shifts for the first time.

Paleo—The Order's secret location where Impures are blood castrated.

Paven—A vampire male of pure blood.

Pureblood—Pure vampire. Powerful, no heartbeat. Will go through Morpho and Meta and find a Pureblood true mate.

Puritita—One who is chaste.

Rain Forest—Secret, magically protected home of the shifter community.

Sacro—Dirty.

Shifters—Humans with animal DNA, who can take the form of their animal counterpart at will.

Similis—The Impure guards of Mondrar.

Swell—Vampire pregnancy.

Tegga—Nursemaid/nanny/governess.

True Mate—The one each Pureblood *veana* and *paven* is destined for. True mates share an identical or complementary mark somewhere on their skin.

Veana—A vampire female of pure blood.

Veracou—The mating ceremony between two Pureblood vampires.

Virgini—Virgin.

Witte—Animal.

1

The hawk shifter flew overhead, circling Petra in the cloudless sky as she stumbled back and forth in front of the mouth of the cave—the same Rain Forest cave she'd pulled a burning, fiercely stubborn Synjon Wise into after he'd tried to follow his lover into the sun seven months ago.

Now it was Petra's turn.

Not to burn, but to feel the constant aftershocks of a misery she couldn't shake.

Tears ran down her cheeks, another great sob exiting her tight throat. She was in so much pain. Unimaginable and inescapable. Her body, her swollen belly, her mind, her heart . . .

No. She had no heart. It was silent. An empty, useless organ.

It was a realization that had once filled her with curiosity. She was a vampire. A *veana*. Not a shifter, like her adopted family. Gone were the perpetual feelings of being an outcast among a society who wanted nothing more than to embrace her. Now she had living proof of her own existence. Now her questions could truly be answered.

Whom did she belong to? Where were others like her? What could she expect from her life? How long would that life be?

He had gifted her with those answers. That male. The dark-haired, dark-eyed *paven* who'd come to the Rain Forest to bury his beloved, and himself if Petra hadn't been there to stop him. Inside the shelter of her tree house so many months ago, Synjon Wise had told her everything, offered her a future. He'd just had to kill someone first. She could hear his voice in her head even now. That deep, rich accent.

"Vengeance before romance, love."

But the one he'd had to kill, the one who had murdered his Juliet, well . . . he was Petra's only connection with the outside world. Her only connection to her blood. He was her father.

Cruen.

Another pained cry wrenched from Petra's lungs, from deep inside, from the place where the ache seemed to originate, and she stopped and gripped the cool, moist curve of the cave's entrance.

She heard her mother's voice somewhere behind her. "What can we do?" Not the mother who had given her life, but the one who had raised her. As part of her pride, a cub to be cherished.

The beautiful lion shifter Wen had been the best mother any creature, shifter or vampire, could hope for. Now she nearly wailed in pain at Petra's distress.

"I don't know," said the other female, the one who had brought Petra to the Rain Forest a week ago. This was her biological mother, Celestine. A Pureblood vampire who was as desperate to make up for lost time and bond with her daughter as Petra was to push her away.

She didn't need another parent. Especially not one who considered her part in creating Petra a grave mistake.

"You're a vampire, like her," Wen continued, her unsteady voice carrying on the breeze. "Surely you've seen this kind of—"

"Never." Celestine's tone was emphatic, impassioned. Fearful. "Her sister, my daughter Sara, is also in *swell*, but she is an Impure. She never went through Meta. Getting pregnant before you're of age, before you experience your transition, is very rare."

"Do you think that's why she's reacting this way?"

"Emotional surges are expected in pre-Meta *swell* . . ."

"But not like this."

Celestine paused before saying, "No, not like this. And not this far along. The surges are purported to be very early on in the pregnancy."

"What are we to do?" Wen said, her own voice breaking with emotion. "She's been here a week, and every day—every hour—it grows worse."

Their impassioned chatter grated on Petra's exposed nerves, searing her mind with agony. Her nails scraped against the rock.

"There must be something we can give her to ease this suffering," Wen continued. "This strange hunger. The pain."

"Blood," said Celestine.

"She won't drink it," Wen returned. "I've tried. You've tried. She—"

"Stop it!" Petra snarled over her shoulder, tears raining down her cheeks, relentless. "Stop talking about me as if I'm not here!"

Both females froze in the glare of the sunlight, their gazes cutting to her immediately. Petra despised the fear and empathy she saw in their eyes. Or maybe their expressions made her feel frustrated . . . or was it desperately sad? She didn't know.

Whimpering, she gripped the underside of her large belly. She couldn't decipher her feelings. There were too many of them, and too much of them. What was wrong with her? And was it affecting her baby?

Celestine moved toward her. "You must drink."

"No," Petra growled. *Blood*. Just the thought of it on her tongue, running down her throat, made her gag, made her vicious. She hissed at the both of them and pressed herself back against the mouth of the cave. She wanted to drink, wanted to feed her growing *balas*, but she couldn't keep anything down. Gods, wasn't vomiting worse for the child?

Tears in her own eyes now, Wen started rolling up her sleeve. "You can have mine, baby. Take all the blood you need. Please, Pets." She bit her lip, the loving childhood nickname swallowed up by a sob of despair. "Seeing you like this . . ."

Overhead, the hawk cried, swooping in low, before returning to the sky. Petra glanced up and growled at the bird. She'd told Dani she didn't want to see her, didn't want a ride over the treetops of the Rain Forest, didn't want the female's looks of sympathy or fear. But her best friend refused to leave, to retreat to her nest.

"Our blood won't stop this, Wen," Celestine said gently. "I'm afraid she needs *his*."

"The father of the child . . ."

"Yes."

Father! Petra silently screamed. *Synjon Wise was no father.* That bastard wanted to kill her, and the baby. She'd seen it on his face in the dim light of the *mutore* Erion's dungeon a week ago, heard it in his voice when he'd repeated her admission about the child she carried being his.

She turned and ran into the cave. Sobs burst in her chest, scraping her throat. She wanted to get away from her mother and Celestine. From everyone. From light, heat, sound. She wanted to search for darkness. Maybe it would claim her.

No. Fuck no. She had to survive for the *balas*. She had to fight her pain and misery, grant this child the home and family it deserved.

"Oh, gods!" she heard Wen cry. "It's not possible to bring Synjon Wise here, is it? To ask him to care for her and the child? After what was done to him, does he even remember their time together?"

"His memories weren't taken, just his emotions," Celestine said, her voice echoing inside the walls of the cave. "He knows about her and the *balas*. He knows that she carries the grandchild of his enemy. The question is, will he care?"

Petra met the back of the cave. It was dark and wet and cold and rough, but it welcomed her. Breathing heavily, panic and sickness and fear and anger rippling through her, she curled up against it and tried to force every thought, every feeling, every memory out of her mind.

But it was impossible.

Along with the staggering emotional and physical pain in her body, her brain conjured her past, flipping by, scene after scene. She saw every bit of her childhood in the Rain Forest. She saw the hunts, the shifters, her friends. She saw her work, helping shifters with their early transitions. She saw her brothers.

She saw Synjon.

Once again, she experienced the desperation and pain of dragging him inside the cave she huddled in now. She felt his interest in her, both mentally and sexually. She felt his kiss, his touch.

She felt the moment he'd placed a child in her womb.

Tears flooded her cheeks. He was responsible for this, what she was going through. And yet he was completely at peace, his brain turned off to any and all emotional connection. She didn't know if she was grateful or pissed off at the Romans for striking the bargain between Cruen and Synjon. She'd hoped for so much more than just being free, her *balas* momentarily out of harm's way as she'd watched Synjon's emotions being bled from his body on the dungeon floor.

She'd hoped for something of the male who'd held her, kissed her, cared for her once upon a time in the tree house that she had yet to return to.

Petra swiped at her eyes and whimpered. As she leaned into the cool, hard rock, growing more and more lost but still blindly determined to do anything and everything to protect her child; Synjon Wise was out there in the world somewhere, devoid of care, of concern. The *balas* and its mother the furthest thing from his mind.

*   *   *

Within his sprawling penthouse of glass and brick, Synjon Wise sat comfortably at his Bösendorfer, his fingers moving quickly across the keys as he played something light and pointless.

The party guests circulated through the six thousand square feet of interior space, leaving the wraparound terraces and 360-degree views of Manhattan to the shard of moon and the cold December night. It was his third party in seven days. The first had been the very night he'd bought the place. The small crowd had been courtesy of his Realtor. Broadway actors, artists, financiers, Pureblood and Impure vampires. He'd never thought much about owning a flat, or dipping into the massive wealth he'd accumulated over the years. He'd been far too busy working, spying, following the trail of vengeance . . .

This was so much better.

This was a blissful nothingness.

And the vengeance? It would be coming to *him* now.

He glanced up from the sheet music he didn't need to read. The dull hum of conversation, the deep thirst of those who continued to empty glass upon glass of Dom Pérignon White Gold, and the females whom he'd instructed not to come near him until he ceased playing. It was a far cry from the manic scene in the *mutore*'s dungeon a week ago. Here, no pleas for mercy pinged off the walls, no shocking secrets were revealed, and no blood was being extracted from his person.

In this house, he did all the drinking.

A flash on the terrace snagged his attention even as he continued playing. Three massive fanged blokes appeared on the flagstones, their eyes narrowed, their expressions grave in the bleak moonlight as they quickly assessed their surroundings, then headed for the glass doors. Synjon knew them, of course. One far better than the other two, and although the memory, the history, he shared with them held a good amount of tension, he knew absolutely that they were not his enemies.

Dressed in black and taller, wider, and far more fearsome than any of his guests, the three males entered the great room, bringing with them the winter chill and a swimming pool's worth of testosterone. Every set of human eyes widened, every pair of human feet drew back. His fingers still sliding over the keys, Synjon tracked the males, waited for them to spot him, scent him. It took no more than a moment before they did, before a pathway was created across the polished stone floor.

Syn continued to play as the Roman brothers approached, stalking him like prey. They appeared rather tense. Syn wondered what that felt like.

The one he knew best, a nearly albino vampire male with a perpetual sneer, spoke first. "Nice party. But I think our invitation got lost in the mail, Brit Boy."

There was a time when Syn had risen to the male's caustic play. Reveled in it, in fact. He had no interest now. "You weren't invited, Lucian. In fact, none of you were."

The male turned to his skull-shaved brother, Alexander, and snorted. "Good to know the guy still has some asshole left in him."

Alexander didn't respond. His focus was entirely on Synjon, his tone serious as he spoke. "We have a problem."

"We?" Synjon asked, his fingers moving into Bach's Concerto in F Minor. He used to despise the piece, had been forced to practice it over and over as a *balas*, but now he felt only the smoothness of the keys against his skin.

Alexander's voice dropped, and his eyes narrowed. "The *veana* who carries your child—"

"Petra," Syn supplied, picturing the dark-haired *veana* and feeling . . . nothing.

"Yes," Alexander ground out. "She hasn't gone through her Meta. We didn't know that before. When we brought her back home . . . We didn't know how a *veana* in *swell* who hadn't gone through her transition would react . . . She's losing her mind, Syn."

Synjon looked up, assessed the male. He couldn't imagine why Alexander was telling him this. "Now that you're here, would you like to stay? Join my guests?"

A growl rumbled in Alexander's chest. "No."

"Perhaps you'd like something to drink?"

"Christ," Lucian muttered, leaning against the piano.

"Some*one* to drink, then?" Synjon caught the eye of one of the humans who enjoyed feeding his vampire guests. She grinned hopefully at him.

"We're not here for a party," Nicholas said tersely, moving around to the other side of the piano. "Petra is ill, Syn. She can't control her emotions. She's in pain. She's going out of her mind. It happened soon after she returned to the Rain Forest. You have to—"

"Attend to my guests," Synjon said evenly. There was so much to do—he had to select his blood donor for the evening as well as his sexual conquests. He had discriminating tastes in both. But first, a little Prelude in C-Sharp Minor. Rachmaninoff used to make him snarl.

Times changed, it seemed.

Arching an eyebrow at the three males, he said, "If you'll excuse me."

"'Excuse me'?" Lucian repeated, giving Syn a disgusted look. "Whatever happened to 'Get the fuck out of my way, you bleeding tossers'?"

Useless. Words with emotions attached.

"I don't react to people and problems with threats and anger anymore, Lucian," he said, his voice even. "I take care of them quietly, quickly."

"That's too bad," Lucian muttered. "Merry fucking Christmas."

"We should go, find another way to help her," Nicholas said tightly. "This *paven* doesn't give a shit about anything. And it's our fault. We made him that way."

"Cruen made him that way," Alex amended.

"We forced him, held him down and allowed that ancient bastard to drink the emotions from his blood."

"We had to." Alex's gaze slid away from Synjon. "He was unreasonable and dangerous. We couldn't risk having Petra or the child harmed."

Lucian growled, pushed away from the piano. "Well, now he feels nothing for them, and Cruen got to run free."

Not free, Synjon mused, closing in on the seven-measure coda. "Well, *gentlepaven*, it was a successful plan all around. I've never felt better."

"You feel nothing," Lucian returned.

"Oh, I feel quite perfect where it matters—all things physical. I'm not burdened with tedious, irrational emotions. It's all very civilized, really." Rachmaninoff ceased to exist, and Synjon glanced up at Alexander. "I appreciate what was done to me."

"What about all that is being done to Petra? All she can't control?" Alexander returned with barely disguised menace. "She needs your blood. Now."

"That's unfortunate for her." Syn jerked his chin in the direction of the great room. "As you can see, I am otherwise engaged."

"He's lost," Luca muttered. "Fucking lost."

Synjon stared at the three faces, all twisted into ravaged masks of worry. It suited them—that intensity, that feral, predatory glare. But it held no interest for him. He was rather relaxed—though he could use a pint or two, perhaps a quick, hard fuck as he continued to wait for the inevitable. The one guest he wished to see above all others. The one who would come begging.

Alexander spoke through gritted teeth, "Syn, your child and Petra . . . they could both die without your help. Your blood."

Done with this repetitive, pointless conversation, Synjon replied smoothly, "Then I suppose they will die," before he returned to the cool white keys and another song from his past: Nirvana's "Drain You."

2

Cruen despised being laid out on his back.

Even if he'd been the one to request it.

Near his ear, the one that was still intact, the one Synjon Wise hadn't gotten around to slicing off with his razor-sharp blade, the female bloodletter's breath came quick and sharp as she sucked. She'd been at it for over an hour. Retrieval and extraction being the primary goal. But it wasn't going well. Bruises painted Cruen's wrists and thighs. The vein in his neck was her final resting place.

He was starting to grow concerned.

Freedom was nothing to a vampire without power. And he was becoming weaker with every moment that passed.

The bloodletter pulled her fangs from his vein, her head from the curve of his neck, and turned toward her metal spit bowl. She deposited a mouthful of blood with a cough and a sputter, then returned to him. Framed by a cap of short black hair, her ashen face and deep-set blue eyes held an almost wry concern.

"You embedded them too deep," she said, blood staining her teeth.

Cruen eyeballed the extractor, his skin itching, attempting to heal. "I didn't embed anything. I removed and released only."

"I don't know what you released, but it wasn't emotion." She snatched a cloth from the table and wiped the blood from her mouth. "That cluster of bubbling intensity inside your mind remains. And it's too far for me to reach."

With excruciating effort, Cruen forced his weakening body to sit up on the stained pallet. Rising anger fueled his thoughts. "I've taken and released emotion hundreds of times. It is a simple procedure."

The bloodletter stood, grabbed the bowl, and walked over to a nearby sink. "Not always."

"What does that mean?" Cruen demanded to her back, his voice sounding fearfully thin.

"Most of the time, the extraction of emotions is transient," she called over her shoulder. "In and out. There and gone. But sometimes it can stick, become a permanent fixture within the mind."

Apprehension washed over Cruen as he watched the female dump his blood into the sink. Permanent? That couldn't be. All he had performed was a basic emotional extraction in Erion's dank dungeon. Taking Synjon Wise's passion to kill in exchange for walking free.

"The one you drained," said the bloodletter, "was he familiar with this type of grab?"

"I don't know," Cruen said tightly. "He used to be a very competent spy for the Order. And a military operative for the government."

The female released a weighty breath, then turned and came to stand before him. Her gaze remained serious. "I don't think this was an accident. Not with the depth of those implanted emotions."

"What?" His nostrils flaring, Cruen growled, a sound that used to have anyone who heard it shaking. Now it felt as feeble and nonthreatening as that of a *balas*. "Are you saying the *paven* whose blood I extracted did this to me on purpose?"

"That is my belief, yes."

Cruen stared at the female, his lips parted. This was madness. Why would Synjon Wise permanently implant his emotions inside Cruen? Yes, the *paven* wanted revenge, had ever since he'd found out that Cruen had not only taken and caged his beloved *veana*, Juliet, but had taken her life as well. But why wouldn't he have just continued with his torture? The bloodletter's assessment had to be wrong.

"Does this *paven* have a beef with you?" the bloodletter asked, as if reading his thoughts.

A beef? Cruen sniffed with lackluster humor. "The *paven* whose blood and emotion I ingested wanted me laid out in the sun—after he made sure I suffered first, of course."

The female's eyes narrowed, her expression tight and resolved now. "You were hoping that by taking his emotion you would be taking his desire to kill you?"

"Let's just say it was a bargain struck. A bargain that was intended to benefit all." *Protect us all.* Cruen, Petra, and the *balas* as well. Even that bastard Synjon Wise. If he had truly hurt Petra or the child, he would no doubt have suffered gravely for it.

The bloodletter was staring at him, her lips rolled under her teeth.

"What?" Cruen demanded, his skin now healed, his mind jumping. His body being stripped of energy with every breath. He needed to find strong, pure blood to bring back his power and his strength.

"The *paven* has done this to make you suffer," she said in a quiet voice. "But also to make you his prey."

"*Prey?*" Cruen ground out. How absurd. "He feels nothing for me now. No anger, no hunger for revenge. He won't come after me."

"He won't have to. Because you'll be going to him."

Cruen lifted his upper lip, flashed his fangs. "Never."

The female shrugged. "You might even fall to your knees before him and beg."

The insolence! Cruen's fangs dropped and he hissed. He had limited strength, but there was nothing he wanted more at that moment than to rip the vocal cords from this female's throat. Clearly, she was taunting him now. Perhaps trying to extract more money.

Pulling on every fiber of strength he possessed, Cruen leaped from the table, and with a fearsome snarl, headed for the door, and for his guards on the other side. The guards that would have to flash him home, as he was quite without the power to manage it himself.

He pulled the door wide and was almost through it when he heard the bloodletter's words of doom on the air behind him.

"One final word, my lord. If you ever want to find peace or strength, if you ever want to function normally again, you'll have to find this male and give back what you took."

*   *   *

"Despite what's occurring with your mental and emotional state, everything within you is working well and is healthy."

"For now," Petra said, pulling her eyes from Brodan and shifting on the bed in her room at her mother's house. Unable to keep herself still for any length of time, and hating to be around groups of people, she'd refused to go to the clinic when her mother had insisted that she see Brodan for a checkup.

The doctor, who was also a bear shifter and one of Petra's closest friends, placed his warm hands on her stomach and gently prodded around the *balas*. "I wish you'd come stay with me, Pets. I'd feel better if I could watch you full-time."

"That's a good idea," Wen agreed, hovering somewhere near Petra's head, along with Celestine. "It's not far, my dear, and with you a few months from your time . . ."

"I don't want to be watched." Petra closed her eyes and attempted to breathe through the waves of misery and depression threatening to consume her. "I'm sorry, Brodan. For acting like a complete asshole most of the time when you're just trying to help me. I appreciate the offer. I just . . ."

"Pets, look at me," he said, his voice clear and strong through her haze. "Please."

It took everything she had to turn back and face him. He was such a great male, handsome and strong and caring. And if her luck didn't completely run out, the male she would turn to when the *balas* was born. But, right now, if she continued to engage with him, be touched by him, scent him, she was going to bite him. Hard. And not out of hunger. Out of irrational anger. Her fangs were already dropping and saliva was pooling in her mouth.

"Tell me what you need, Pets." His eyes implored her. "You know I'll do whatever you ask."

"Can you find a way to stop this?" she said, her tone pathetic even to her own ears. "Turn off this insanity inside me before I explode or lose my mind? Or gods help me, do something terrible. Hurt you or my family. I don't know how long I can keep this anger and sadness and manic energy penned."

He reached out and brushed a few strands of hair back from her face. The gesture repelled her. Like every touch she'd experienced in the past week: her mother, her brothers, her best friend. It all made her recoil.

Brodan acted as if he hadn't noticed. He was also incredibly kind. And she was a great fool for not giving herself to him ages ago when he'd made it clear he wanted to be more than friends.

"We've known each other for how long, Pets?" he said, his voice low and masculine but gentle.

Petra forced a bleak smile. "Forever."

"And you've always trusted me."

"Of course. What are you asking?"

"I want to try something." He left her side and dug into his medical bag, which was propped up against some books on her dresser. When he returned he was holding up a bag of blood.

Petra cringed, her insides recoiling, panic rushing through her. "I've tried drinking blood. I can't make myself swallow it. And what I do manage to force down comes right back up."

"I know." He gestured for Wen and Celestine to hold the bag and tubing. "I want to try putting it directly into your vein."

"Oh," Celestine exclaimed. "That could work."

"Yes, indeed," Wen agreed.

Hope flared inside Petra, and she quickly pulled up the sleeve of her shirt. There was nothing she wanted more than to shut off these overwhelming feelings racing through her, controlling her. "Whose is it?" she asked him.

"A combination of donors." He swabbed the inside of her wrist with a square of wet cotton. "I want to see if you have a reaction to this first. If you do, we'll give you the blood of each donor separately until we find a match."

"And if there's no match?" She hated to ask the question, but couldn't stop herself.

Brodan gave her an encouraging smile. "Let's not go there yet, okay?"

She nodded, her breath hitching in her lungs. *Please let this work. Please.*

With skilled fingers, Brodan quickly inserted the needle into the soft skin of her wrist, then followed up with a tiny plastic tube into her vein.

She bit her lip. Not from the pain. There was barely any. Whatever little pinch occurred on her wrist was drowned out by another onslaught of emotion. Tears scratched at her throat and she gritted her teeth against them and silently screamed. She was so fucking sick of tears! She was not this weak . . . But even with the effort, the admonishment, the salty bastards still came. Bubbling up. Blinding her. Escaping. Sliding down her cheeks.

In the moist blur, Petra saw Celestine, a cloth in her hand. The older *veana* leaned down and dabbed at Petra's tears, while Wen whispered soothingly, "It will be all right, my Pets."

"Did I hurt you?" Brodan asked, his warm hand on her arm, his tone heavy with concern.

"No." Petra shook her head, blinking to get rid of the new tears forming in her eyes. "No pain, just fear. I'm scared, Brodan. I feel so completely out of control. This *balas* . . ." She turned her head away and cried softly for a second or two. "I'm already a terrible mother and the child hasn't even been born yet."

"That's bullshit."

The new, though familiar, voice made Petra turn. Behind Brodan, standing in the doorway wearing only jeans and matching severe expressions, were her brothers. Big, tough, blond lion shifters, Sasha and Valentin had always been her closest allies and her biggest supporters. They made her laugh and protected her. She was so grateful to them—and she couldn't wait to see them as uncles to her child.

"If this blood thing Brodan's cooking up doesn't work, we've got another plan," Sasha told her, a slight sneer on his full mouth.

"Damn right," Valentin agreed with a punch of feline ferocity. "We love you too much to see this continue."

"This plan of yours is to be our last resort only, boys," Wen said in her strongest maternal tone.

"Yeah, yeah," Val said.

"I don't want that piece of shit male here," Brodan said tightly, watching the blood move through the tube toward Petra's waiting vein.

"None of us do," Sasha said with true venom.

Valentin growled. "But you know as well as we do that we're going to have to take some drastic measures if this doesn't work."

"What are you talking about?" Petra asked, her insides growing cold with confusion and worry as she gripped the edge of the mattress with her free hand. "What drastic measures?" She looked at each male in turn.

Wen turned back to Petra and put her hands on her daughter's shoulders. "Just a backup plan, my Pets."

Inside Petra, anxiety mixed with confusion and a lack of control for one seriously potent cocktail. "For what?" she demanded, looking from her brothers to her mother.

"Shit," Brodan said gravely. "For this." His gaze met Petra's. "Your vein just closed up. It won't even allow the blood inside."

Celestine cursed, and Wen squeezed Petra's shoulders.

Brodan stripped off his gloves, then glanced over and nodded at Sasha and Val. "Do it."

"Do what?" Petra cried out, trying to sit up.

But her mother held her down, whispering words of love, while her brothers released terrifying twin growls and rushed out of the room.

* * *

The party's over.

Or was it just beginning?

Synjon took off his shirt and draped it over the black leather piano bench. He loved to fuck, needed the release to keep his muscles content, and though he didn't allow anyone to touch him, undress him, or speak to him, he made sure that the females who spread their legs and bent over the polished black surface of his Bösendorfer came in ways, durations, and decibel levels they'd never known existed.

"Are we going to your bedroom or what?"

The female who had spoken out of turn, the female he'd chosen for tonight, stood near the glass doors that the Roman brothers had walked through only a few hours ago. Her arms were crossed over her chest, and she had one hip cocked in an I'm-the-bloody-shit kind of way. Her small, strong body was encased in a simple black minidress that paired well with her short blond hair, nose ring, and dark eyes. Blond hair and dark eyes. It had become his routine shag. For some reason, his body refused to take any female who sported the combination of dark hair and blue eyes.

It was bloody irritating.

He gestured for her to approach him. "Come, female."

She didn't move. "A little premature, don't you think?"

His nostrils flared. Perhaps he'd chosen wrong with this one. Perhaps he needed to fill her mouth with something.

"I want to see where you sleep," she said, her tone close to defiant as she started walking toward him.

"I don't sleep. And no one enters my bedroom." *Or my bed*. It was sacred space. As was the room that lay beyond. The one he'd constructed for a very special, long-term guest he hoped would be arriving soon.

"Turn around and put your hands on the piano," he commanded.

Her eyes flashed and her nostrils flared as she drew nearer. "So you don't have to look at me? Is that it?"

With every look, every word she uttered, this female was growing more tiresome. In fact, Syn was wondering why he'd chosen her in the first place. With all the willing and wet hopefuls, why had he gone for curt and derisive? Both were heavy with emotional undertones—and he didn't do emotions. Only physical, animallike need. Hot, hard, release-filled fucking.

He regarded her with a lift of one dark brow. "Your choice, female. And it's a very simple one. The piano or the door."

Her mouth twitched. "You're really something—you know that?"

He glared at her. Was that humor in her expression? He didn't think so. In fact, he was starting to believe this encounter was a grand mistake. He cocked his head. "I'll walk you out. My driver's downstairs. He'll make sure you get home without a problem."

"I don't need a driver, asshole." She grinned wide. "I've got wings."

Before Synjon could draw his next breath, two males rushed him from opposite sides of the room. Growling and snarling, they bodychecked him so bloody hard he lost his vision for a few seconds. *What the hell . . . ?*

Widening his stance, he shook his head, trying to clear his vision. He was a natural fighter and a seasoned killer, but over the past week, ever since Cruen had bled his emotions, his instincts had been slightly off. He was slower to react. And it showed now.

"I want to kill him," he heard the female say.

"We can't," said one of the males.

"No," said the other. "But we could hurt him a little."

Even without full use of his sight, Synjon felt the steady heat come up behind him. He whirled around and shoved his elbow into the neck of one of the males, followed by a fierce head butt to the face. He heard a whoosh of air, and the male's bloodscent rushed into his nostrils. *Familiar. Not vampire.*

But whether enemy or estranged ally he wasn't sure.

Someone grabbed his arms, pinned them behind his back. Syn growled and slammed his head back, meeting flesh and bone.

"Fuck!" cried one of the males.

"Don't let go!" yelled another.

Cuffs were snapped around Syn's wrists and he was hit from behind by something hard, maybe metal. Not once, but twice. Then something smacked into his skull, and his vision went gray. He went down, knees, belly, head. Again he shook his head, willed his eyes to open and focus. His vision returned just as he was flipped over onto his back. He was about to shoot to his feet when one dirty, black boot clamped down on his windpipe while the other slammed him mercilessly in the groin.

Stars glittered on his retinas as one of the males loomed over him and uttered tersely, "Do you remember us, vampire?"

"Cats," Syn hissed through gritted teeth. "Fucking pussycats."

"That's right. Val and I are taking you back to where it all began." He pressed harder on Syn's throat. "You're going to feed our sister."

No air was getting through. He fought to keep his eyes open, his brain functioning.

"And your cub."

The glass door opened and Synjon felt a blast of cold air move over him. Weight lifted off his airway, and he was shoved to his feet.

"Ready to go for a ride, asshole?" the female said, moving out onto the terrace.

"Not interested anymore, love,' Synjon rasped. "Not sure if I ever was."

Suddenly Synjon dropped down, and in a series of quick, powerful moves, he sent his foot into the gut of one male and his knee into the other.

The pussy brothers were bloody well kidding themselves. Even with the fucked-up vision and the slow reaction time, he wasn't going anywhere. He had a very important guest arriving soon. A guest who would beg him for mercy, and a quick death before he baked slowly in the sun.

A needle slammed into his neck then, cutting off all thought, all fantasy. Instantly, the room started spinning. *Bloody bastards . . .* Synjon braced for a fall, forced his fangs down and a growl from his throat.

The female on the terrace sneered at him. "I can't believe she wasted her time on you."

Seconds before Synjon blacked out, he saw the blond female leap from the ledge of his penthouse balcony and shift into a glorious, massive, and highly pissed-off hawk.

3

With the sun warm on her skin, Petra circled the tree, then raced toward the stream. Thank the gods for her mother's suggestion to get some air, some exercise. It was how pregnant shifter females brought on their labor. Hours of sprinting through the Rain Forest. Granted, Petra was no shifter and she wasn't trying to bring on labor, but the running did something for her. Something miraculous. It released some of the intense and debilitating emotion that had been holding her hostage for a week.

When she reached the stream, she leaped to the other side and continued along the water's edge. As she ran, she spotted creatures moving, courting, and mating under the surface of the shallow water. It was a sight she'd grown up with and was used to. A sight that meant a new year approached. New beginnings . . . new life.

Ever since she'd woken up to the understanding that she lived in a rain forest with an entire species of shape-shifters, Petra had wanted to be like them. She'd been somewhere around ten years old when she'd realized she wasn't. Even the young who hadn't shifted yet could run like the wind and scent prey. It hadn't made her feel like an outcast exactly, but like she was missing something amazing.

And then, just seven months ago, everything had changed. When he came. He came and made her feel understood, not like a freak. He unleashed the truth, showed her what she was capable of if she embraced it, trained it—fed it.

Her fanged nature.

And in some odd way, embracing her vampire had made her feel closer to her family, as though she had more in common with the shifters than she had ever thought possible.

Breaking into a sprint, she passed a bear shifter who was trying to climb a tree and get to a nest tucked into one of the branches. It growled playfully at her, then returned to its task. Petra found that the faster she moved, the less pain she experienced. It was as if the overwhelming feelings didn't have time to fully fuse to her insides.

And the *balas* liked it.

She wasn't sure how, but she could sense it. And moving so quickly provided one of only a handful of times when she'd been able to connect with the little life growing inside her. If she could just give it nourishment now . . .

If she could just give it blood.

Bile rose in her throat as she picked up speed, leaving the stream behind and taking off across the flat land toward her lion shifter family's sprawling one-story compound. Somehow she would find a way to protect her *balas*, feed her *balas*, give her *balas* the loving and proper family it deserved.

Even if she had to spend the remainder of her *swell* running.

Just a foot over the property line, she nearly collided with a massive blond male.

"Damn it, Val," she said, jerking to a halt. "You could've hurt the baby."

The blond male with shoulders as wide as the doorframe of their family house backed up a foot just to show he wasn't in her space. His dark eyes moved over her curiously, concerned. "You're sweating. Breathing heavy. What are you doing?"

"Whatever I have to do to keep sane."

He frowned. "My poor Pets."

"What do you need, Val?" She jogged in place. She wanted to hold on to this moderately contented feeling for as long as possible. Maybe she could try drinking blood as she ran. Maybe the movement would curb her disgust.

"I need you to come with me," Val said, his mane of blond hair escaping the tie at the nape of his neck.

"Where?"

"Back home. I have something to show you."

"I don't want to go home. I don't want to stop, talk, look." She shook her head, pain rising within her, clenching her belly. "The speed makes me feel better. Or maybe it makes me feel nothing, I don't know." Tears choked in her throat. *Goddamn it.* "It's starting to come back, Val. I gotta go." She began to move past him.

He blocked her way. "Pets, wait."

She snarled at him. "I can't."

"We have something for you," he insisted, his eyes shifting from her chin to her ear. "Something we think might help."

"Nothing helps. Don't you get that? Except for this. Moving, sweating. It's just going to have to be pure survival mode until Little Fangs here is born."

He made a face. Disgusted or embarrassed, she couldn't tell. "You're not really going to name it that, are you?"

"I'm going." Groaning, she took off again at a fast jog.

"Pets, wait. Please." In seconds, Val was at her side. But this time he was in his lion form. He kept pace with her, snarling, tossing his incredible mane, giving her the "cat eyes" that as a child always got him what he wanted.

That wasn't happening today.

"Go home, Val," she called out. "I appreciate your concern, but this is my problem to deal with."

She sped up, hoping he'd get the message and take off for home, but he was clearly determined. With a massive roar, he shot out in front of her, and the minute she slowed to avoid crashing into him, dipped his head, pushing her off balance.

"Goddamn it, Val!" she cried, stumbling, trying to right herself.

But the lion shifter knew exactly what he was doing. When one of her legs jacked up, he lowered and shoved his body underneath. As Petra straddled his back, instinct gripped her, and she fisted his mane in both her hands to keep herself steady as he rose to his full height.

Not waiting for a response or permission, he took off, barreling over the stretch of land at a shocking pace, kicking up dirt. She couldn't believe him. What was he trying to prove?

She curved over him and leaned into the wind. "I should bite you for that," she called near his right ear as they raced across the pride's lands. What the hell was Val thinking? What was so freaking important that he had to practically abduct her? And who else was in on it?

Her gut twisted. Why couldn't her family and her friends understand and accept that this was going to be her existence, her reality, for a little while? She knew they cared deeply for her. She knew they wanted more than anything to stop her suffering, and she loved them to death for it. But at some point they had to realize there was nothing to be done but to ride it out.

And speaking of riding it out . . .

"What the hell are we doing here, Val?"

The lion shifter had come to a dust-kicking halt outside the River House, the one-story cabin on stilts that bracketed the rushing water below. The structure had been built by Sasha, Valentin, and their father many years ago to use when the weather grew unbearably warm. Petra couldn't count the number of times she'd stretched out in the shade underneath the house, in the water, or on the bank. It had been perfect and relaxing. Completely the opposite of now.

Valentin quickly shifted into his male form, grabbed a pair of jeans from the stair railing, and pulled them on. "Come inside, Pets."

Inside? This was crazy. What she wanted to do was turn around and run, keep running until she lost her breath. But she knew Val—his stubbornness and that look on his face. He would just come after her again. Better to see what he had inside the house, appease him for a few minutes, and then take off.

The pain of hunger rushed through her as she followed Val up the short flight of steps. Maybe she could talk with Brodan later, see about the blood-as-she-ran idea. Granted, it was a long shot, but the *balas*—

Her fangs dropped suddenly and saliva pooled in her mouth. The scent blasting into her nostrils as she walked through the front door of the cabin was not only familiar but despised. Chills broke out on her skin, but instead of wanting to run away, she had an irrepressible urge to run forward, deeper into the house, stalk the scent, and seize its owner.

A low hiss exited her lips. It wasn't possible. It couldn't be. How could Val have done this to her? He loved her, and yet he now tortured her.

Her mind screamed at her to turn around, get out, get as far from the scent and all the memories that surrounded it as possible. But her need, her hunger, the vampire *veana* inside her, refused to let her retreat.

It wanted that scent.

Breathing heavily, she stumbled after Val, licking her lips as she passed familiar furnishings and the framed watercolors that she and her brothers had made when they were little.

With every step, the scent grew thicker, and she felt her fangs vibrate in her mouth as the hallway became increasingly dark. She followed her brother into the smallest bedroom, the one she normally used when they stayed in the house. The room where all sunlight was absent. The only illumination coming from the small lamp on her bedside table.

Even though she'd scented blood the moment she walked into the house, *familiar blood*, she wasn't prepared for its origin—for the massive *paven* who was sprawled out on the green-and-blue floral quilt atop the queen-size bed.

"Oh, my god," she rasped, reaching out to grip Val's arm, her gaze lifting to see both Sasha and Dani enter the room and head for the hand-carved teak headboard and tightly sealed window. "Why? What is this?"

Sasha grinned. "Vampire. Freshly caught."

Petra's insides recoiled. He was smiling? He thought this was funny? Her breathing became erratic, and her gaze shot to Dani. Thank gods her best friend remained sober. In fact the blond female looked pissed off.

"He is a total bastard, Pets," she said, her nostrils flaring, the action making her nose ring vibrate. "After you're done with him, please rip that shit apart, okay?"

"Done with what?" Petra said, her voice high-pitched and panicked. Her fangs wanted out, down, and in. Hunger like she'd never known surged in her blood. Her nails dug into Val's biceps. "What do you think I'm going to do with him?"

"He's your blood donor, Pets," Dani said, as though this were the most obvious thing in the world.

And shit, maybe it was. Synjon Wise was the father of her child, and his blood had been the only blood she'd ever been interested in tasting. But he was a monster. A killer. A male interested only in vengeance. A male with absolutely no soul, heart, empathy, or conscience. A male who'd been forced to the dungeon floor a week ago, held down by four massive vampires, and drained of his bitter and dangerous emotions. She didn't want him in her precious world again. She didn't want him in her mouth or her bloodstream.

He was a toxic substance.

Her wide, manic gaze slid to the bed. Synjon was lying on top of the pretty, feminine blanket she'd had since adolescence, unconscious, spread-eagled, clad only in a pair of dark blue denim jeans that hung just below his hipbones. He was leaner than she remembered, which made the continuous ripples of muscle on his arms, shoulders, and abdomen all the more obvious. His dark hair was cut short, his skin had remained a pale bronze, his cheekbones were prominent, and there was a light sprinkling of stubble around his full lips.

He was every bit as beautiful as she remembered.

Time rushed backward and claimed her. She'd seen this male unconscious before, in pain and desperate, and had wanted more than anything to save him. Now, as she stared, as she started to shake, as saliva pooled in her mouth and her fangs begged to do what they were meant to do, all she wanted was to attack, bite, and pull every last drop of blood from his veins into hers.

Dani chuckled wryly from her spot beside the bed. "Not to worry, boys. I think she likes her prezzie."

Synjon came awake to the scent of unfamiliar surroundings and the sound of a female's rage. Though his instincts were to jump to his feet and execute everyone in the room, everyone who held him hostage, he kept his eyes closed, his ears open, and his muscles flexed and ready. He would not be a prisoner. Not when he had to return home to Manhattan to welcome a prisoner of his own.

"Like it?" the female cried again, hunger, violence, and pain threading her tone. "I can't believe you did this, Dani! I can't believe you brought him here!"

Though Synjon felt no emotional connection to the female who spoke, he knew her voice instantly. He knew her body intimately.

In fact, he could see her with his eyes closed.

Black hair. Light crystalline blue eyes. Irresistible smile. Pink flush to her cheeks when she got excited.

It was an image his skin, cells, and muscles craved, yet wanted to forget, reject.

"Petra, come on," came a male voice. "He's what you need."

A tremor went through Synjon. He knew that voice too. It belonged to one of his abductors, one of Petra's brothers. He'd met them both many months ago in the Rain Forest community where they lived. Had battled with them inside their house as he'd tried to find the female who'd rescued him from the sun. This time, Synjon would make sure the bloody git and his lion brother paid for the cuffs and body slams with a little torture of his own. After he finished with his long-awaited guest, of course.

"He's the opposite of what I need," Petra growled. "Shit, Sasha, what anyone needs. He's an empty, soulless, gutless bastard."

"Fine," Sasha returned. "What the *balas* needs, then."

Balas.

Something about the word scratched at Synjon's insides, but he quickly shoved back the sensation. The truth in the male cats' words, the need Petra might have of him, meant nothing to the ultimate goal of vengeance that was nearly within his grasp. A vengeance that could finally be carried out without the inconvenient second-guessing and guilt that had once plagued him.

"Why are you hesitating, Pets?" It was the female hawk shifter again. Dani. Synjon knew he'd failed on that account. How had he not seen through that blue-balled facade of his to what truly stood before him? What had tricked him?

"It's clear you want to tap that, Pets," Dani continued with an almost audible sneer. One of the males laughed, and the sneer quickly became a growl. "Shut up, Val."

"You're just such a guy sometimes, Dani," he remarked with another low chuckle.

But Dani was all about Petra. "I want you to take stock, Pets. You're losing your freaking mind. Your emotions are out of control. You can't eat or sleep." She sniffed. "I mean, the vampire's right here for the taking. I say drain him dry and leave his shell in the sun."

"You have no idea what you've done," Petra said in a pained voice.

"Hell, yes, I do," Dani returned. "And if you don't want to do it for yourself, then do it for the baby."

Balas.

The correction came swiftly to Syn's mind. He wondered why that would be.

"He'll fight me," Petra said.

"So what?" Dani returned. "Fight him back. You're ridiculously strong. I've never seen anything like it. Is that like a pregnant vampire thing or something?"

"I have no idea. I don't know anything about being a *veana* in *swell*. Or being a *veana* who hasn't gone through Meta."

"Well, whatever the cause, it's kick-ass and you need to use it."

"Even when he does wake up." The male spoke again. Petra's brother. *Sasha*. "He can't leave this room. It's morning now. Sun's bright and hot and ready to soak up some male vampire skin, so you have a good amount of time to get what you need."

Synjon kept his body ice-still. These shifters were in for a rude awakening if they believed a *veana* could hold a *paven* like him hostage.

"What's your plan?" Petra asked, her voice heavy with intensity, need, hunger.

"We're going to lock you both in the cabin," Dani said.

"Oh, gods," Petra uttered. "This is insane."

Synjon's mouth twitched. He agreed with that assessment. *Locked in*. Did they not know what world he came from? What profession? The disaster he could create with just a twig and a firecracker? Petra's brothers had gotten lucky back at his flat in Manhattan. That wouldn't happen again.

"But if you need us, if you need anything," Dani continued, "there's a two-way radio in the bathroom. We'll be here in seconds."

"Except for this room," Sasha added, "there's sunlight all over the cabin. After you take what you need, leave him in here. He can't follow you. We'll be back to get you before the sun sets."

"Get me?" Petra repeated, slightly panicked. "What do you mean?"

"You're not staying here with him at night," Sasha said tightly. "Soon as the sun goes down, he'll try to escape. Val and I will be here to make sure he doesn't. Although with what you've become, I'm pretty sure you could tame his vampire ass."

Synjon heard retreating footsteps, then Petra's voice outside the door. "This is crazy. We can't just take a member of the Eternal Breed."

"We already did, Pets."

Synjon fought the instinct to crack a lid and see where he was and if anyone remained in the room. And he was glad he did. He heard a door close several feet away, then locks bolted into place, then after a few long moments, movement near the bed.

His entire body flared with warning.

The mattress dipped on his left side and the scent of something floral mixed with female sweat entered his nostrils. His cock stirred. He, however, did not. He felt a breeze move over his face, then warm breath and the tip of a nose against his neck.

"Should I tame your vampire ass, Synjon Wise?" she whispered. "Or just go straight for the jugular?"

He moved with the speed and grace of a trained killer. He had her pinned beneath him in under five seconds. "You won't touch me, love. Unless I wish it."

Black hair spread out wild against the pillow, nostrils flared with contempt, arms trapped above her head and belly exposed, she stared murderously up at him. He'd seen her only a week ago, in the dungeon of the *mutore* Erion. She'd come to rescue her father, Cruen, soon to be caged and tortured, and had ended up hearing the terrible and undeniable truth about him. And she'd felt Synjon's hatred, rage, contempt, and lust for vengeance. Then she'd witnessed the Romans holding him down while her father took his emotions.

Syn's gaze moved over her. Taking in each feature, each change. She was physically extraordinary-looking. Far more beautiful, far more desirable than any of the other females he came in contact with. And the fact that she was in *swell* made her even more attractive. He wasn't sure why. He wasn't sure why his dick was so smitten, filling with blood, pressing against his zipper, trying to get at her.

Maybe his body was remembering their night together. Her mouth on his. His fangs inside her vein. Her skin smooth and hot under his palm. Her tight pussy squeezing his cock until his body refused the comfortable existence of control.

It was a memory he normally chose to ignore. But with her beneath him, with her scent wafting into his lungs, it couldn't be helped. Or stopped.

"I was told you wouldn't come here even when you knew how bad off I was," she whispered, her eyes narrowed, her body shaking beneath his.

Syn's gaze rested on her upper lip and the tips of her fangs. "True."

"Or how the life of this *balas* was in danger."

His gaze traveled down her neck and breasts to the rise of her belly.

"*Your* balas," she added with a hiss.

That thing, that something strange he'd felt before at the mention of the *balas*, moved through him once again. The physical sensation was almost like desire, but stronger. Without his consent, his hand reached for the base of her abdomen and remained there.

"What are you doing?" she said, a low growl ending the query as she shifted beneath him, trying to get free.

He didn't answer her because at that very moment, he felt something press against the center of his palm, then retreat. His brows drew together. *What the bloody hell was that?* He waited a few seconds for it to return, but when it didn't he moved his hand just a little to the right. His breath hitched, held in his lungs. He wanted it again. Whatever it was.

"Get off me!"

Sudden, shocking pain accompanied her cry, and Synjon gasped, falling to the right, falling off her. For the second time in twenty-four hours, he saw stars. *Foolish prat,* he scolded himself, his cock screaming, heat shuddering in his groin. *Paying more attention to the swell of this* veana's *belly than to planning your escape.*

The breath completely yanked from his body, his balls on fire, Synjon coiled into himself and cursed. The pussy brothers and the hawk shifter were right; Petra had some serious strength. Far greater than any *veana* he'd ever heard of or encountered. Was such a thing normal in *swell*? Or was she somehow different?

"I would say sorry." She scooted off the bed. "But I'm not a very good liar."

"Fuck," he breathed, shaking off his pain, wondering if his dick was permanently scarred.

"Don't want you making any more babies, do we?"

From his fetal position on the mattress, his gaze flipped up to find her. She stood just outside the door. In the hallway, where shafts of sunlight hit her neck and hair.

"I won't be held here," he told her through gritted teeth. "By you, your family. Even that hawk shifter who was only a few hours ago working her way into my bed."

Shock registered on her face. She paled. "What?"

"She didn't tell you?" he said evenly. Though he felt no emotion, he knew exactly how to extract it from others. Years of psych training in the military hadn't been bled out of him. "Your small blond viper of a best mate, Dani?"

Petra shook her head. "She was there helping my brothers. Helping me."

"Your brothers came later, love." Recovered from the knee to the nuts now, Synjon pushed off the bed. He stood in the darkness, his eyes narrowed on the female who'd nearly turned him into a eunuch. This was going to be far trickier than he had thought. Her strength was amazing, strange, and couldn't be matched. He would have to outwit her instead. An option that would take far more time and planning.

She crossed her arms over her chest. "Whatever happened with Dani was just an act to get you off your guard, and you know it."

"Well, she certainly fooled me. And I'm not easily fooled." Synjon smiled coldly. "Must've been that black minidress, those come-shag-me heels, and the phrase 'Where would you like me?'" His gaze moved over Petra again. "No *paven* alive can refuse that."

Petra's mouth thinned and she shook her head. "You really have no shame, no care, no feelings for anything, do you?"

No. He did not.

"'Tis compliments of your father, love," he said tightly. "Now, step aside."

Her expression changed to near amusement. "Where do you think you're going? The sun's shining. It's day."

"It's still night in New York. I may get a bit singed on the departure, but nothing a few *veana*s can't take care of."

Her mouth dropped open and she just stared at him.

"I'm asking you to step aside." His eyes locked with hers. "I will only ask once."

She lifted her chin. "And if I refuse?"

"I shall make you," he said simply.

Petra took a breath, then released it as she moved into the very center of the doorway. "Make me, Syn."

His brow furrowed. It was a response he hadn't expected. It was illogical.

She continued, her tone filled with an almost feverish excitement. "Make me get out of your way. I've dreamed of it—this clash—and everything inside me is begging for it. I've wanted to deny this new strength I possess. Or just not deal with it because I didn't understand its purpose, and shit, maybe it even frightened me a little. But I think it's the perfect time to see just how powerful I am."

"The *balas* . . . ," he began slowly.

"You won't touch the *balas*." She grinned, her eyes flashing with heat. "I won't allow it. Ever."

Again the strange sensation scratched at his insides,

and again he forced it back. "I will show no pity, love. As you know, it doesn't exist in me anymore."

She sniffed, dropped into a fighting stance. "Trust me, Syn. It never did."

He moved first. But Petra was only a second behind him. Fangs bared, blood surging in their veins, they collided in the center of the room: cold and lethal versus savage and ravenous.

4

Cruen stood where so many lesser beings had stood before him. Where he had called to them, pulled them into his reality, rejected them.

The Hollow of Shadows.

Under the spotlight of a full moon, Cruen wanted to sneer at his predicament. But the action and the emotion behind it would steal the minimal energy that remained inside him. And though he grew worse with each moment he breathed, he had to appear capable and highly functioning before Feeyan and the others. For now, for today, he would tell them his only issue was a glitch in his ability to flash, the reason most frustratingly undetermined. He remembered something similar happening to another member of the Order many years ago. He hoped at least seven of the ten members would recall it now.

The temperature around him dropped another five degrees, the cold gripping his bones, weakening them further. It was truly disgraceful. The once all-powerful, feared, and respected vampire reduced to this. Begging for entrance to the plane he had created. Begging for an audience before the table he used to rule.

Damn Synjon Wise for his trickery, his treachery. What was his reasoning for this? Why not keep him in Erion's dungeon? Why not just kill him outright?

An owl screeched overhead as Cruen walked toward the mouth of the cave. If he could just sit for a moment, find and collect his breath, save his strength. He wondered if Feeyan and the Order were ignoring him, his call. After all, they were a new, modern bunch now, and he had abandoned them for greater things. His self-serving agenda was common knowledge. And yet, even as he worked out the thought, he felt their almighty hand reaching for him, their strong and faithful energy wrap around him and pull. A weightless sensation moved through him as the Hollow of Shadows grew smaller and further away, while in his mind anger flared with the knowledge that even if he'd wanted to, there was no turning back. Feeyan had the power now. She was great. She was the leader of the Order.

And he was only a shell of the *paven* he used to be.

An even deeper, more bitter cold assaulted him as his feet hit compacted snow. At first Cruen was confused. Had the Order changed their reality—his reality—from sand to snow? Then, as Feeyan appeared at his side, tall and imperious, and the clouds parted before him to reveal several glorious white-capped mountains, he knew where he was and why.

"It is good of you to call, Cruen," Feeyan said, her eyes matching the snow that surrounded them, while her expression mirrored the cold. "To what do I owe this unexpected pleasure?"

He matched her crisp tone. "I was hoping for an audience with the Order."

She smiled, but it didn't reach her eyes. "I am the Order."

It was like looking at himself only a few years ago. Ambitious, arrogant, secretive. He quite admired her in that moment. "So I'm to have a private audience?"

"I think it best to start there," she said, studying him. "Don't you?"

Cruen hesitated, handpicking every word that was to come out of his mouth. His successor was a complex *veana*. Not unlike him, she went beyond the boundaries of the Order to further her agenda, seek power and alliances. He had counted on standing before the group of ten and stating his case, his concerns. Now, with just their leader, perhaps he needed to play this game a little differently.

"We have a problem," he began, the cold invading his bones, looking to weaken them further.

"We?" she repeated disdainfully.

"The Eternal Breed," he said evenly, forcing calm, coolness into his expression. "I come to you as a concerned Pureblood."

Her brows drew together in surprise, interest even. A small victory that gave Cruen the minute shot of mental adrenaline he needed to get attention, and action, for this lie he had conjured.

"A Pureblood looking for assistance," he added.

Her mouth curved into a dangerous, disbelieving smile. "Since when do you need the Order's help for anything, Cruen? You are all-powerful, remember?"

Yes. He remembered. *And I will be back there again. As*

soon as I get to Synjon Wise. As soon as I dispose of this emotional disease inside me.

"This isn't a personal issue," he said, his eyes locking with hers. "It's a problem for our kind."

"What problem would that be? And why would you care?"

"Perhaps because I might be responsible for it."

She fell silent, her narrowed gaze moving over his face, searching his expression, his body language. Cruen knew the intimidation tactic she was using. It had been one of his favorites. He nearly grinned. She truly had been his best pupil.

"Responsible how?" she said at long last.

It wasn't the most optimal route to Synjon Wise, this lie he was about to tell Feeyan. No doubt Celestine and Petra would be caught up in the coming madness. But he couldn't see any other way. He didn't have the power the job required.

"It all began when I was creating the Breeding Male," he said, his gaze shifting to the skiers on the mountainside. "As you know, I used not only the DNA of Pureblood vampires, but also that of demons—"

She hissed at his side. "And animals. One sits on the Order. I must look at her every day. Despicable."

Perhaps, he wanted to snarl. But the "animals" and the demons had been the route to the Breeding Male they all revered so. He would agree that they were not on par with the vampire breed, but they were serviceable, respected for their blood and all that it offered.

He continued to stare out at the snow, imperiously, unfettered. He had never wanted to reveal this secret to the Order. Doing so meant his research would be open to others. With a heavy breath, he said, "The DNA samples were not from animals."

"What?" Her voice was very low.

His lips tightened around his teeth. Perhaps this was a mistake. Perhaps he should've come up with a different—

"Look at me!" she screamed.

Cruen had no choice but to obey. His head came around fast and sharp, his vision momentarily blurred. In seconds, he caught her fearsome gaze, and knew his willing body had just revealed some of its weakness.

Her eyes narrowed and she licked her lips, studying him. "If you didn't use animals," she said slowly, "how do we have the *mutore* and Order member, Dillon?"

The words, the revelation, hovered on the tip of his tongue. This was it. If he revealed them, their sheltered world, it was over. For them, and for him and his research. They would never grant him samples, test subjects, anything, ever again after this.

Feeyan was glaring at him with equal parts suspicion and gleeful curiosity. At his ear. Or lack thereof.

"What happened, Cruen?" she asked. "Animal bite?"

No.

Synjon Wise.

Nearly debilitating shame drained Cruen of any scrap of concern he might have had for his relationship with the Rain Forest and its inhabitants. The *paven* who had tortured him, skillfully removing his ear before setting his skin to flame under the light of the sun, must be found. His emotions returned.

His life extinguished.

"There are shape-shifters in existence," he began,

barely feeling the frigid air swirling around him. "They have a hidden world in the Rain Forest. They were once peaceful. Incapable of posing a threat to our kind."

Feeyan's eyes turned an emotionless stark white. For a second or two, she didn't speak. Then her fangs lowered and she spat out, "And you kept this from us?"

Of course he had. And he'd have continued to do so if that hidden world didn't now contain Synjon Wise. "I was trying to protect them. But they are no longer peaceful. They've taken our own."

Her eyes widened. "Taken?"

He nodded. "Purebloods. A male, and a female in *swell*. The shifters keep them as prisoners."

Nostrils flared, Feeyan ingested this news. "Abducting Pureblood vampires," she said thoughtfully. Deadly. She turned to face the mountain just as a group of thick gray clouds approached. "Well, we cannot have that, can we? I rather prefer blood at mealtime, but I'm willing to try a little raw meat in honor of the Eternal Breed."

Petra stood in a blinding-white patch of sunlight, panting, sweating, thrilled, hungry, irritated. Basically, too freaking close to being out of control for her liking.

Three feet away, taking up residence in the doorway of the dark bedroom, his stance cold and calculated, his sharp-angled face sporting a nasty burn near his left temple, was her adversary.

The one she'd grabbed, clung to, pulled—not to keep him out of the sun this time—but to get him into it.

Her eyes moved over him, dark blue jeans that hung on narrow hips, wide, smooth, lean-muscled chest, broad shoulders, thick column of neck and a hard, set jaw. She lifted her gaze to connect with his iron stare. "You look a little afraid, Mr. Wise."

"I don't feel fear, *veana*."

"Right. It's an emotion. I keep forgetting you're practically a machine."

"I am impressed, though," he said, the burn at his temple still smoking slightly.

"Machines don't get impressed."

He lifted his hand to his temple, hissed as his fingers made tentative contact. "Acknowledging skill, strength, and cunning in one's opponent is not an emotion, but an understanding, a reasoning of events." His brow lifted. "Do you wonder why you're suddenly so powerful?"

Yes. "No."

"I don't believe you. You, who wanted to know everything about your vampire self."

"That was before."

"Before what?"

She placed her hands on her belly. "Before I had to survive, fight." She cocked her head. "Nice battle scar, by the way."

"Not my only one, I think." He took his hand from the burn. "Day's still young and you look hungry."

Her mouth watered at his words, his suggestion. The struggle to keep him from bolting had only aggravated her hunger. Being near him now, scenting him, was torture on her system. And to think, just hours ago the thought of blood on her tongue, running down her throat, made her gag.

Of course, she hadn't been thinking about Synjon's blood then.

Her mouth twitched at both the irony of the situation and the emergence of her fangs.

"So what's the plan?" he said, leaning against the doorframe. "You wanted me here, Muscles. Now you have me. For a few hours at any rate."

A tidal wave of emotions, anger, and lust barreled through her. Needing his blood was one thing, but what he'd just implied was another. She abandoned her sunlit patch and moved toward him. "Let me make something very clear, Mr. Wise. I don't want you here." Confident in her strength, she came to stand within an inch of him. "I don't want *you* at all."

He smiled, but there was no true humor in his expression. "You're practically drooling as you stare at me."

"I don't drool."

"Open your mouth, let me see your fangs."

"Fuck you."

He pretended to be shocked. "Not in front of the *balas*, love."

"Don't pretend you care anything for the *balas*," she said through gritted teeth.

A sudden gust of pain assaulted her then, and she shuddered and winced before reaching for the wall to steady herself. This was bad. This whole mess. He was right. The bastard. She was drooling. She wanted so desperately to control herself around him, but her body, and the *balas* inside her womb, knew what it wanted. And it would go to any lengths—even the humiliation of its host—to get it.

"I'll tell you what," Syn said in a soft, calculated voice. "You want my blood? Take it."

Her gaze flipped up to meet his. Just the words, the suggestion, the offer, pained her.

"You *do* want it?" he said.

Her eyes narrowed as she glared at him, and her entire body shuddered with need. She hated the thought of blood in her mouth. But his blood . . . "Yes, I want it," she ground out. *Shit, I crave it. I obsess over it. I lust for it.*

He leaned closer, whispered, "Why do you hesitate, then?"

"Because, Mr. Wise, what I crave is toxic." Her top lip trembled. "Despicable sludge. Poison."

Dark brows lifted above intrigued eyes. "You speak of my blood."

A grunt of sarcastic amusement came from her throat. "The *paven*'s a genius."

"Are you in love with me, Petra?"

"What?" She recoiled. "Shit, no. Never!" The thought made her sick. Or was it hunger and need raging inside her that twisted her empty belly? It was so hard to decipher what emotions coincided with what situations.

"Then why does it matter to you if my blood is moralistically toxic? It's not logical. If you need it, you take it."

Logic. Christ, logic had no place within her. Not now. Not this week surely. She couldn't reason that way. She drew on lust and pain and hunger and angst. "What I don't want to take is you inside my body."

Syn's eyes shifted to her belly. "Too late, love."

She hissed at him, and the *balas* moved and stretched

against her skin. Automatically, she placed a hand there and started rubbing in slow, soothing circles.

"I'm here," he said evenly. "Only until the sun sets. Take it now while it's available to you."

Her fangs dropped completely, pressing against her lower lip. Gods, she hated this, hated her brothers and Dani for bringing him here, making her face him.

Want him.

This male who would've killed her and her child if Cruen hadn't bled the desire out of him.

She growled deep in her throat and gripped the wall tighter. No child should have a father like this one—a father who didn't want them or care about them. After she brought this child into the world, after the madness inside her ceased to reign, she was going to make sure she gave her new little life a true family.

"Your hesitation is foolish and a waste of time," he said. "The *balas* clearly wishes to feed."

"Don't speak of my child." She inhaled deeply, trying to control her hunger and a new wave of melancholy. "If it actually happens, this transaction of blood is between you and me. But first I want to know what it is you want."

His brows lifted.

She sneered at him. "You don't work on empathy, Mr. Wise, or understanding or kindness, remember? So what is it you want?"

His nostrils flared as he pulled in a deep breath. "When the sun goes down . . ."

"I let you leave?" she finished for him.

His eyes filled with amusement and he laughed softly. "Even with that glorious new strength you possess, you won't be able to stop me in the dark. But looking the other way, calling off the cats if they pose a problem." He shrugged. "That I will take."

She stared at him, this *paven* before her. Someday her *balas* would ask about its father, and she would be forced to remember that Synjon Wise hadn't always been a heartless, emotionless shell. That in fact he'd been generous and funny and irreverent and sexy as hell once upon a time. For the good of her *balas*, she would remember how close she'd felt to him the night they'd conceived. How he'd asked her to come with him, promised to teach her, show her the world of the Eternal Breed.

And for the good of the *balas*, she would leave out the fact that he'd wanted to kill not only Cruen but perhaps even Petra herself.

"Shall I make it easy on you, love?" Syn said, cutting into her thoughts with the rusty blade of reality. "On the both of us?" He brought his wrist to his lips, and with his eyes pinned to her, bit down. "After all, I have guests coming at midnight."

The scent hit her like a tree branch to the face. Knocking her out, sending her to heaven. She could almost taste it on her tongue, luscious, sweet like nectar. And she was so thirsty.

She stared at his wrist. Thick, strong, and oozing that wondrous, yet toxic, blood. This would satiate her, calm her, feed her.

This would save her *balas*.

Never in her life had she wanted something as much as she wanted what flowed in slow, mouthwatering twin lines down his wrist.

She reached out, snatched his arm, and pulled it close. Fool or forager, she couldn't help herself. Her gaze narrowed on his forearm as her fangs dropped lower. Gods, she remembered how it felt to be bitten, to be drunk from. Sweet pain and intense pleasure. She didn't want to feel that again with him. She wanted no connection to this male who cared nothing for her and her child.

But unlike the *paven* himself, his blood was impossible to resist.

When her fangs entered his vein, Synjon's breath caught in his throat. But when she began to suckle, taking his blood into her mouth, her fingernails digging into the back of his hand as she worked, he lost his breath completely.

He'd fed others in the past, a simple, sometimes sensual contract. After all, it was the way of the vampire. But this . . . blood exiting his veins at a rapid pace, and what blood remained heading straight for his groin, making his cock stand at attention. Well, this was a problem.

One feed.

That was all he was giving her.

A soft, almost guttural groan escaped Petra's throat as she changed the angle of her draw, as she gripped him tighter. His wrist felt weak and wet, and irrepressible desire flooded him. Unfortunately for that moment, intense sexual desire hadn't been taken from his blood. Only his emotions, past and present. Only what Syn had allowed that piece of shite *paven* to take.

He sagged into the doorframe, his eyes drifting closed, the burn near his temple all but forgotten. This was trouble, what raged inside him. Perhaps more trouble than the desire to kill, to torture. He wanted to take her. Fuck her. Right now. Again. His fingers vibrated and his mouth filled with saliva. He saw it clearly playing out in his mind. He wanted to strip her naked, ease her to her hands and knees on the rug behind him. He wanted to look her over, see her round bottom lift toward him in anticipation—see her juicy, pulsing sex. He wanted to position himself behind her, slide his cock to her entrance, then thrust deep, pressing against her womb as his hands gently cupped her belly.

The belly that housed, cradled, and protected the *balas*.

He pulled in air. This wasn't good. In fact, it was bloody madness. Considering the child inside Petra's womb as anything more than fact could ruin his plan. It was why he'd stopped fighting midway through Cruen's bloodletting. He'd seen a new path, a better way to exact his revenge.

And a bargaining chip in the form of a child could cost him that revenge.

A hiss escaped his lips and he opened his eyes to see her pull back from his vein, her lips delectably blood-stained. Just inches away, her gaze lifted to meet his and though Syn's instinct was to lean forward and clean his blood from her mouth, lap at the excess with his willing tongue, he held himself in check. Not just because any further intimacy between them would be foolish and would weaken his resolve, but because there was something glistening in her eyes that intrigued him. Concerned him.

Calm, calculated ice-blue fire.

"The *balas* likes your blood." Her tone was as cool as her stare, and in one swift movement she brought his hand to her belly. "Feel. If you can."

The sensation lasted only a second—from inside her body, through her skin and into his palm—but Syn could not deny its impact.

Was that a shock of emotion?

. From a small, satiated being?

He ripped his hand from Petra's belly and stated flatly, "We're done here."

Petra didn't move. In fact, she was so still, it was almost eerie. Then she grinned. "I don't think so." Blood stained her teeth. "I think we're just getting started."

5

Euphoria had claimed Petra. She leaned back against the doorframe and sighed.

After months of insecurity and fear, and a week of utter insanity and raging hunger, she could finally breathe without pain and sadness, move without tears.

"I want more," she uttered, her eyelids lifting to find Synjon several feet away, deep in the bedroom, nearly plunged in darkness except for his arm, the one that had just fed her.

"You've had enough," he said, his tone even but resolute.

Petra barely heard him. She couldn't stop staring at his wrist, illuminated by the sunshine at her back, and the gaping twin wounds that called to her like a lover. The anger and emotional pain had subsided, but now something new and strange had taken its place.

Possessiveness. Over his blood.

No.

My blood now.

"I didn't know it could be like that, taste like that,"

she said, sounding deliciously drugged even to her own ears. "I must have more."

Synjon pulled his wrist from the light. "Greedy *veanas* don't prosper, love."

"And selfish *paven* must pay for their mistakes," she returned.

"Are you calling your *balas* a mistake?"

She grinned, feeling absolutely no anger. Only calm seas and ocean breezes. He was trying to bait her into rejecting him. And that may have worked a few minutes ago. But times had changed. She could never reject him now. Even with all she knew about him, all she'd experienced. He had the blood. He had what she craved, the magic elixir that could keep her sane and satiated.

She shook her head drowsily. "No, Mr. Wise. The only mistake I made was pulling you into that cave, saving your life."

"On that we can agree," he replied.

Like the cat she'd always wished she could be, Petra slid away from the doorway and stalked into the room. Her insides completely relaxed, she moved toward Syn until she could see him clearly, until her eyes adjusted to the dim light. He stood beside the bed, feet apart, arms at his sides, ready to spring, his eyes narrowed. She couldn't help herself. Her gaze followed the ridges of muscle in his abdomen up to both the hard planes of his chest and the well-sculpted breadth of his shoulders until she reached what truly interested her. What made her mouth water. What made a guttural moan of need escape her lips.

His neck.

And the long, thick line of pulsing vein beneath.

"You owe me, Synjon," she said softly. "You owe *us*."

"I gave you the blood you require."

She nodded. "True. You gave me blood."

"But it's not enough."

She shook her head, her lips twitching into another satisfied smile.

"You will break our bargain, then?" he asked, every muscle in his extraordinary body tensing.

"My loyalty is here." She stopped before him and placed her hand on her belly. "Will always be here."

His gaze dropped and his nostrils flared. "I suppose I cannot fault you for that."

His vein called to her. A siren song she could never refuse. Didn't want to refuse. Saliva filled her mouth in anticipation. She *would* feed again. Soon. "Until the *balas* is born, you will remain here."

"As your prisoner?"

Her eyes lifted to meet his. "No. As our food source."

Though his expression was as calm as the river outside, something flashed in his gaze. But it was gone in an instant. He shook his head slowly. "I won't allow it, love. I cannot."

"We'll see." Breaking into a broad grin, she turned and walked away, out of the room, down the hall, and into the sunlight, feeling—for the first time in months—fucking fantastic.

The moon was obstructed by heavy clouds as Phane landed on his perch on the roof of the warehouse in SoHo. It had taken several months, but he'd built the thing himself. Not your ordinary two-by-two redwood block, the massive perch was erected out of steel and sported a feeding station, an all-weather leather nest, and a high-tech sound system. Nearly fifteen feet in the air, it overlooked the city, and the long, heated swimming pool that was Helo's sanctuary.

Still in his hawk form, Phane blinked, his beak twitching as he watched the water beast move back and forth along the brightly lit bottom. They had created a world for themselves here. He and Helo and Ly. An existence. Granted, it wasn't perfect, but at least it was on their terms, and that was all that mattered in the end.

As if his thoughts had summoned the lone wolf, the roof door burst open, and the large, shaggy gray male stalked out. His eyes trained on the water, he went directly for the pool, then when he reached the edge, tilted his head back and howled.

The sound was purposeful, and caused Phane to screech in return, his feathers rustling. In seconds, he broke from his perch, and took off. He didn't bother circling, trying for a gentle landing. He dove low and quick, touching down a little too roughly near an unlit torch just as Helo emerged from the steaming water. They all shifted at once in the cold night air.

"Button up, Beasts," Lycos said, grabbing a pair of jeans off one of the deck chairs and yanking them on. "We've got company."

Helo followed suit, pulling on his own dark blue denim. "Is that what your howl was about, Ly? Are we having a party tonight? I could use some female company, but that call of the wild you just released is supposed to be reserved for dire circumstances."

"This is dire," Lycos said. "In my opinion anyway."

Helo snorted.

"And there will be females, yes," Lycos added with a smirk. "But they'll all be mated."

"Well, what's the point of that?" Helo said, turning to Phane as the door to the roof opened once again.

"Gotta love family," Dillon said, walking out onto the deck. The jaguar shifter and new Order member was followed by her mate, Gray, and most of the Roman clan. "They really know how to make a person feel loved," she added.

"Oh, it's you," Helo said with a disappointed chuckle.

Snarling halfheartedly at the water beast, Gray pulled out a chair for Dillon to sit in. "Don't worry, baby. Later on tonight I'll make you feel real loved."

"Okay," said Lucian, who was the last to enter the rooftop oasis. "Let's not start down that road. I might lose my dinner."

His mate, Bronwyn, welcomed him on the chaise where she was already seated, then cuddled up next to him. "You used to be such a romantic, Luca."

"That's right," Nicholas agreed with a wide grin as he stood behind his mate, Kate. "Sweet, romantic, lovable Luca."

While Kate bit her lip to keep from laughing, Lucian flashed his fangs at his older brother. "You. Shut it." Then he turned back to Bronwyn. "And you, my beautiful raven-haired vixen," he said in a far gentler tone, nuzzling her neck. "Don't pretend you like all that sappy shit. When I know the truth. When I know exactly what you prefer."

He leaned in then and whispered something in

Bron's ear. Instantly she gasped, her cheeks turning bright red. Bringing a hand to his mouth, she tried to silence him, but Lucian only growled playfully and nibbled at her fingers. Pulling her hand free, Bronwyn broke out into a fit of laughter.

Phane watched the entire display, his gut aching. He turned away from them and focused on Helo and Lycos. This was becoming too familiar. This jealousy, this growing need for a mate of his own. He wanted what his Roman brothers had. What his Beast brother, Erion, had. Shit, he would even go into Hell and remain if it meant he had a chance of finding someone like Hellen or Bron or Sara or Kate.

His gaze moved back to the family, to Dillon in particular. His half sister, the one who had also been headed for the Dumpster when Cruen had decided to rescue them, adopt them. Use them. She was eyeing her own mate, the Impure male Gray, but not with flirtatious abandon. Instead, the female *mutore* looked thoughtful, concerned even. Phane crossed his arms over his naked chest and waited for whatever was to come. Because clearly this wasn't a social call, no matter how much the couples were using it as one.

"Dillon?" He said her name softly, but firmly.

She looked up, found his gaze.

"What's going on?" he asked her, his voice carrying above the small crowd, snagging their attention.

When all conversation had ceased and all eyes were on D, she puffed out her cheeks and blew a weighty breath that caught in the cool night air.

"We have a slight problem," she began. "Unfortunately or fortunately because of my illustrious and very unwanted position on the Order—"

"We get it, baby," Gray said, giving her a smile and a squeeze on her shoulders, trying to ease her tension. "You have a love/hate thing going on with those Pureblood bastards."

She turned and glared at him. "Yeah, laugh it up. It should've been you."

"True that," Gray said. "Mouth closed over here."

She shook her head and turned back to the group. "Anyway. The Order has learned about the shifter community where Sara's sister and her adopted family live."

"Shit . . . ," Helo muttered. The Order had only recently found out about the trip into Hell, and the origin of Erion's *mutore* side. What would their reaction be to another group who'd had influence over their vampire blood?

"How?" Phane asked, drawing closer.

"Feeyan informed us," Dillon said. "I don't know how she found out. But that's not the problem. Well, not the biggest part of the problem."

"What do you mean?" Helo asked.

Lycos sneered. "Are the big, blustering vampires scared of the wee animals?"

"The Order can't see the shifters as a threat to the Eternal Breed," Phane said, wondering where this was all going. "Not like the *mutore* were."

"Are," Lycos corrected, his tone dripping with ire. "*Mutore* will never be accepted by the Purebloods even if one happens to be on the Order."

Dillon turned her gaze on him, but said nothing.

"The shifters have kept to themselves forever," Helo said, remaining close to the water. "They're peaceful beings. It was Cruen's interference that started this, taking their DNA, using it to make a more perfect specimen of vampire."

"Now she knows where the *mutore* came from," Lycos said. "If that isn't a threat to their perfectly pure blood I don't know what is."

"It's not about the blood," Dillon said at last. "At least not yet. Feeyan believes the shifters aren't so peaceful after all. In fact, she believes they're holding Pureblood vampires against their will."

"You mean Petra?" Phane said. "That's bullshit."

Seated beside Alexander, a very pregnant Sara nodded. "Of course it is. Petra wants to be there. Her family"—she paused for a few seconds—"the family she grew up with, at any rate, is there."

"Do they know this?" Helo asked Dillon. "Do they know the truth of the situation?"

"No." Dillon took a deep breath, shook her head. "I didn't want them to know the connection between Petra and our family."

"Why not?" Lycos asked coldly. "What is there to hide besides her asshole of a father, and how he conned Celestine, a desperate *veana*, into screwing over her mate and fucking him instead?"

A low growl rumbled in Alexander's throat, but Sara put her hand on his arm to quiet him. She looked at Lycos, her eyes steady, her voice clear. "My mother made a mistake, a grave mistake, going to Cruen for help. She's paying for it. We're all paying for it. But the Order isn't going to profit from it. Do you understand?"

The female held the wolf shifter's narrowed gaze, her chin lifted. Sara was a tough female, and loyal above all else. She took no shit, and every male gathered around the pool thought twice when going head to head with her. Even Lycos. Growling, he nodded and turned away.

"We need to go to the Rain Forest," Nicholas said, breaking the tension with a call for action. "We need to speak with the shifters."

"I say we explain things to Petra," Helo suggested. "She can come here. At least for a while. Until the Order understands that she's not being held captive."

"Problem is, it's not just Petra," Nicholas said tightly.

Phane's brows drew together. "What do you mean?"

It was Gray who spoke this time. "It seems one of our elite Purebloods was abducted from his home and taken there by shifters."

"Who?" Helo and Phane said at the same time.

Lycos growled. "Syn, right?"

Lucian turned and glared at him. "How'd you know?"

The wolf shifter rolled his eyes. "You three couldn't get that British bastard to go help poor little Petra, so a few of her loyal family members did it."

"Cool it, Lycos," Alexander warned, his eyes dimming with irritation as he pulled his pregnant mate closer.

"Yes, it's Synjon," Dillon confirmed. "And the Order is demanding his release."

"So what do you want from us?" Lycos asked, his jaw twitching with tension.

"You know what they want," Phane said without looking at the male. "We're part shifter. We should go. The community might take it better coming from their own."

"We're not their own," Lycos said.

"What is up your ass today, Ly?" Helo asked with irritation. "Christ."

"Not a thing," Lycos said, pulling off his jeans. "Just opting out of the visit to the homeland, that's all."

Once naked, the male shifted, his wolf springing forth easily. The powerful animal snarled at them all, his eyes snapping with irritation, his gray pelt bristling. Then he took off past them, disappearing inside the house.

"We don't need Ly. I'll go," Helo said, then turned to Phane. "It's a helluva lot warmer there, and I wouldn't mind seeing where we began. What about you, Phane?"

Phane didn't say anything at first. He wasn't siding with Lycos, abandoning the whole mess, but he wasn't sure he wanted any part of where his cells originated. The idea filled him with unease. Then again, how could he refuse his family? Their call for help? And, truly, that's what the Romans were to him now.

Family.

He turned to Dillon, lifted one sharp eyebrow. "When do we leave?"

He listened to the water running as she showered.

Then waited when it shut off.

He listened closely for the sounds of cotton brushing wet, heated skin.

Then abandoned the bedroom when the door to the bathroom silently crept open to reveal five and a half feet of naked female.

Now, Synjon stood just a millimeter outside the patch of sunlight that had burned him not long ago, the patch Petra had once occupied, with his narrowed gaze taking in every bit of perfect flesh he could manage to see through the open doorway down the hall.

Unable to stop himself, he moved his gaze over her, pink and smooth and lush as she stood near the small bathroom window, gazing out, towel in hand. Her long legs gave way to a tight, round ass, and her beautiful belly was the perfect complement to large, heavy breasts with puckered, succulent, rosy nipples. *Swell* agreed with her. So did his blood. It was a good thing he had no emotional feeling—a brilliant move by all parties involved—or the sight before him, coupled with the recent memory of her fangs inside him, might have caused him to reconsider his plot to torture and kill her father.

And that long-held goal would be met at all costs.

She eased the towel between her legs and patted her inner thighs and her sex. His tongue felt dry in his mouth. He knew just where he could wet it.

Behind the zipper of his jeans, his cock was straining and pulsing, begging to get free—to get at her.

Never going to happen, prat. You've been there once before, remember? It's a terribly addictive place to be.

As soon as the sun sank, as soon as the sky turned from lavender to gray, he'd be off, past the pussy brothers and that witch of a hawk shifter, and back to his penthouse balcony. An emotionless *paven* seated behind his white and black keys waiting for fate to find him.

"Admiring your handiwork or cursing it?"

He glanced up, caught that pale blue stare. "Neither."

"Oh, yes." She wrapped the towel around herself. "It would take an actual working heart to feel one or both of those things."

"You know you don't have a working heart either, right?"

Decently covered by the long white towel, she left the bathroom and walked through the living area toward him. "I may not have blood pumping through that particular muscle, but I have and give and show the true meaning of the word. Goodness, kindness, thoughtfulness."

"I remember," he said evenly.

"What?" She came to stand in the patch of sunlight in the hall, her skin pink and glowing. "What do you remember? Me pulling you into that cave? Feeding you? Taking care—"

"I remember the night we created the *balas*." The words weren't said in a soft, sentimental, romantic tone. It was only fact. Though he wasn't sure why he would bring up such a fact.

Petra's eyes were shuttered as she stared at him. Perhaps she didn't like it when he spoke of the child. Or perhaps it was about sex. The memory of the two of them together. He couldn't tell.

He shouldn't care.

"I also remember waking up to an empty tree house," he added. Once again, fact.

She sniffed. "You couldn't possibly be looking for sympathy."

He hesitated in answering. Was he? He didn't think so. But there was something about the memory that poked and prodded at that dead muscle behind his ribs. "I told you who I planned to kill and you ran away to warn him."

"Yes. Of course I did. He's my father." And with that, she walked past him into the bedroom.

He turned and watched her. Watched as she pulled out a drawer and dug through a stack of clothing.

"How do you call that *paven*, that monster, torturer, and wreaker of havoc, 'Father'?" he asked evenly.

"Because that's what he is."

"No matter what he's done?"

"Yes."

"What will you call me, then?"

She froze, her hand deep within the drawer, her wrist covered in denim. For a moment she just stared straight ahead, breathed in and out.

"What will you tell the *balas* I am?" Syn continued, unemotional but oddly curious.

She didn't answer him.

"That I'm a cock-up without feeling, but Cruen is a good and worthy parent? Is that what you're going to say, Petra?"

Finally she released a breath. "I don't know what I'm going to say. I don't know what Cruen is. I never got the chance to know." She glanced over her shoulder at him, her eyes stormy. "But I do know this: I won't let my child go through anguish and pain."

"What does that mean?" Syn asked, walking over to the dresser.

She grabbed a pair of jeans and a blue tank, then turned to face him. "The child won't even know about you, Syn."

His brows drew together and he looked down, at her *swell*.

"This *balas* will have someone else to call Father. Someone who knows how to love. Someone who wants a family, wants . . . us."

His breath caught in his lungs and his eyes returned to hers.

"Feeling something now?" she asked softly.

He wasn't sure. He wasn't sure what was happening inside him. It seemed that even though his emotions were no longer there to access, his physical body was throwing off some serious sensations. His mind told him there was nothing here to care about, no anger, no sadness, no love. Her words were only that. Letters, syllables strewn together, her version of facts. But his hands weren't acting right. They were clenched into fists at his sides, and his gut was pulled in uncomfortably tight.

What was this? What was happening to him?

"Pets!"

Both Synjon and Petra turned toward the door, expecting to find someone in the hall. But no one stood there.

"Petra?" called the female voice again.

They both went to the door, stared out into the hall.

"Come pick up the two-way!"

"Who the hell is that?" Syn said. But Petra was already out of the room, running down the hall and through the living area.

When she reached the bathroom, there were a few minor crashes before Synjon heard her speak.

"Hey," she said, then paused a moment before explaining, "I was taking a shower." There was another pause. Longer this time. "No, he's fine. I'm fine. We're getting along splendidly and he never wants to leave—" She was cut off. Synjon stood in the doorway, straining to hear. Maybe there was something he could use later. Something about the brothers or the hawk female. "What?" she said, her tone different, quiet now. "Why? Oh. Okay, fine. Yeah, I'll come. But I don't like it."

For several long seconds the only sound was the river trees gently scraping the exterior of the house. Synjon wondered if Petra was still listening on the two-way.

When a good minute had passed, he called out to her. "Problem, love?"

Supreme quiet met his query, then a sigh and, "The Romans are here."

Syn's skin hummed with tension. "For you or for me?"

"Not sure. But either way they're going to be leaving this place alone and unhappy."

And with that, she closed the bathroom door. Completely and forcefully this time.

6

"You drank from him, didn't you?" Dani called over her thickly feathered shoulder to Petra as they flew past a stand of teak that housed three of the Avian's twenty-two nesting grounds.

Avoiding her best friend's massive wings, Petra leaned forward and wrapped her arms around the hawk's neck. "Of course I did."

"Well, I hope you drained him dry. I hope he could barely breathe. I hope he was coughing and sputtering and losing consciousness—"

"I get it, Dani," she shouted over the wind. "You want him to suffer."

Dani glanced back, her hawk eyes flashing with ire. "Did he tell you how close he came to having sex with me?"

"No, you told me, remember?" Petra returned.

"Of course, for me," Dani went on, "it was all part of the act. We needed to get him alone, get him as vulnerable as possible. He's a total manwhore, and last night I made sure he chose me."

This wasn't a subject Petra felt all that comfortable with. Especially a second time. And yet she couldn't seem to stop herself from asking, "So, if Sasha and Val were late or hadn't shown up, were you actually going to—"

"Fuck him?" Dani called back, sounding appalled before she actually snorted. "Hell to the no."

"You make it sound like a fate worse than death, Dani. The guy's incredibly hot. And the things he can do . . ." *What the hell am I saying?* She shook her head. It felt like someone else was running her mouth.

"I don't want to hear about his magic tongue," Dani shouted.

Heat flared in Petra's cheeks. "You can stop now."

Dani laughed. "Fine, then. His magic penis."

"Okay," Petra said, completely mortified now. "I think we should play the quiet game. Don't you?"

"No. I don't." And just to send that message home, Dani dive-bombed into the forest, pulled up right before they would have hit the ground, and then started serpentining through the trees.

Petra gripped the hawk's feathers, her mouth dry as she panted with fear. "That was unnecessary," she called through gritted teeth.

"I don't think so," Dani called back. "You need your brain shaken up, reworked. You're talking about this guy being all hot and everything, and all I can think is he screwed my best friend, got her preggers, and couldn't care less."

Petra winced. Her best friend's words cut deep. As they were meant to. "You know my father took away his emotions. He couldn't feel a thing now even if he wanted to."

The hawk made an irritated sound. "Are you seriously defending him?"

"No." And she wasn't. That would be insane. That would make her foolish and optimistic, and worse yet, a glutton for punishment.

"You totally are," Dani returned. "Please tell me that blood you took from him didn't shatter the reality of the here and now, and his major dickhood."

Jeez. Sometimes Dani could be a major pain in the ass. "Rest assured I haven't suddenly become blind to reality. But his blood did calm me down. Made me able to think and feel, without pain and depression along for the ride."

"Well . . . I suppose I am glad of that." Dani was quiet for a moment. Then, "You think he'll try to escape?"

Absofreakinglutely. "He tried once already."

"What?" Dani cried, dropping about eight feet, making Petra's gut fly up into her throat.

"Christ, Dani! Pregnant back here."

"Sorry." She quickly leveled out.

"He got burned, okay? Stepped right into the sun, trying to get past me. Didn't work out very well. Skin started smoking and all that."

Dani snorted. "Nice. Wish I could've seen that."

"He's not going anywhere. Val and Sasha are standing guard inside the cabin."

"That should be interesting."

"Yeah."

"You hope he doesn't go, don't you?"

"What?" Then she sighed. "Oh, Dani, my love, he has the blood."

Dani's hawk made a screeching sound at that, then started circling the waterfall below and the gathering stones beside it. The stones that marked their borders, and that welcomed all outsiders to their world. "All right, vamp girl," she called back. "Before we land, I really need you to repeat after me."

Petra rolled her eyes. "What is it?"

"*I. Hate. Synjon. Wise.*"

Petra laughed. "Fine. Simple enough." She raised her voice to the wind. "I hate Synjon Wise."

"Barely convincing," Dani drawled. "And this too: *I will never let him touch me again.*"

Petra's laughter petered out. Now that one wasn't so simple, and Petra didn't want to even look into why that might be. She'd had enough worrisome admissions today.

Dani squawked at her. "You're hesitating. You shouldn't be hesitating. Hesitating will get you into trouble."

"Shit, Dani. Look at me. I'm already in trouble. Seven months' worth." She laughed. "And I kinda have to touch him if I'm taking his blood."

Dani glanced over one feathered shoulder. "Yeah, but he doesn't have to touch you."

"Look out! The tree!" Petra called, pointing ahead. "Jeez. Come on, Dani, focus. Mom and baby don't have the ironclad shifter belly."

Smooth and easy, Dani banked around the massive tree, then came in for a landing just outside the rock wall of the gathering stones. Petra slid off her back, spotting her mother already seated beside Sara on several small, flat boulders in the center of the stones. Pe-

tra's blood sister. She still couldn't get used to that
concept. Neither of them had noticed her yet. They
were deep in conversation, and for one second Petra
felt a splash of jealousy move through her. Sara already
had one mother. She didn't need Petra's too.

"Hey, Bestie," Dani called out to her.

Petra stopped, realized she'd been walking toward
her mother and Sara, and glanced over her shoulder.

Dani's hawk eyes narrowed. "You never repeated
that last bit."

No, she hadn't.

"I will never let him touch me again," Dani urged.

Petra gave the hawk a quick grin. "Thanks for the
ride, Bestie. I owe you." Then she made her way toward
the gathering stones and the family she barely knew.

Phane couldn't take his eyes off the female hawk. He
stood on the very top of the highest rock within the
gathering stones and stared. Every member of his family that could handle sunlight—except Ly, of course,
who had once again refused to come—was seated and
waiting a few feet below him. Like Helo, Phane had
also been curious about the Rain Forest and its creatures. After living all of his life among vampires,
Phane had wanted to know about that other part of
himself. The one that had never been discussed or revealed. But in all that time—hell, even back at the
house in SoHo—he'd never contemplated another being like himself.

He felt his hawk scratch inside his skin as he watched
the female shift from avian form to human. In the air,
gliding, swooping, touching down, she'd been fucking

magnificent. But on land, in her female form . . . Shit, he'd never seen anything or anyone so hot. She was the perfect height, not too tall, not too short. Her body was a mix of athletic strength and dangerous, supple curves. Her blond hair was cut in a short and sexy style that accentuated her beautiful, sharp-as-shit face, and mysterious black eyes and a ripe mouth that she seemed to work well and often. But it was the piercing—the small ring through her nose—that made Phane's entire body erupt in possessive desire.

He wanted to lick it, run his fangs over it.

Maybe while she bit his neck.

His cock strained against the zipper of his jeans. Then went steel hard as before his very eyes the last shreds of hawk feathers disappeared and she was completely and totally nude. His obvious, lecherous gaze raked over her spectacular body just seconds before she slipped on a thin electric blue dress.

She'd been naked. In front of anyone who cared to look—and Phane was pretty damn sure there were many who wanted to look—and she didn't give a shit.

That was his kind of female.

Fuck, he might be in love with her already.

He thought about shifting into his hawk and gliding down to stand beside her. He needed to stake his claim, let her know he planned on mating with her. Not today. Not unless she agreed to it, of course. But soon.

Unfortunately, the dark-haired *veana* who looked so similar to Alexander's Sara stepped into the center of the stones at precisely that moment, drawing everyone's attention. Phane knew the female was in *swell*, but he hadn't realized how far along she was. Five, maybe six months. She looked good though, healthy, her face and eyes bright—far better than when he had seen her last.

"Why have you all come?" she asked the small crowd of Petra's mother, the Roman females, Helo, Phane, and Dillon.

The last was the first to speak. "This land, Petra, your existence—it has all been a closely guarded secret for some time."

"Try forever," said the hawk shifter female, who stood in the shadows of a massive boulder, just a few feet behind Petra.

Damn, she was tough. Phane liked tough.

"Right," Dillon amended. "Well, it's a secret no longer."

"Do you speak of more than yourselves?" asked Petra's mother, Wen, who sat beside Sara.

"I do."

"Humans?" Wen asked.

"No," Dillon said. "Our kind. Vampires."

Wen looked momentarily relieved. "Didn't they already know? With Cruen as their leader . . ."

"He held this secret pretty damn close to the vest," Dillon explained. "He didn't share anything about you with the vampire community, and he told you nothing about us."

"So is that the only reason you're here?" Petra asked. "To let us know about this development?"

"We wish," Sara said tightly, her eyes locking with her half sister's. "They know Pureblood vampires are here. They think they're being held against their will."

"That's right." Dillon ran her hand over the smooth

surface of the rock. "And by this new species they've just heard about. The head of the Order, Feeyan, is running on paranoia and nerves, if you get my meaning."

"I'm not here against my will," Petra informed her, crossing her arms over her chest. "I'll be happy to tell them that. Anytime they want to come here to the gathering rocks—"

"You'll have to go to them, Petra."

"No." She shook her head. "I'm not leaving the Rain Forest. Not until the *balas* is born."

Dillon sighed. "You don't want them to come here. You don't want us—the Order—involved in your world. Trust me."

As the forest winds blew around them, Petra seemed to consider this. "If I go to them, tell them the truth, that I'm a free and independent being and I wish to remain here, can you guarantee that they'll not only accept what I say but allow me to return?"

The wind died, and everything, everyone, within the gathering rocks grew still, eerily quiet as Dillon pondered this. The *mutore* female looked like she'd rather be anywhere else, and dealing with something far less problematic.

"I can't guarantee anything," she said finally, her tone unabashedly melancholy. "Not when it comes to the Order."

Petra put her hands up in a defensive posture. "Then I'm not going."

As the female hawk shifter broke from the shadows and came up alongside Petra in a blatant show of support, Phane dropped down from one rock to the next until he stood just inside the flat, grassy oval where the pair was.

"Here's the problem." It was Kate who spoke this time. Nicholas's mate had been pretty quiet lately, keeping to herself since her nephew, Ladd, had gone to the Underworld to live with his father, Erion, and his father's mate, Hellen. Everyone knew how hard the move had been on the *veana*, and it was good to hear her sharp, steady voice again. "If the Order comes here to see you, they're going to want to see and question the other vampire who's here."

Petra's lips formed a thin line and her face paled.

"What other vampire?" said the female hawk shifter with a sneer.

"We can't skirt around this anymore," Kate continued. "Is Synjon here, Petra?"

Petra was silent, but Phane noticed her hands had gone to her belly. The hawk female's eyes narrowed on Kate. Damn, she was fierce. He wanted her eyes on him like that.

"Is he here against his will?" Kate asked, her gaze unmoving as she sought Petra's attention.

"You don't have to answer them, Pets," said the hawk shifter. "You don't have to answer to anyone—"

But Petra couldn't be quelled. "The baby needs him."

"Pets!"

She shook her head. "No. It's okay, Dani." With a slow exhale, she walked forward, toward Dillon and the small crowd seated on the rocks behind her.

Dani. So that was the female shifter's name. *Hot damn,* Phane mused, wanting to try it out on his tongue but knowing he had to use only his mind for now.

Dani.

He liked it. He liked it a lot. And so did his hawk.

"I sympathize with what you're saying, Petra," Dillon said. "I know what Synjon's put you through, what a complete and total shithead he's been over the past week. I was the one who told Alex, Nicky, and Luca to get into that penthouse of his and talk some sense into him. But right now, I speak for the motherfucking Order—not my favorite thing to do, mind you—but there it is. They won't rest on this until they have the truth."

"Look, *veana*." It was Helo who spoke, his gaze on Petra, his voice calm. "Let us speak to Synjon. If he's cool with being here, all he has to do is tell the Order that and we're done."

Petra turned her attention to the water beast and sighed. "He's not cool with it."

"Oh, shit," Dillon muttered.

"You need to let him go, Petra," Kate said.

"No."

"Then at least let Helo or Phane speak with him."

"No."

Kate turned to Sara. "Please talk to her. You're her family. Her blood."

"And say what?" Sara asked, her tone very different from that of the rest of them. It was coarse and strained. "'Let your baby suffer, die because his emotionless father wants to go back to his fuckpad and party'?" Sara looked around at her family, who were all staring wide-eyed at her. "If Alexander was acting like this, if I needed his blood, and my baby was at risk, would any of you ask me to hand him over?"

Kate fell silent. Dillon and Helo too.

"So, it's settled," said the hawk shifter. "The asshole isn't going anywhere."

Phane turned to regard her. Tough, tantalizing, she completely fascinated him, and he didn't want to leave. Syn was one lucky male. How could he get Dani the hawk shifter to take him "against his will," show him the nest she was going to keep him in? Feed from him anytime she chose?

"You understand," Dillon said over Phane's pornographic daydream. "If he's not either released or telling the Order that he stays here of his own free will, the entire ruling vampire force might descend on your private world."

Petra's jaw was tight and her eyes were strained. She glanced at her mother. The one who'd raised her. Wanted her.

Wen gave her a broad smile. "Let them come!"

"Double shit," Dillon muttered.

"That's right," Dani called out. "We'll protect Petra and this child."

"You would protect a vampire?" Phane said, addressing her outright for the first time.

The female hawk shifter, the hot little blond bird with metal in her nose, turned to look at him.

"Incurring the wrath of the Eternal Order?" he continued.

Her eyes narrowed as she moved her gaze up and down his body, pausing for only a second when she spied the bulge between his legs that he couldn't conceal, or refused to conceal—he wasn't sure which. "We always protect our own, bloodsucker. And Petra's our family."

The bulge quickly upgraded to steel. "You may have to fight."

She grinned, and the megawatt heat that smile put out nearly sent Phane to his knees. "Nothing I enjoy more than a good dirty fight."

"You mean a good clean fight," Phane corrected.

"No. That's not what I mean." With one last look in his direction, she turned back to the crowd.

"We appreciate the warning," Wen said to them all. "If they come we'll deal with them."

"You're sure?" Petra asked the older female. "I don't want to bring a problem here—"

"They're bringing the problem, my Pets," said the older female.

Petra turned then, her gaze resting on Dillon. "If you must tell them something, tell them the truth. A vampire *balas* needs his father's blood to survive. Let's see if they truly value the Eternal Breed or not."

Just two hours until sundown.

Two hours until he was back in New York. Where he belonged. Where Cruen's body would soon find shelter, pain, suffering, misery . . . then death, if he was a model prisoner.

Synjon continued to wear out the floorboards in the large, lightless cabin bedroom. The pussy brothers sat in the direct sunlight at a table in the living area just ten feet away, playing cards. Every so often, they'd glance his way and remind him they didn't appreciate having to babysit his deadbeat vampire ass.

They were really getting on his nerves.

Before he flashed to the penthouse, he was going to

flash directly in front of the pussy brothers and do some facial rearranging.

"Huffing and puffing in there, bloodsucker?" Sasha called, amusement lacing his tone. "I thought you didn't have emotions."

"I think he's been faking it," Valentin said.

"Bet he's learned how to do that from all the women he's conned into his bed."

Synjon nearly rolled his eyes. These two were truly the feline equivalent of human teenage boys. And clearly Sasha was the instigator. The male would be first in line for the fangdown at sunset tonight.

"When is Petra returning?" Syn asked as he passed the open bedroom door. "She's been gone a bloody long time."

"Miss her, do you?" Sasha said with a chuckle.

"Sure," Syn returned evenly. "Or it could be that I grow weary in the company of grown children."

"I think he just insulted us," Valentin said with mock injury.

"Hard to tell with that accent," replied Sasha. "Listen, bloodsucker, Petra'll be back when she's hungry." He laughed. "I like that."

"Still can't believe our little sister's a vampire," Val said, his tone now slightly melancholy.

"Makes sense, though, doesn't it? Those games we used to play. She never attacked like an animal. And during snack time she always wrinkled her nose at our raw meat cakes and criticized us for our less than perfect table manners."

"She still does that," Val said. "But, shit, brother, I

refuse to use a knife and fork. I was given canines for a reason."

"I hear that."

Synjon stopped pacing. "Perhaps you blokes can reminisce outside."

Sasha tipped his chair back so he could see Syn. "Not sure we're ready to risk that."

"Sun still shining, eh?"

"Hard and hot."

"Then I'm not going anywhere, am I?" Syn said before continuing his pacing.

Val pressed his chair back too. "Doesn't matter, bloodsucker. Sun, moon, dusk. We're going to make sure you stay here until our sister is done with you."

"That's right," Sasha piped up. "Don't wanna have to make the trip back into frozen New York City to pick up your pale ass again."

It was truly his grand shame. The pussy brothers catching him off guard, knocking him out, dragging him here. He'd have to make sure that didn't get out, in the spy community, the military, or his home *credenti*. "How *did* you manage it?" Syn asked. "I'm curious."

"What? Breaking in your place and stealing you?" Val grinned. "Dani's such a pisser."

"Forget Dani," Sasha remarked. "It was our skill and incredible brute strength."

Synjon's nostrils flared at their idiocy. "What drug did you use to get me to this hovel? That's all I want to know."

Both chairs dropped back into place with a crash, and Synjon couldn't see them anymore. "Did he just call the playhouse that you and me and Dad built with our bare paws a hovel, Val?"

"I believe he did."

Sasha growled softly. "If his blood wasn't needed inside our sister, I might have to spread it around the hovel right now."

"Please don't make any messes, boys," Petra said, walking through the front door. "I spent way too many years picking up after the two of you."

"Thank Christ you're back," Synjon said, coming to stand in the bedroom doorway. "The pussy brothers here are trying out material for their comedy act. So far I'd say it's a glorious fail."

For one brief moment, Syn was sure her lips twitched with amusement. It reminded him of her smile. The happy one, the well-pleasured one. He saw it on the lids of his eyes when they were closed. That particular smile made her eyes light up, and glow with blue fire.

She eyed her brothers. "You can go."

Sasha raised a blond brow. "You sure?"

"He's not going anywhere. Sun's still high."

"All righty." Sasha kicked the chair back and stood. Val too. "So, what happened? With the meeting?"

"Mom will tell you," she said, her voice softer than before. "She's back at the house." She tilted her chin in the direction of the door. "Go."

"Fine." Val walked past her.

But Sasha hesitated in the hall, his eyes on Syn. "We'll be back in two hours."

"Lovely," Synjon said overpolitely. "Can't wait."

There were grumblings of irritated comebacks, but Petra managed to shuffle her brothers out the front door. When she returned, Synjon was leaning against the doorframe, his back to the dark bedroom.

"You were gone a long time."

She shrugged. "There was a lot to discuss."

"Like . . ."

"Dillon was there."

"The Order." *Interesting. And quite possibly problematic.*

Her eyes turned a crystal blue as she walked toward him. She licked her lips. "She and Gray and the Roman brothers' mates and even a few of the *mutore* wanted to make sure you were being well treated."

Even in jeans and a tank, she was unbelievably sexy. Or maybe it was because of the jeans and the tank. He tried to keep his gaze off her belly. It bothered him that her *swell* intensified his desire for her.

"And what did you tell them?" he asked.

She stopped just a few inches from the doorway and inhaled rather obviously. "That I was doing my level best to locate and drain every bit of shitty attitude from your person."

He grinned. Couldn't stop himself. It wasn't just her *swell* that was making his cock twitch. It was her voice too, her attitude, the hunger in her expression. Bloody hell, he might not have emotions, but his body was on fire and ready to go.

All she had to do was say the word.

"I'm surprised they didn't want to see me," he said.

"They did."

"And you . . ."

"Told them no." She leaned in then, breathed in, and ran her nose along the ridge of his collarbone.

What the hell? Synjon's hands fisted around the door-frame. *Do that again, little* veana, *and the next time you take my blood I'll be taking your cunt.*

She spoke against the skin of his neck. "I told them you were mine until the *balas* is born."

"And they didn't insist?" he said in a hoarse voice.

She laughed softly. "No one's going to fight a pregnant girl over her food."

"Is that why you stand so close, *veana*? You want my blood—"

She jerked back then, and speared him with her gaze. "Not *want*, Mr. Wise. *Need*. Don't ever mistake the difference. I don't."

He stared at her, his skin twitching with desire. He'd never seen a female so famished before. He couldn't help himself. He leaned in and lapped at her upper lip with his tongue.

Again she jerked back. "What the hell was that?"

"You had a little of my blood on your lip." His brow lifted. "I wanted it back."

She brought her hand up and swiped at her mouth. "Don't do that again. You don't get to touch me."

"Why? Because it excites you?"

"It disgusts me," she said far too vehemently.

"I very much doubt that."

"Do you?" Her eyes narrowed.

He couldn't keep standing there, scenting her, his dick a pulsing stone behind his zipper. He turned and headed into the dimly lit bedroom.

To his surprise, she followed him. "Why? Because the rich, sexy, emotionless Synjon Wise has only to lay a finger on a female and she's panting and parting her thighs for him?"

He turned around, shrugged. "Well, it might require more than a finger."

"Pig."

"I never claimed to be anything but, love."

She clamped down on his chest and shoved him hard. He fell back on the bed, taking her with him in such a controlled way it was clear he hadn't been caught off guard.

Shocked by where she found herself, poised above him, straddling his waist, Petra glared down at him. "How many females have you taken to your bed since we were together?"

"I never take anyone to my bed." When her eyes lit with something far too soft, he amended the statement quickly. "Now, if you're talking about a casual shag over the back of the couch, well, then . . ."

"That's disgusting." She tried to get up, get off him.

But he held her ass tightly. "No, *veana*. That's normal, healthy fucking."

"No, Syn, that's just you. Screw 'em and leave 'em."

His fingers dug into her ass and his voice dropped without his permission. "*You* walked out on *me*. Let's not forget that."

Her jaw worked and she stumbled slightly over her words. "I haven't. I don't."

"Good."

"Just like I won't forget that you wanted to kill my father."

"Wanted to?" He started to laugh. "It may not have

happened in that dungeon as I'd planned. But it will happen."

"I won't allow it."

"You won't be able to stop it."

Her fangs dropped. "I could kill you right now."

"Shhhh . . ." He grinned. "No empty threats in front of the *balas*."

Practically growling, she swatted his hands away and climbed off him. "It's a promise. One I make to the *balas*. Protection from the evils of the world."

"Then we are both saying the same thing, Petra." He watched her turn and walk out of the room, his body screaming for her to come back, make him warm again. Maybe even make him feel again. "Because like it or not, love," he called after her, "accept it or not—grandfather Cruen *is* the evil of this world."

7

"They remain in the Rain Forest?" Cruen asked calmly, his gaze moving down the table, taking in the face of each member of the Eternal Order. "Why have they not been rescued?"

There was no more mountaintop. No more snow, or Feeyan solo at his side. This time, Cruen stood before the ten, his feet ankle-deep in the very sand he had once conjured. Yes. *Before* the Order. Not behind the table where he'd ruled for so long. The shame was not lost on him.

His jaw tightened. Gods, how had he fallen so far? How had he allowed a piece of British tripe to best him? Make him so weak and ineffective that he had been forced to piggyback to the Hollow of Shadows on one of his Pureblood guards?

A fact he would never allow the members of the Order to learn. To the ten, he was only here on Eternal Breed business. His concern for one of his brethren, and his desire to protect the pure blood. And perhaps even his need for redemption for not only keeping the shifter world a secret but using their DNA to enhance the vampire race.

"The Order has just returned from the Rain Forest," Feeyan informed him coldly. "All I have heard is that one of the Purebloods is not a prisoner."

"And from whom have you heard this?" Cruen asked. "Who did you send?"

"Me." Dillon grinned from her seat, farthest down the table. "Hello, Daddy Dickest."

As the other Order members muttered under their breath, Cruen's gaze narrowed on the vampire and jaguar shifter he'd adopted so long ago. The one who had run from him when she claimed one of his guards had touched her. Cruen had never been sure of what happened. But he was sure of Dillon's penchant for deceit, and for turning the other *mutore* against him. This time, however, she would not interfere with his plans. "You are one mongrel I wish I had left in the ditch."

"Awww," she said with heavy sarcasm, her head cocked to the side. "You're still such a sweet-talker."

Feeling his blood heat to a dangerous, energy-stealing level, Cruen ripped his gaze from the female and turned back to face Feeyan. "What of the other Pureblood? Has he professed his wish to remain as well?"

"Why is this any of your business?" Dillon continued brusquely. "Why are you even here? Because we all know altruism is not your thing."

His fangs started to descend. He should've drowned her when he'd had the chance. "So the Order is now being run by not only its newest member, but a *mutore*." He spoke to Feeyan, and liked the flash of embarrassment and unease he saw in her eyes. "How far we have fallen."

"Oh, that's rich coming from you," Dillon snapped back. "You who created us."

This time, he did turn to look at her. "Mistakes are part of any experiment."

She hissed at him, pushed away the gentle, calming hand of the Order member beside her. "Calling yourself a mistake, huh, Pops? How many species are you now?"

"I was born a Pureblood, mongrel." He sneered, but inside, the weight of his physical and emotional exhaustion threatened to fell him. "What I did to myself, how I used my own flesh, my own blood to test the DNA of other species, was for the good of our race, to better our race. My sacrifice makes me a hero. But your birth will always make you trash."

"Fuck you."

"That's quite enough," Feeyan interrupted smoothly.

"Look how he speaks to a member of the Order," Dillon said hotly. "You know he doesn't give a shit about the Eternal Breed." Her eyes narrowed on Cruen. "Do you have a personal reason for wanting us to infiltrate the Rain Forest shifters, Daddy Dipstick?"

Growing weaker by the second, Cruen was doing his very best not to collapse, drop like a stone—his backside into the sand. "Do you have a personal reason for keeping the Order out, mongrel daughter?"

She leaned forward on the table and grinned broadly. "Shall we talk daughters?"

"Enough!" Feeyan cried, standing, her hands outstretched.

Cruen eyeballed Dillon with new interest. The *mutore* female clearly knew about his connection to Petra and the *balas*. She knew Petra was his daughter. But why wasn't she revealing it? Why wasn't she using it against him?

Why didn't she want the Order to know about the relationship?

"Synjon Wise has not been in contact," Dillon told the others with forced calm.

"What does that mean?" Looming above them all, Feeyan turned to look at her. "He's no longer there?"

"He's there. But we haven't been given access to him."

"Haven't been *given*?" Cruen repeated with a painfully forced laugh. "A Pureblood is being held captive and the Order remains silent."

"He is not captive," Dillon returned hotly. "He is there feeding his unborn *balas*."

Feeyan was silent for a moment, closing her eyes and muttering incantations under her breath. Exhausted, both mentally and physically, Cruen watched her. He knew this game. He'd played it many times. Gathering silence, gathering attention, showing his power. He wondered why the new leader of the Order hadn't developed her own tricks of the trade.

When she opened her eyes again, they were a stark and shocking white, and her voice boomed when she spoke. "I want the Purebloods brought here, Dillon. If what you say is true, they need only claim their situation and I will return them."

"But," Dillon began, looking more nervous than Cruen had ever seen her, "the *veana* is late in her *swell*."

"Flash does not impact *swell* in a Pureblood *veana*." Feeyan lifted her chin and added imperiously, "But that is not something you would know, is it?"

Dillon's nostrils flared, and her jaw went tight, but she said nothing.

"You have twenty-four hours to bring them before me, or the Order will see this as a true Pureblood abduction, even an act of war by the shifter breed."

"Perhaps I can help this situation along," Cruen offered. "Go with Dillon to speak to the shifters."

Feeyan turned her attention on him.

"No way," Dillon said quickly before the leader could answer. "I don't want him there. The shifters won't want him there. Not after he revealed them, betrayed them. I'm trying to do this with diplomacy."

"Don't you think your presence there will cause more pushback?" Feeyan asked Cruen. "Better to let the Order handle things."

"The Order," he began in a calm voice, "specifically one Order member, Dillon, tried to handle things and failed. I care about the Purebloods held hostage not only because they are Eternal Breed but because one of them carries my blood."

The world around him fell into utter silence. The Order members sat up straighter, all of their eyes on him as they waited for him to reveal more. For one moment it felt like old times to Cruen. He was all-powerful. Their leader. He captured their attention and respect, then used it to further his cause.

Perhaps he would have that again someday.

Feeyan didn't seem to possess it.

For now, though, he needed access, a valid reason, and a ride into the Rain Forest community.

His gaze connected only with Feeyan. "The Pureblood *veana* in *swell* happens to be my daughter." Through his emotional pain and physical exhaustion, he lifted his chin and smiled. "I will make sure she and the *paven* held captive are returned."

Petra dove under the water and swam downriver a few yards. The sun was sinking, staining the sky a beautiful ripe mango color. Sasha and Valentin had arrived at the cabin a little while ago for their evening shift. Confident almost to the point of cocky, they'd told Petra all was handled and she didn't need to return until morning.

For breakfast, they'd added with sneers in Synjon's direction. A dig that Syn completely ignored.

Right before she'd walked out the door, she'd pulled Sasha aside and warned him that arrogance was a dangerous mind-set to be in with someone as experienced and cunning as Synjon Wise. But Sasha had only reminded her that he and Val had already bested the cunning Brit, and on the *paven*'s home turf no less. Containing him would be far less complicated.

They were tying Syn up as she closed the door and headed for her parents' home.

A loud roar met her ears as she broke the surface of the water. Shifting from bear to male on the bank, Brodan gave her a grin, then dove in beside her. They'd seen each other naked for years. It was just part of the shifter way. But there was something different about it now, and Petra wasn't sure why. Without making a big deal about it, she floated back a few inches, keeping space between them.

"Where's blood boy?"

His hair wet, and his eyes flashing in the dying rays of the sun, Brodan looked incredibly handsome.

"Back at the house."

"You tie him up?"

She shook her head. "Sasha and Val took care of it."

Brodan's sharp eyes narrowed. "I hate that you need him."

"Me too," she said, though the words weren't as quick to leave her tongue as they should've been. "But it won't be much longer."

He splashed water on his face. "It should've been me."

His words stilled her. "What do you mean?"

"I should've been the one to help you."

"Brodan—"

"I know. I know. I get the biological connection." He took a deep breath and blew it out. "I just wish . . . shit . . ."

"What?"

His eyes came up and locked on hers. "I just wish it could've been me."

Her insides tightened. It wasn't a surprise to hear, and in fact she'd thought the same thing a million times over the past few months. Brodan would be an incredible father. Loyal and loving. Fun and generous with his time and attention.

"Hey," he said, dropping his chin, giving her a soft look.

"What?"

"I didn't say that to make you feel uncomfortable."

"I know. And I'm not." She gave him a small smile. "You'll be an incredible father. And mate."

"To some lucky shifter female?" he said with a grin. "Is that where you're going, Pets? Because if you are, I'm not sure I'm ready to hear it."

She shook her head. "No, that's not where I was going."

His brows lifted. "Interesting." His eyes warmed. "So, have you decided what you're going to do after the baby is born? Where you want to be? And with whom?" His eyes roamed her face. "What would be best for the cub?"

"Vampire," came a male voice behind her.

Petra gasped, her gaze flying to the bank, her hands flying to her chest as she scrambled to cover herself. *What the hell?*

Backlit by the intense white moonlight was Synjon Wise. "Not cub," he said. His arms were crossed over his chest, his broad, heavily muscled chest.

"Syn—," she breathed.

"You remember my name, love," he remarked dryly. "Even as you float around naked with the doctor here. Well, I suppose that's something."

"How did you . . . ?" She glanced past him to the house in the distance. Panic bubbled within her. "Where are they? Sasha and Val? What did you do to them?"

He shrugged. "I told you, as I told them, that I'm expecting guests this evening."

Brodan, who had been farther away from the shore, was hauling ass out of the water, nearly in midshift.

"No!" Petra called out to him. "Brodan, wait."

The male paused and looked back at her, gave her a quick growl.

She shook her head at him. "No. Please. I don't want anyone hurt."

Synjon nodded, his tone and manner utterly controlled, as emotionless as always. "She's a wise one, Dr. Feelgood. The blood of a bear has always intrigued me."

Tearing his gaze from Petra, Brodan inched closer, growling with menace.

"Syn," Petra said warningly. "My brothers."

"Are fine. Just a bit tied up at the moment." He shrugged at the easy joke, then pulled in a breath. "They really are decent blokes. Protective of their family. I respect that. But the jokes, love, and all that male braying. Gets tedious."

They weren't hurt. Only tied up. Relief spilled through Petra and she sank an inch farther under the water. It wasn't as though she was surprised. Somehow she'd known he would find a way out of his captivity. Somehow she'd known that even with that moment they'd had that afternoon, his hand to her belly, feeling the movement of the *balas* beneath his palm—even though she'd swear she saw a hint of emotion, connection, in his eyes—he wasn't tied to her . . . to their *balas*. Not even by the thinnest of strings.

She looked up, found his gaze, and held it tightly. "So, what is this? Your visit to the river's edge? You came to say good-bye?"

He didn't answer. And for a split second he looked confused.

"Or to interrupt two people enjoying a swim?" Petra

pushed, wishing he weren't so close and she wasn't so hungry.

His brows lifted and he said with a streak of arrogance, "I interrupted something, did I?"

"Yes," Brodan ground out, his eyes flashing with irritation, as he stood in the shallow end of the river halfway between Syn and Petra.

"Planning your future?" Syn added, his eyes locked on Petra.

She shrugged, "Maybe," the tops of her breasts surfacing at the water's edge.

An action that didn't go unnoticed by either male.

"With the good doctor here," Syn continued. "Home every night for dinner. And you serving up a lovely raw steak." He lowered his voice. "While you're secretly dying to drink his blood."

"No secret required, Pets," Brodan said, though his gaze remained on Synjon. "My blood is yours. Always has been. And the cub's."

"Vampire!" Syn snapped. He glared at Brodan, his fangs descending.

Brodan froze and so did Petra. Only the sound of the river slapping against the rocks could be heard. Within a few seconds, Synjon's fangs retracted, along with any expression of anger.

It was almost as though it had never happened.

Almost.

"What the hell was that?" Petra said, shivers moving up her back and into her neck. Shivers that had nothing to do with the cooling night air.

"What?" Synjon found her gaze again, the mask of emotionless male back in place.

"Your emotions . . ."

He stepped back. "I have no emotions."

She shook her head, her mouth dry. "I saw—"

"You saw nothing."

"I don't understand, Syn—"

"Enjoy your swim," he interrupted. "And a healthy fuck, if you're so inclined."

And with one last look in Petra's direction, he flashed from the riverbank.

Petra wasted no time in pulling her shaky body out of the river, yanking her clothes on, saying a hasty good-bye to Brodan, and rushing back to the cabin. She had to see it for herself. See that her brothers were safe and unharmed. Synjon's word meant so little to her now. He had no reason to keep her family in good health.

Especially if the ones in question had attacked him twice already.

She jogged up the steps, dashed into the silent house, and ran down the hall. "Sash? Val?" she called, searching the hidey-holes of each bedroom. Finally, inside the small closet in the main bedroom, she found them. Both Sasha and Val were just as Syn had claimed: fine, tied up, with a bit of their pride squashed.

Petra made quick work of the gags and rope. But when they were free, both sat unmoving inside the closet.

"I'm so sorry, Pets," Sasha said mournfully.

"Stop."

Val grimaced. "We totally failed you."

"No, you didn't." She gave Val a pat on the back. "He's a trained spy, in the military . . ."

"But we took him down in his apartment," Valentin said, shaking his head.

"By surprise," Sasha amended. "We've been fools. Arrogant asses. Didn't prepare. Not in any real way. Wise was right when he called us the pussy brothers."

"Hey," Val said.

Sasha tossed him a look.

Val shrugged. "Yeah, all right."

Petra heard the door to the cabin burst open, and seconds later Dani entered the dark bedroom. "I was doing a moonlight flyby and saw that bastard by the river with you and Brodan."

"You're too late," Petra said.

"No, she's not." Valentin eyed Sasha as he pushed to his feet, then offered his hand to his brother. "We're going to fix this. We're going back to his apartment, taking him again."

"Hell, yes," Sasha agreed, slapping Valentin's palm and jumping up. "And this time, we're keeping him in the clinic, sedated. You can feed from him like that. Coma Vamp."

"Yeah, drugs in Pet's blood would be real great for the cub, idiots," Dani said with a snort.

"Oh, right," Sasha said, walking out of the closet. "Then we'll knock him out the old-fashioned way."

"One, two, three!" Val added. "Four, five, six!"

The brothers chuckled as they started for the door.

"He's not at his apartment," Dani called after them.

"What do you mean?" Petra began, turning her attention to the hawk female. "How would you— Oh, gods, Dani, you didn't fly into Manhattan. It's broad daylight there. You could've been shot at."

Dani put her hands up. "Ease up, bestie. Didn't go to New York, though I'm really starting to dig that place. It's all dressed up for the holiday they celebrate. The one with fir trees and snow and reindeer."

"Dani," Petra said tightly. "Synjon?"

Her gaze locked on Petra and softened a hair. "I didn't leave the Rain Forest, and neither has the vampire."

The words sank in, but their meaning didn't. Petra didn't understand. Syn was still here? Had he lost his ability to flash? No, that wasn't possible. She'd seen him flash from the river.

"You know where he is, Dani?" Sasha asked her.

The hawk shifter turned to the brother and shrugged. "Where he was headed."

"And you didn't dive-bomb the bastard, scoop him up in your talons?"

Dani's gaze returned to Petra. There was no typical bluster or hard-ass hawk attitude glistening in her eyes now. Only the solid intimacy of a best friend. "Tell me what you want. Personally I'd like to forget he exists, but I'll do whatever you want me to do."

What she wanted. Shit, that was a big and constantly changing question. Maybe it would be better if she could just forget he existed too. But that wasn't practical, was it? The effects of his blood were pure magic. She and the *balas* still needed him, so for now there was only one answer.

"We're going," Val said before she could open her mouth.

"No." Petra pointed at them and said in her most resolute, most authoritative voice. "You're not. This is my business, my blood to go after. I'll handle it."

His face tensing with unease, Sasha was first to object. "Pets—"

"There's a reason he hasn't left." She moved past them all and out the bedroom door. "I need to find out what it is."

8

"Unbelievable," Nicholas Roman growled, stalking forward.

Alexander was right beside him. "What the hell is he doing here?"

Though feeling weaker and more emotionally lost than ever after such a jarring flash, Cruen stood his ground outside the gathering stones as the Roman brothers and two of the *mutore* came to stand before him. Nostrils flared, hands balled into fists, the four glanced back and forth between him and Dillon, who stood beside him.

"Mommy made me bring him," Dillon grumbled, then amended her statement with a shrug. "He told Feeyan about his connection to Petra."

Nicholas glared at Cruen, his lips forming a sneer. "So now you want to claim her? After all these years?"

All I wish to claim is that British bastard who glued his emotions to my insides. All I want is my power back. Perhaps even my chair on the Order. But to the Roman brother he said smoothly, "I have a right to know where my

Pureblood daughter is. If she's being held here against her will."

Alexander chuckled bitterly. "The old *paven*'s getting sentimental. How sweet."

"So sweet I might lose a fang, right into his carotid," Helo added blackly.

"Where is Petra?" Cruen asked, ignoring the males. "Where is my daughter?"

"*My* daughter." The female lion shifter who'd raised Petra from near infancy left the gathering stones and headed his way. "She's my daughter, Cruen. She wants to remain here, in her home, her homeland, around her family."

As the shifter closed in on him, Cruen recalled the day he'd brought his and Celestine's infant here. In his time spent gathering blood samples in the Rain Forest, he'd witnessed all manner of selflessness. Each faction helped the others, looked out for the others. It had actually started to irritate him. Such goodness was tiresome. But when Petra was born, when he'd taken her from Cellie, he'd known the perfect place to keep her safe while keeping his connection to more blood samples open.

Wen's eyes were fierce as she stared him down. "You don't belong here, vampire."

"Perhaps Petra doesn't either," he said. "Perhaps it's time for her to learn about her own kind."

"She'll make that decision, not you."

Cruen nodded. Yes, he'd chosen well with this female. Protective, but in a quiet way. He'd heard of her desire for a daughter, and her failure to produce one. She'd been so grateful.

"Don't you have some Frankenstein monster to create back in your lab?" Helo asked him.

Cruen's gaze shifted, ran over the water beast, who had once called him father. "I think I made enough monsters for one century."

Helo's expression darkened.

"Now I come directly from the table of the Order," Cruen said in the calmest of voices. "Unless you want Feeyan here in my stead, I suggest we get on with this."

Both Roman brothers turned to Dillon with an incredulous look.

"Gahhhh, I can't believe I'm saying this," Dillon rattled with a sigh, "but he's right."

The guard behind Cruen leaned in and spoke directly into his ear. "Shall I go with you or wait outside the stones, sir?"

"Wait outside."

"Very good. Sir."

Was he imagining things, or did he detect a thread of disrespect in the guard's tone? Cruen mused as he walked past the Romans, the *mutore*, and Wen, and into the circle of stones. The male had been with him for only a few months, and had always acted completely servile. Perhaps, with the circumstances being what they were, with his power nearly gone, he himself was projecting that feeling of insolence.

"Let's get started," Dillon said, following him.

"Shouldn't we wait for Petra?" Cruen suggested, sitting down opposite the rest of the group. "And the *paven* she holds hostage?"

"No one's being held hostage," Alexander said through gritted teeth.

"So you all keep saying."

"You know exactly why Syn's here, Cruen," Lucian snarled, his body ready to spring. "I'm surprised you can't feel it, seeing as how you sucked down all his emotions a few days ago."

Cruen fought the urge to drop his fangs and hiss. Existing in a weakened state was acute misery, but being reminded of the act by Lucian Breeding Male Roman was a complete and total embarrassment.

This could not continue a second longer.

"Cease this game," he said with forced authority. "Where are they?"

"Petra's not coming," Wen informed him.

"Syn either," Alex added.

Cruen's blood began to heat. He tried to stop it, knew it would steal his energy, and what little power remained inside him, but he couldn't. He whirled on Dillon, fangs bared. "I suggest, Order Member Nine, that you take control of this situation. Unless you want the destruction of this lovely shifter world and every heartbeat in it on your conscience."

Home.

New York City.

Wraparound balcony with a view of the park.

That's where he'd wanted to go, where he'd aimed his flash. Where he should be. But something inside him had refused the call. Instead, he'd ended up in the last place on earth he'd ever expected to be again.

He bent and stepped inside the cave. It was dark, only the spent light of the moon illuminating the first five feet or so. As he moved inside, scented the familiar dank odor of the walls, he remembered the day he'd been saved. He should've died. Gone with Juliet into the sun. Instead, he'd not only been rescued against his will, but had gone on to create life.

He felt no emotion with this memory. Not even a twinge at the thought of Juliet, her death, his grief. And yet, not long ago, standing beside the river, watching Petra and the bear shifter float naked below the water as they discussed the future of the *balas*, he'd felt something.

He'd gotten angry.

Or was it possessive?

He didn't know. Without past emotions to guide him, he couldn't decipher what was what. But he did know, did understand, that with that small, poignant surge came a reason to worry.

How was it possible? He'd had every emotion bled from him. He'd made sure of it. Bloody hell, after the Romans had held him down, made it clear what was about to happen, he'd made sure it all left his body, went inside that mad vamp prat, and stuck like flypaper.

Forever.

Or at least until it strangled the energy and sanity from him, then led him straight to Synjon for help.

He pushed away from the wet rock wall. He had to go. Now. No matter how his body seemed to wish him to remain, there was only destruction here. And truly, the only one who was meant to be destroyed in all of this was Cruen.

"You goddamn British bastard."

He whirled around, and instantly his skin tightened and his insides flared with heat. How the hell hadn't he sensed her? Scented her? What the bloody hell was going wrong inside him?

Standing directly in the mouth of the cave, backlit by the moon, Petra looked gorgeous and appetizing as she glared at him. "Here. Of all places. Seriously?"

Yes, he'd said the same things to himself. "It's not where I had intended to be."

"And where is that? On the balcony of your penthouse or pressing some idiotic female up against the piano?"

His mind went rogue and conjured that image, but it wasn't some foolish chit whose hips he fisted as he moved behind her. In fact, in his mind it never was. "Your feathered friend tell you about that?"

Petra moved into the cave. "Either that or you're just so grossly predictable."

He glanced past her.

"Yes, I'm alone."

Syn couldn't help but find that strange. After all that had happened, past and present, wasn't she worried about her safety around him? Even with her shocking strength, she was no match for him in the dark. And where was her little army? The pussy brothers and the hawk? Following her every movement, fighting to bring back her blood meal.

"Why did you come here?" he asked. "Why would you think to come here?"

"Don't go there in your head. This was anything but sentimental. You were spotted. By my feathered friend, no less." She crossed her arms over her chest. "The question is, why are *you* here? *Still* here. And at the site of the first of many mistakes on my part."

"If you mean to force another emotion out of me, that's not the way to do it."

Her eyes widened. She dropped her arms and moved toward him. "So you admit it. You felt something back at the river?"

He didn't answer.

Which, in truth, was probably an answer in and of itself.

"But how is that possible?" she said, coming to stand before him, her belly nearly brushing the waistband of his jeans. "I saw Cruen take all of your emotions. Did he leave something behind?"

Impossible. Fuck, it had better be impossible. He knew what he was doing, had been meticulous in his actions on the floor of that dungeon. He'd made sure every thread of emotion was gone from his mind and superglued elsewhere. He held her gaze. "What happened by the river was nothing. A moment's irritation for your bear shifter."

She shook her head. "I don't think so."

"Perhaps you don't want it to be so. Perhaps you're looking for something that isn't there, will never be there."

Her face contorted into a mask of disbelief and then after a moment she broke out laughing. "Oh, Syn. What do you think I want? What do you think I'm looking for? For you to care about me?" She placed her hand on her belly. "About us? Fall in love with us? Be bonded to us?"

Her words sank deep into his gut, and they seemed to want to remain there. "That would be the logical desire for a female in *swell*, yes."

Her laughter died, and the light he'd always seen

glowing within her incredible pale blue eyes went out. There was nothing but emptiness. Not unlike his own, he imagined.

It bothered him.

In fact, he had an irresistible urge to take her in his arms, kiss her, tease her—anything to bring that light back. It didn't have to be happiness or curiosity. Anger and hatred would do just as well.

"Do you really think I'd be stupid enough to hope for such a thing?" she said after a moment. "Believe that you're a worthy male, emotions intact or not?" She stepped forward, got in his face, the curve of her belly now pressed against him. Her eyes locked with his. Dispassionate to detached. "I think there's something happening inside you. Some kind of reaction to the baby."

The cool night air rushed into the cave, moved over Syn's naked chest. He wanted to deny it, her suggestion, but even as he attempted to summon the words, his hands itched to reach out and touch her swollen belly.

"What are you feeling right now?" she whispered.

His eyes met hers. "Nothing."

"Liar."

He couldn't stop himself. The urge was the greatest he'd ever felt. Yes. *Felt.* In seconds, before he could say a word or defend himself, his hands were on either side of her stomach. For a few long seconds, he held her, felt the firmness of the world that surrounded the growing life inside her. Was that how he'd begun? How she'd begun? It was bloody amazing to—

His fingers froze, his body too, and his skin started to heat up again. His mouth going dry with shock, his gaze dropped as under his hands he felt movement, a stirring. Then, almost in slow motion, he felt something small and hard press into his left palm. Petra must've felt it too, as she groaned and shifted her position.

Inside him, his chest, his lungs, air seemed to hold, then expand, making him feel as though he couldn't catch his breath. His mind warned him this was dangerous, warned him to pull away and never touch this female again. But he couldn't. He just bloody well couldn't. His hands, fingers, skin, muscles . . . they all refused to move. It was as if his body was beyond his mind's control.

He looked up, caught her staring at him.

"I feel," he uttered.

Her nostrils flared. "Should I say I'm sorry?"

He slowly shook his head. "No."

"Then what should I say, Synjon?"

"Bloody hell, *veana*." He grabbed her, gathered her in his arms, and kissed her hard on the mouth.

For one moment, she seemed to struggle internally, about pushing him away or giving in to what they couldn't seem to deny themselves. But before they took their next breath, the latter won. Her arms went around his neck and she kissed him back, followed him as he changed the angle, moaned with him when he parted her lips and stroked her tongue with his own.

His hands raked up her back and plunged into her hair. It felt like silk. Yes. He could feel it. Just as he could feel the warm, wet heat of her mouth, and the smooth skin of her neck, the curve of her belly, and the slight back-and-forth movement of her hips as she simulated what her body wanted from his.

Could he touch her here? Have her here? On the cold, wet floor of this cave?

Fuck. *This* cave.

His hand swept around her side and palmed her breast through her tank and bra. He groaned with the feeling. She was so heavy, so warm, her nipple rising against his palm, begging to be touched, gently twisted, insistently suckled.

She whimpered, pressed herself closer into his hand. "Oh, yes. Gods, that feels good."

The cave filled with a new scent. Her scent. And he wanted to lap at the walls, taste her arousal in every drop of condensation.

He ripped his mouth from hers and dipped down into the curve of her neck. He suckled her vein, then kissed her hard and hungry. There were so many places on her body he wished to drink from. If she would allow it, he'd start from the bottom and work his way up.

Just to make the point that he wanted what pressed so eagerly against him, his hand left her breast and journeyed down to cup her sex.

He nearly lost his mind.

Hot, wet, and pulsing.

In one swift and impulsive move, he lowered his head and suckled her breast through the fabric of her tank, while slipping his hand inside the waistband of her jeans. He found her smooth pussy drenched in arousal and eased two fingers inside her.

She cried out. Froze for a full five seconds. Then, like a female possessed, started bucking against his hand. Back and forth her hips swayed as she moaned and groaned, as the walls of her sex squeezed around his fingers and released more blazing-hot cream.

What was he doing? What the bloody fuck was he doing? His cock was so rock hard inside his jeans, he thought it might burst. But he refused to release it, give in to what it craved. He couldn't take that from her again. Not now. Not yet. Here, in this cave, with the moon bathing her in its light, Synjon had only one thought, one goal. He wanted Petra to feel, release. He wanted her to come. Against his palm, his fingers. Against him. He wanted it like he wanted his next blood meal. As if he wouldn't survive without it.

This wasn't emotion.

This was pure physical desire.

As he teased and nipped at her breast with his teeth, he found her swollen clit and circled the bud with his thumb. She was so hot, her breathing so labored as she writhed and whimpered against him.

"Come for me, love," he uttered against her soaking-wet tank. "I can't wait to feel your tight, hot pussy shake and quiver around my fingers."

She moaned.

"I remember how it felt around my cock."

It happened in an instant. Total disconnect. It was as if the moon had extinguished her light and a cold wind blew through the cave. Neither was true, but the sudden gasp from Petra's throat, and the way she jerked out of his hold and backed up a few feet, made it feel true.

Stunned, Synjon stared at her, his fingers wet, his dick hard and pulsing as the moon illuminated her dark hair, making it seem as if she wore a halo.

"What's wrong?" he asked, breathing hard. "Did I hurt you?"

She shook her head. "I won't be that. Not that female."

"What female? What are you talking about?" He was so physically amped up, he thought his head would explode. He needed blood.

He needed her.

"One of those many emotionless nothings you screw and send home."

Oh, bloody hell.

"I refuse to be that."

You're not, love. You could never be.

The words played hide-and-seek on his tongue. If he said them out loud he was admitting not only to her but to himself that he had an emotional bond, however slight, to her and the *balas*. And he couldn't afford that connection. Perhaps after he took care of Cruen. After the male paid for his innumerable sins. Maybe then. If she could forgive him . . . But right now, if he felt even the slightest bit of connection to them, they could become a bargaining chip. They could sway his choices, change his reactions.

He couldn't allow that.

He might not have his emotions anymore, but he had his memories. All that time mourning the loss of his female, thinking her dead, when in truth Cruen had taken her, caged her, called her the Breeding Female and forced her to feel pain and sexual misery until Lucian Roman could be brought in to service her.

Then holding her in his arms, watching the light leave her eyes as Cruen killed her a second time.

No. Nothing. Not even this female and her child could break his resolve for vengeance.

Petra stood several feet away, her arms wrapped around her chest, trembling. "I deserve a male who loves me, wants me for more than just a shag."

His eyes found hers in the near darkness. "The doctor. The bear shifter."

She nodded. "I hope so. I think that would be best. He's always been there, offered himself. He wants to be our family. Me and the cub."

A cold stillness crept over Syn, and he couldn't stop himself. "No."

"You don't get to say no," she said, her voice tight and small. "You don't get to have an opinion about me and this child at all."

Despite the implacable resolve he'd had a moment ago, he felt it again. Scratching inside him. So small, barely noticeable. But it was there. His connection to the *balas*. "You need my blood."

"I'll survive. Just as I have been. It won't be long now."

"I can't allow it."

"You don't have a choice."

"The *balas* will be fed by me."

Her lip curled and her fangs dropped. "Do you hear yourself?"

"Yes," he said with unmasked domination. "Unfortunately I do."

Phane stood beside Helo, Nicky, and Lucian as Dillon and Alex continued their efforts to persuade Petra's mother to see reason. Well, the Order's reason. Clearly his *mutore* sister was hating her job right about now, wishing she was anywhere else. Having to do the Order's dirty work *and* having Cruen along for the ride sucked serious ass.

He turned to look at the ancient *paven*. For the most part Cruen had remained pretty quiet throughout the discussion. Like he was waiting for something. Phane couldn't help but wonder about the male he used to call father—what did Cruen want now? What was he working on? What schemes, what manipulation?

After being held and tortured in Erion's dungeon by Syn, getting his ass kicked out of Hell, losing his place on the Order, one would think—and hope—that the mad vamp had learned his lesson about playing with the lives of others. But Phane knew him well enough to believe that no doubt the only thing he'd learned was how to deceive better, cheat better, manipulate better.

"The Order is adamant about seeing Synjon," Dillon said, her tone clearly displaying her frustration.

"We can't take him away from Petra and the baby," Wen said in an equally irritated voice.

"It's only for a moment," Alex added calmly. "Then they will return him."

Wen looked first at Alex, then at Dillon. "You can't guarantee that. You said so yourself."

Showing her irritation and frustration at the situation she had no choice but to facilitate, Dillon released a weighty breath. "I understand how you're feeling. Wanting to protect your child." Dillon's eyes flickered in Cruen's direction, then returned to Wen. "But you will have a war here. They're not kidding or bluffing about that."

Wen shrugged. "If that's the price of keeping Petra and the child safe and satiated, then so be it." She looked down, thoughtful for a moment. "I'll just have to go and see the faction leaders."

Another voice, a truly unwelcome voice, entered the conversation. "Let me speak with Synjon and Petra."

It was Cruen. He straightened against the boulder at his back and continued, "Perhaps the Order might forgo their battle plans if I assure them that both Pure-bloods are here of their own free will." His gaze rested on Wen, and he said in the gentlest of voices, "Where are they?"

The female shifter's jaw twitched. No matter what had happened in the past, how Petra had come to be her daughter, it was crystal clear that the lion shifter felt nothing but hatred for the male now. In fact, Phane was pretty sure that if she had the chance, the female might challenge Cruen to a fistfight. Or a fang/canine fight. Phane grinned as that image flashed through his mind. Petra's lion of a mother seemed pretty damn tough.

"No one is seeing Synjon Wise," Wen said with complete and total rigidity. "You can tell your Order that."

Gone was the gentleness. Cruen's upper lip trembled into a sneer. "So he *is* here against his will."

"No one said that."

"No one had to. Who took him?" He leaned forward and hissed. "Who guards him?"

Before Wen could answer, the sound of a large and pissed-off bird rent the air. Phane glanced up, as did the others. Coming in for a glorious moonlit landing was his sexy hawk shifter female. She carried two males on her back. And Phane's own hawk scratched at his insides in warning until he realized they were Petra's brothers.

Both males leaped off her back the minute she touched down and came running toward them. Phane watched, waited, for the hawk to shift into her glorious female form, but she didn't. Instead, she stretched her wings and tossed her head, while remaining grounded.

"We screwed up," Sasha said breathlessly, not noticing their newest guest. "Wise got away, and Petra went after him."

Everyone within the gathering rocks turned to stare at him. The Roman brothers came to their feet.

"Are you kidding me?" Alex growled. "How did that happen?"

"Oh, shit, this is bad," Dillon muttered.

"Do you know where?" Lucian asked, eyes narrowed.

"Dani does," Val said, running a hand through his blond hair. "The caves, I think. But Petra didn't want anyone following her."

"Well, she can forget that request," Lucian said.

"Your daughter is very stubborn, Wen," Nicholas remarked dryly.

"Tell me something I don't know," she answered with a worried look at her sons. "You should've followed her anyway."

"Dani took her," Val said. "It was impossible to track her movement at night."

"So they're still in the Rain Forest," Helo said. "That's something."

"She shouldn't be running after anyone," Wen said

miserably. "She's pregnant. Oh, my baby, my cub. I'm going to find her." She started toward Dani, then glanced over her shoulder. "Who's coming with me?"

Alex and Nicholas were at her side in seconds.

"We'll follow on foot," Sasha said, then quickly shifted into his lion form, as did Val.

"We could use another Avian," Dillon said as they reached Dani, who was waiting impatiently, fluttering her feathers. She gestured to Phane. "Take me, Helo, and Lucian?"

The hawk shifter instantly turned her sharp gaze on him.

Striding forward, Phane gave the female a quick wink, then stripped out of his clothes and shifted into his hawk.

As all three of his passengers climbed onto his back, Phane ventured a glance in the direction of the female shifter. Intrigued, she was checking him out, her bird eyes moving over him, from feather to head to beak, then finally to his eyes.

He cocked his head at her, letting her know he was ready to follow her lead. She narrowed her eyes at him, then gave a glorious screech, and with wings spread, kicked off into the starry sky.

Yes, she would belong to him someday, Phane thought, taking off after her, reveling in her strength, her soar, and her steely beauty.

Below, on the ground, no one had noticed that the gathering rocks were now silent and empty and Cruen was gone.

9

She'd allowed him to touch her.

No.

She'd practically begged him to touch her.

As she stood in the mouth of the cave, staring at Synjon, trying not to follow the path of moonlight that washed over his naked chest and the hard waves of abdominal muscle, she realized that no matter what she told herself about him, what she knew to be true about him, she would never stop wanting him.

It was her curse. One she would take with her into any subsequent relationships. She just prayed that when her baby was born, the hunger she had for his blood would subside. Maybe with that need gone, there was a chance for love and desire with another.

With Brodan.

She looked up then, locked eyes with the male who tormented her in so many ways. She couldn't allow it. Couldn't let him stand there after he'd touched her, called out for her climax, then declared that her *balas* would have only his blood. It wasn't fair. Or right.

"Try again," she said.

His brows drew together. "What?"

"To flash home." She swallowed thickly. "Try again to flash home."

His jaw tightened and he raised his chin. "You don't mean that."

"I do."

"My blood . . ."

"I want it," she said, tasting it even now as she spoke. "But the price is too high."

He moved toward her, long, hard, muscular limbs, ripped stomach muscles bunching, flexing. Again she swallowed.

"You don't worry about the child now?" he said.

"I'm starting to think it might be more dangerous for the child if you stay."

He came to stand before her. "For the child or for you?"

The scent of him snaked into her nostrils. It was a poison aphrodisiac. It made her knees go rubbery and her mouth water. She licked her lips in the hope that even a drop of his blood still remained.

His voice dropped low, his eyes bored deep into her. "Hungry, love?"

Petra felt her fangs descend. With just those words, she fell into a dangerous haze. Her brain felt slow and fuzzy and refused the information it knew as truth—as a warning. She inched toward him, toward his neck. His scent beckoned her. *Come. Bite. Drink.*

Maybe just a mouthful? Something to ease the pain of a dry throat?

Suddenly Synjon's head came up, and his gaze darted past her. "What is that?" he said warily.

"What? I didn't hear anything." She shook her head, tried to clear it.

Synjon stalked past her, was out of the cave in seconds.

Still reeling, her belly growling with hunger, Petra followed him, followed his gaze to the sky. Oh, yes, *that* sound. Before she even saw it, she knew. She knew what was coming.

"Hawks." The word came out on a growl of irritation.

"Your friend," he said dryly, "is becoming a pain in my arse."

Petra fought the urge to agree. She had to pull herself together, get her mind back to the reality of what was before her and beside her. "She's not alone. That's two sets of wings on the wind."

Syn turned to look at her. "The cavalry has been called. To rescue the princess from the evil pirate."

She hated the words even before they came out of her mouth. "If you want to leave here, you'd better do it now."

He laughed softly, confidently. "I'm not worried about them. I'm untouchable when I want to be."

"Yeah. I know." *I remember*.

He shook his head at her, then reached out and grabbed her hand.

She snatched it back. "Go, Syn. Now."

"Bloody hell."

Above them the sky was filled with feathers and flight, but Synjon hardly noticed, or hardly cared. He reached out again, but this time he grabbed Petra around the waist. Within the blink of a hawk's eye, he had her flush against him, and they were gone in a flash.

The birds would've been quicker.

But Cruen knew that even if they found Synjon and Petra, the two of them weren't going anywhere but back to their hideout. And that was exactly where Cruen was going to wait for them.

"You sure you know where we're going?" he asked his guard as they trudged through the forest.

The male nodded. "I received the information from a reliable source."

"Let's hope so, or you'll both be feeling my wrath."

"Do you need assistance, sir?" the guard asked him, concern darkening his gaze. "You look . . ."

"I look what?" Cruen ground out.

"Nothing, sir."

Although the male didn't know Cruen's history, or about his decline in magical power over the past several years, or how Synjon Wise had tricked him, trapped him inside a mental and physical nightmare, he did know about Cruen's inability to shift. He had been told that the problem stemmed from Cruen's DNA, the experiments he'd conducted on himself in service of the Eternal Breed.

It was all the explanation a hired hand needed.

When Cruen's powers returned, he would no doubt have to dispose of the male. He couldn't risk having anything about this side trip leaked, to either his staff or the Order. But for now, he mused as they broke through the trees onto flat land, he needed all the help he could get in order to contain Synjon Wise.

"How much farther?" he rasped.

The guard moved solidly beside him. "Just across the plain and to the river."

One moment Petra felt the cool darkness of night and the next she slammed down on a hard surface, dawn breaking all around her.

In the span of a breath, she was pulled out of the dawn's light and through an open door into a dark, sprawling penthouse.

The effect was utterly jarring, and she reached out to grab the one beside her to steady herself.

"It's all right, love," Synjon said, holding her close.

Panic ripped into her as she realized where she was, whom she was with, and what he'd just done.

She pushed away from him, her eyes narrowing, her fangs dropping. "How could you?"

"How could I?" He stood there in his opulent living room, wearing only the faded jeans he'd come into the Rain Forest with, his expression completely at ease. "Did you not do the very same thing to me?"

"For the *balas*," she nearly shouted at him. "For your blood, for the *balas*."

"This is also for the *balas*."

"Bullshit."

His brow lifted and his voice dropped. "Please don't curse."

"You're kidding me, right?" This wasn't happening. She was not going to be kept here against her will. She headed for the open glass door, went out onto the balcony and stood directly in the rising sun. The cold air chilled her to the bone, so completely unlike the Rain Forest that she instantly started to shake.

"Take me home," she said through chattering teeth. "Now."

Remaining in the shadows, Syn crossed his arms over his chest. "Come back in here before you freeze."

"Everything I have is there!"

"Not everything."

"My family, my friends, a male who cares about me."

"And what about what you need?"

She shook her head, hissed at him.

"What you need is here, and you know it. Inside my veins. Red. Sweet. Hot."

Around her, the wind picked up, sending her hair one way, then the other. His words made her mouth fill with saliva and her fangs dropped farther. She hated her vampire self in that moment because it made her weak. To his words, to his offer, to the imagery he had just plastered on the canvas of her mind. Maybe even to the thread of possibility that had been lying dormant inside her since the night in her tree house.

The night they'd made the *balas*.

"You don't want to go," he called out, his eyes locking with hers. "Look at you."

"Don't tell me what I want," she said, weakly now, her tongue running over the surface of her lower lip.

"You're hungry, Petra."

"I'm always hungry."

"So stay and feed from me."

She shook her head, her chest tight with emotion—

something she'd been relatively free of for the past twenty-four hours. "Why are you doing this?"

He seemed to struggle with the question. Even more so with a response. Finally he just shrugged. "Instinctual reaction. My *balas* is inside you and my instincts call for me to take care of it."

"How clever—and convenient." She wrapped her arms around herself, rubbed her exposed skin. "And when did this new and exciting reaction kick in?"

"Come inside," he said.

"When, Synjon?"

"When I fed you, and perhaps even when the *balas* moved under my hand. All right, love? There it is."

She stilled. Even in the cold air, her entire body stilled.

He tossed his hands up and turned away, calling out, "Yes. I admit it. A connection was forged." He turned in a small circle, faced her again, his body still in shadow. "Not emotional. That is an impossibility. But instinctual."

Her teeth started chattering again. "You sound like a shifter."

"Well, perhaps we all have animal in us."

"I won't be your prisoner."

"Then be my guest."

This was madness. That she was even standing here, having a conversation about staying with him in his penthouse in the sky. If he wouldn't take her back in a flash, she should walk straight past him to the door. Leave. Leave him again.

He moved to the very edge of the darkness. "Please come inside, Petra."

She wasn't sure, couldn't swear to it, but there might have been a brief glimmer of apprehension within his gaze. As if he'd heard her thoughts, her plans. But was the apprehension for the *balas* alone?

Snow began to fall the moment she left the terrace. She walked back through the glass doors, closed them behind herself, then moved into the shadows with Syn.

Instantly, he threw something black and warm and soft around her shoulders. She wanted to melt into it. Into him. And she despised herself for all of it, for being so weak.

"Stay," he said, his voice soft near her ear. "Stay until the *balas* is born."

"This is insane," she whispered as much to herself as to him.

"I will give you my vein whenever you need it."

"So obliging."

"No. I just realize my duty now."

Why was she doing this? Standing here, listening to him? "Maybe it's too late."

"Don't sacrifice the *balas*'s well-being for unnecessary pride."

She whirled on him, nostrils flared. "Don't do that."

He had the audacity to look confused. "What?"

"Go the manipulative route with me. I've been caring for this child since its conception."

With a slow release of breath, he sat down on the arm of a rich brown buttery-looking leather couch. "You're right. I apologize."

Still bristling, Petra stared at him. What the hell? An apology from Synjon Wise? Was the world coming to an end? Or did he truly have a change of heart? Had this connection he believed he had with the *balas* altered him somehow? And so much that he was willing to feed and keep her until it was born?

She didn't know what to think about that. What to believe. What to hope for. She had so much anger and resentment inside her for him, for what he'd done to her father in the dungeon of Erion's castle. Gods, what he still wanted to do to her father.

Her breath caught as, inside her womb, the *balas* moved, stretched, warned her that if she didn't give it what it required soon, things would return to normal.

And that normal had been pretty much a living hell.

She pulled the blanket closer around her, keeping out the chill and the strange notions of a male changed. But notions still managed to push through, their hopeful warmth poking at her to believe, to accept. "This would be only until the *balas* is born."

Syn nodded, his eyes flashing with momentary satisfaction. He'd won.

"After that, I'm going home."

He nodded again. "To the Rain Forest."

"Yes."

"To the bear shifter."

She sniffed with melancholy. "If he'll have me."

Synjon's gaze moved over her face. From lips to cheeks to eyes. "Oh, he'll have you, love. Who in their right mind could resist you?" Then he stood and gestured for her to follow him. "Come. I'll show you where you'll hang your hat."

10

Synjon knew as he led her through the penthouse that what he'd just proposed, what he'd just done by stealing her away and offering her his home and his blood, was practically begging for trouble.

The one and only goal he'd had was to bring Cruen here, and instead he'd brought the *paven*'s daughter.

Forget emotions. Clearly he was without intelligence as well.

When he reached the door of the spare bedroom, he stayed where he was and let her pass. "You should find everything you need here, except of course for clothing and personal things. But we'll get that tonight, yes?"

She stared at the large, modern bed in the center of the room, with its steel frame and pale gray linens, then turned to look at him. "We're going back to the Rain Forest?"

He didn't like the shimmer of eagerness, of hopefulness, in her blue eyes. "No. We can get it all here in Manhattan."

She shook her head. "No. I don't want you buying me anything."

"Oh, for fuck's sake, love," he replied, laughing at the absurdity, "I have more money than I could spend in a thousand lifetimes. Don't put a meaning on it that's not there. I took you from your closet—you'll need another."

"You're going to get me a closet, eh?"

"You know what I mean." His gaze moved over her. "We'll go shopping tonight."

That shimmer of hopefulness changed to a glint of wickedness. "I thought you had guests coming."

Guests.

Right.

He was expecting the usual suspects at midnight. And one special friend, if the *paven* had news to share. His gaze moved about the room. It looked so sparse. Cold, even. He hadn't noticed it before. Shite, he'd been in here only once or twice since he moved in. Would such a dim, modern room displease her? Make her uncomfortable? Make her miss the rustic warmth of her home in the Rain Forest?

He would have to fix that.

That, and other things.

"No guests tonight, I think," he said. "And what color do you fancy?"

She stared at him, looking as confused by his behavior as he was. "You mean, what's my favorite color?"

"Yes."

"Green. I like green."

"Good." He cleared his throat, nodded in the direction of the bed. "Call your family. They'll be worried."

Her eyes were as wide as plates and her lips were parted as if she couldn't figure out what to say. She glanced over her shoulder at the phone, then back at him. "I don't understand you."

Join the bloody club, veana. He didn't know what had gotten into him, what was spurring this sudden need to make her comfortable, make her feel at home. He just knew he couldn't fight it.

"Get some rest, Petra." He turned around to leave.

"So, what? You're not afraid I'll have them come and get me?" she called after him.

Synjon's lips twitched. Saying anything more about favorite colors—now that was a legitimate fear. But keeping Petra and the *balas* by his side? Not so much.

"Just let me know when you're hungry, love," he called before closing the door and heading for his study.

"Now they're both gone!"

After finding the caves empty, Phane and Dani had flown the party back to the lion shifter's land. While the Romans searched the river cabin, Phane, Helo, Dillon, and Wen returned to the family home.

"The bastard took her somewhere," Dani said, bursting through the front door. "I know it."

"Why would he do that?" Phane asked, following her. "He's only wanted to get away from her."

"I don't know." She charged into the first bedroom, nose lifted, eyes narrowed. "Who can explain asshole?"

Phane heard Helo chuckle from the room next door.

Once the house was searched, they all met up in the living area. Everyone except Wen. The older female had told them she was going to contact the faction leaders, let them know the situation. But Phane wondered if she truly just needed a moment alone. She'd looked stricken after leaving the caves.

Hands on her hips, Dani surveyed them all expectantly. "Well? What're we going to do? Where are we going to look first?"

"We should split up," Helo said. "Take different sections of the forest."

Once again, the door opened and both the Romans and Petra's brothers entered the house.

"Nothing at the river cabin," Nicholas said. "But Lucian stayed behind just in case they show up."

Dani nodded. "Good." She turned to Sasha and Val. "What about you two?"

"We're going to search on foot," Sasha said. "Ask every shifter we come across if they've seen either one of them."

"I'll take the sky," Dani said. She glanced at Phane. "I could use some help up there. You interested?"

Phane's hawk stirred. "Very interested."

"I need to buy time with the Order," Dillon said. "Cruen's disappeared. He wasn't in the caves with us. I lost track of him. That's not going to go over well. Especially if he's back, standing before Feeyan and telling her that two Purebloods are missing on shifter land."

"We'll help with ground cover," Alex said, "then flash into Manhattan when it gets dark. Check out the penthouse."

Dani smirked. "He wouldn't take her there. Not to his den of—"

"Wait!"

Wen came into the room. She looked disheveled, wide-eyed, but the fear in her expression had dimmed somewhat. "She's not here, not in the Rain Forest. She's with him. He took her—"

"Unfuckingbelievable!" Dani called out. She headed for the door. "I'm out of here. I'm going to kick some douchy vampire ass!"

"No, Dani," Wen said, going after her. "Stop. She doesn't want us to come."

With a low growl, Dani turned to face Petra's mother. "Wen, that's the douchy vampire talking, not Pets."

The older female shook her head. "I heard the truth in her voice. She's agreed to stay with him."

Dani shook her head. "No."

"I know my daughter."

Dani stared hard at the female. "Goddamn it." She turned away, then back. "Why? Why would she be so freaking stupid? He's a jerk. He's a whore. He's a—"

"He's got the blood," Phane said simply.

The female whirled on him, her eyes narrowed. She sidled up to him, her finger pointed in his face. The heat coming off of her was so damn intense, Phane nearly reached out to grab her. But Dillon's words stopped him.

"This changes everything, you know?" The jaguar shifter sighed as she headed for the door. "God, I hate this job."

"Yes," Dani called after her, turning away from Phane. "Go appease the vampire Order. But what about us? What about the shifters? One of ours has been taken now. From shifter land to bloodsucker territory.

Maybe we're the ones who'll have to infiltrate to get her back."

"She's not yours," Phane said, watching her, admiring the passion in her. Her ferocity, her loyalty, made his hawk scratch and stir. "She's not shifter."

"This is none of your business," she warned him. "My best friend is out there, pregnant and with a male who doesn't truly care for her. I don't know why she's agreeing to this—if it's really about blood or something far more problematic—but I'm sure as hell going to find out."

Petra woke feeling groggy, emotional, and hungry. She lay on top of the covers in the bed she had agreed to sleep in every night until the *balas* arrived.

She blinked and rolled to her other side. The room was dimly lit, but she could make out the dark gray walls, stark white molding, expensive leather chairs, antique dresser, and the door to her own private bath, well enough. She'd already been in the bathroom. Massive stone shower, white towels everywhere, and a whirlpool tub. It was like a fancy hotel. Not that she'd been in all that many fancy hotels during the months in New York, when she was looking for Cruen, but the one she had been in reminded her an awful lot of this one.

A wave of melancholy moved over her and she moaned against it, then took a deep breath into her lungs.

She didn't want that back. The intense, overwhelming wave of feeling. The pain. The tears she couldn't control no matter how hard she tried. She looked over at the closed door. Where was he? Her sexy prick of a blood donor. His bedroom? The living room? If she called to him, how fast would he be at her side?

She moaned again. Not from the emotional waves crashing through her this time, but from the foolishness of her thoughts. If she dared to attach romance or sensuality or connection to this agreement, she was basically inviting him to hurt her again. What she needed to keep in the forefront of her mind at all times was that he didn't want her in the way she deserved to be wanted.

It was as simple as that.

She sat up and swung her legs off the bed, wondered what time it was as she padded across the room and opened the door. There wasn't a clock in her room, and with all the shading to keep the sunlight out, not to mention the time difference, she was a bit turned around.

Silence greeted her as she headed down the hall and entered the living area. She couldn't help but look around at all the beautiful, yet starkly cold furnishings. Even with the warm light of three or four table lamps, the emotionless space felt dead. The walls, though painted a rich cocoa, were bare, except for one near the kitchen. On it were six gigantic slabs of pointed metal. *They look like fangs*, she thought.

She moved toward it, feeling both intrigued and intimidated by its audacity. *Why this piece?* she wondered, following it past the kitchen and down another hallway. When all the other walls lay bare, why such a blatant scream of ferocity? Looking closely, she saw that the final shard of metal was the color of caramel and longer than the others. She reached out to touch it, then hissed as her skin met the surface.

"Not what you'd expect, is it?" Synjon said, coming up behind her.

Instantly, her body reacted to his nearness: fangs down, skin going tight, breath hitching in her lungs. *Damn it.* This was not a good start to her plan for keeping herself detached.

"It's hot," she said, touching the metal again.

"Yes."

"I thought it'd be cold. Metal is supposed to be cold."

He chuckled softly. "It's a lesson in quick judgment. A cautionary moral."

"Don't judge a book by its cover?" she said.

"Exactly."

She turned around to face him, bracing herself for the heat of his stare, the strength of his presence. But he was no longer behind her. For a second, she wondered if he'd been there at all. Then he called out to her from another room, "Hungry, love?"

She followed his voice, past the hot caramel metal and down a dark hallway. Warm yellow light grew brighter and wider, and she seemed to step inside it, or through it, into a shockingly spacious bedroom suite.

Oh, gods, this was bad.

Petra desperately wanted to take in every inch, every color, fabric, chair, lamp, fireplace, and headboard, but her gaze refused to part with the six-foot-three-inch hard-bodied male who stood in the very center of it all.

Clearly he'd just come from the shower. His black

hair was wet and slicked back from his sharp-angled face, making his dark eyes and heavy mouth pop. A white towel was wrapped loosely around his hips, and a few remaining droplets of water glistened on his broad chest and ripped abdominals. It was probably the worst thing for a female trying to pretend she wasn't hungry for more than blood to see.

She swallowed the saliva that was pooling in her mouth. Pressed back on the tips of her fangs with her tongue as they started to descend.

His eyes flashed with heat. "Do I have time to throw on some clothes?"

"No." The word was out of her mouth before she could bite it back.

He grinned. Then brought his wrist to his mouth and bit down.

Just the action made her moan, made her knees soften, made her insides turn to liquid.

His eyes lifted to meet hers. "Apologies, love. Maybe you would've liked to bite."

In that moment, it was as if Petra were two beings: the emotionally injured female who wanted so desperately to be cared for and loved but knew she'd never find it here, and the hunter, the vampire, the starved *veana* in *swell* who wanted to drink the blood of this male until he begged her to stop.

"Lie down," she said, her tone almost foreign to her own ears.

Dark brows lifted over darker eyes.

"On the bed," she continued. "Back to the sheets."

Syn's nostrils flared. "Is this feeding time or something else?"

"This is why I'm here," she said, moving toward him, stalking him like prey. "The only reason I'm here."

When she stood before him, she took his wrist, cradled it in her hands. She brought it to her mouth and lapped at the blood. One slow stroke with her tongue across his skin. She heard his sharp intake of breath. Oh, gods, the taste was heavenly.

"And I must lie down why?" he asked in a guttural voice.

She looked up and grinned. "I don't want you to get dizzy."

"Dizzy?" He chuckled, low and sensually. "Crikey, *veana*. You underestimate my stamina if you think one feed from my wrist will render me heady."

Her grin widened. "I'm not just going to feed from your wrist."

His smile evaporated.

She pushed him back on the bed, upsetting his towel. He didn't seem to notice—his eyes were locked on her. But Petra noticed. Her gaze flickered to the heavy muscle between his legs. It was surrounded by dark hair, pulsing with thick veins and standing straight up like steel, only the head still covered by the white cotton. Her fangs dropped low and she crawled onto the bed after him. Blood dripped from his wrist and she wanted it.

Gods help her, she wanted everything he had on display.

In her mouth, inside her sex.

She shook her head, tried to think clearly through her fog of feral desire. But it was useless. Hunger ruled every part of her. Only feeding would satiate her now.

She knelt beside him, took his wrist once again and thrust her fangs deep into his vein. She heard him curse, then moan, then curse again. Blood rushed into her mouth, cascaded like the most delectable waterfall down her throat. She gripped him tightly, suckled his skin, pulled and gorged like he was her lifeline, and goddamn it, maybe he was. Maybe that was exactly what he was.

As the hot metallic liquid moved down her throat, catching every inch of her insides, heating them, cooling them, her outside tingled with arousal. She remembered when he'd drunk from her in the tree house. This was the same. The sensuality, the need to be close, the desire to feel him inside her as she thrust her fangs deep.

Was this how it was going to be every time she needed blood? Would she be able to curb this desire? Would she be able to remember who this male was? What he was? And gods, what he was not?

Feeling his vein close, Petra pulled her fangs out and lifted her head. She licked at his wound and watched it heal instantly. It never ceased to amaze her how the power of a Pureblood *veana* could heal a male.

She lifted her head, found him watching her. His eyes were nearly black, and his own fangs were resting sharply against his lower lip.

"Dizzy yet?" she asked him.

"Not from the blood loss, love," he uttered darkly.

Her hunger barely satiated, Petra dropped his wrist and leaned in close. She wanted his neck. She loved that vein. The blood from that vein was always the sweetest.

Before she struck, she caught his gaze. It was threaded with desire. But unemotional desire. Detached lust.

She hated it.

And yet her fangs and her belly and the *balas* all pushed her onward. They didn't need this male to have emotion or care. They just needed his blood.

"This won't last, *veana*," he whispered suddenly.

Her lips parted, fangs completely descended, she nodded. "I know. Until the *balas* is born—"

"No. That's not what I mean. I mean *I* won't last. Feeding you." A soft growl rumbled in his throat. "I need to feed too, or I'll be an empty husk of shite in a few days."

Petra shivered at his words. Not with repulsion or irritation or dread, but with awareness. As if her body were separate from her mind. As if it knew on a very basic level what it was meant to do with a male vampire who requested blood.

She'd felt the beginnings of it in the tree house so many months ago.

Now it was a driving force.

"I could take animal blood," he said. "But you're vampire. How does animal blood sound to you?"

She must've made a face because he laughed and said, "Yes. Exactly. I will need a female's blood, Petra."

Her entire lower half went tight and tingly. How was it that just his words, a suggestion, a request, could send her body up in flames? It was so dangerous, how ready and willing her body was to give this male what he wanted. What he required.

"Yes, Synjon," she said, her breasts tightening at the

very thought of his fangs inside her again. "After I take my fill, you can—"

He exploded. "Bloody hell! Never!" He jerked away from her, his eyes going completely black.

"What? You just said . . ."

"I'm not drinking from you."

It was ice water on a blazing fire, quick and painful. The heat inside her drained out, and she flashed him her fangs. "Something wrong with my blood, *paven*?"

He didn't answer.

"Are you kidding me with this?" she hissed. "I'm sitting here, offering myself—"

"There are females available for the task," he interrupted. "You wouldn't be right—"

She reached out and slapped him across the face. Hard. Then gasped at her action—her reaction. Stunned, shaking her head, nostrils flaring, she started to scramble off the bed.

"Oh, my gods," she muttered, embarrassed, sickened. "I'm so sorry."

"Goddamn it, Petra." In one easy movement, Syn picked her up and placed her on top of him, her legs straddling his hips.

She refused to look at him. She was such an idiot. She got her feet under her and tried to get away again, but he held her backside firmly in his hands.

"Listen to me, *veana*. I cannot feed from you."

Oh, my gods, this was torture. "I know, okay? You've already made that clear. So why are you keeping me here?" She struggled to get free again, but his grip was like steel. "I'm done."

"No, you're not. You want the vein in my neck, and bloody hell, I want you to take it."

For the first time since he'd placed her on top of him, Petra realized that she wasn't just straddling his hips—her sex was resting on his cock. His hard, nearly uncovered cock.

Heat surged into her lower half, and she squeezed the muscles in her pussy. She couldn't help herself. It was such a goddamn tease. She wanted him inside her. Deep. Like he'd been before. Like she remembered. All the way to her womb. Until she lost her breath.

"Take it, Petra," he commanded, his fingers gripping her tightly.

Her eyes found his and held.

"Drain me."

She bit her lip. "So you can go find that female to feed from?" she whispered. Christ, she sounded like a meek little mouse, not like a Pureblood vampire with razor-sharp fangs and impossible strength.

Synjon's eyes filled with heat, and he sat up quickly, catching her when she jerked backward. When they were face-to-face, he gripped her ass in his palms. "I cannot feed from you," he said through gritted teeth, "because it would take from the *balas*."

Her head tilted to one side as if she hadn't heard him correctly. "What?"

"I won't steal blood from the *balas*."

She stared at him. His eyes were so intelligent, hard, filled with passion, and she realized just what he was saying. And what it meant. He did truly care about her child. The idea equally worried and enchanted her, and before she knew what she was doing, she buried her hands in his hair, pulled his head back, and bit his neck. Hard.

"Fuck," he groaned, gripping her, his fingers pressing into her lower back.

Blood poured into Petra's mouth, and she drank greedily. Gods, if she could just have his cock inside her while she fed. If he could pump slowly in and out as the blood ran down her throat.

But she couldn't have that.

He cared about the *balas*, not about her.

His hands raked down her hips and cupped her ass, drawing a moan from her throat in between swallows. His cock pressed against the seam of her covered pussy, begging for access. And while she continued to drink, she ground herself against him until they were both breathing hard.

"Petra," he uttered in the sexiest voice she'd ever heard.

Her belly more than full, she eased her fangs out of his vein, then licked the wound until it closed. When she lifted her head and locked eyes with the *paven* who'd just fed her, she nearly gasped. It wasn't the Synjon she'd known in the past few days. This one with his curled lip and glowing eyes was still ultrasexual and sharp as a polished blade, but his expression also revealed vulnerability.

Vulnerability that he was attempting to mask.

But Petra could see it was there.

What did it mean? How was it possible? His emotions were gone. Vulnerability was the very root of emotion, wasn't it?

And then, as if the expression behind his eyes weren't

enough, he brought his hand between her legs and touched her. Lightly, gently, he ran his fingers up and down the seam of the jeans covering her pussy. She stared at him, knowing he felt just how hot and wet she was.

It was too much. The power he had, the desperation she felt. In that moment, with his hands on her body and his eyes claiming her soul, she knew she'd do whatever he asked of her. Anything. Anything to continue to feel this way.

She pushed away from him, scrambled off the bed, and ran out of the room. Her body was on fire, her breasts ached, and juices ran from her cunt like honey from a jar. She knew she was acting irrationally, but she had to get away from him before she melted into a puddle.

She hurried down the hallway, through the living area and into her bedroom. Breathing heavily, her cheeks flaming from his blood, she slammed the door behind her and went into the bathroom. Thank gods it had a lock. She leaned forward and cranked on the water in the shower, then dropped back against the door and slipped her hand into the waistband of her jeans.

She didn't know if he'd followed her. She didn't care. All that mattered in that moment was coming, and coming hard. She pushed past her underwear, wished she could rip it off, and found her wet slit.

"Ahhh," she whispered, turning her head so her cheek rested against the cool wood. "Gods, yes."

She sent her other hand too, and while one opened her lips wide, the other circled her swollen clit. What she wouldn't give for Syn's long, rock-hard cock inside her right now.

Just the thought had her moaning, juices running down her thighs. She stopped the circle movement and started working the ridge of her clit, up and down until her mind went blank.

She heard something on the other side of the door. A knock or a scratch. She couldn't tell. She didn't care.

"Getting wet, Petra?"

His voice. That sexy growl carried, even over the on-slaught of the shower water hitting the tiles.

"I scent you," he called. "Through the wood. Fuck, I followed you down the bloody hall like a dog in heat."

She pulled herself wider, flicked her clit so lightly she groaned with irritation at herself. What was she doing? Prolonging it? Drawing it out as he talked her through her climax?

"I would've gladly taken care of that problem, love. All you had to do was ask."

Panting, she pressed down on her clit.

"Are your eyes closed, *veana*?"

Moaning, she slipped the fingers that were holding her sex open deep into her pussy.

"Do you see me on my knees before you?" he called. "Do you see my fangs descend? Do you see them bracket your swollen clit as I lick you? My strokes so quick, you lose your breath . . ."

Light flashed on the backs of Petra's eyelids and she cried out.

"Do you see my tongue sliding all the way down the ridge of your clit? Do you feel it thrusting up inside your cunt, fucking your drenched pussy until you come? All the way down my dry throat."

Impaled on her fingers, her thumb pressing hard on her clit, Petra screamed. She didn't mean to. But the feeling, the shock to her system, the words, his voice, it all sent her rocketing out of her body and into the heavens. Convulsing, moaning, she pressed back against the door and just let the waves of climax roll over her.

11

Standing on the other side of the door, his hand wrapped around his cock, Synjon stroked himself in time to the breathy moans of Petra coming down from climax.

It wasn't what he wanted, how and where he wanted it, but hearing her, scenting her—verbally fucking her—had made him absolutely mad with desire.

He wanted.

Her.

In a way he didn't understand.

Couldn't quantify.

Fuck, what was happening to him? he wondered as he let his head fall forward against the wood, his hand moving quicker now. Getting off was a purely physical act. No connection, no intense desire for anything more than a body to move against. And yet . . .

He groaned, feeling the early shocks of climax.

"I hear you," Petra called through the door.

His dick swelled just from her voice.

"I scent you too," she said.

"Good," he muttered. She should know. She should know how physically insane she was making him.

"It makes me hungry."

Come leaked from the head of his cock. "For blood?" he asked through a throaty groan.

"No."

"Oh, bloody hell, woman . . ." His strokes quickened.

"For you," she fairly whispered. "In my mouth."

That was all it took. Just that simple yet erotic admission for his body to shake and his dick to explode. He cursed and sucked in air as he stroked the come from his cock.

With the last few groans of release, he rubbed his forehead on the door. Back and forth. What were they doing? And what the hell had he allowed inside his home—the very place he was supposed to be welcoming a captive?

"Syn . . ."

Her voice was breathy and pained. Hunger raged within him, and he knew that if she opened the door he was going to pounce, thrust his fangs into her throat like he wanted to thrust his cock into her sex. Even now, the urge to knock down the wood that stood between them and take what his body felt belonged to it was dangerously strong.

He needed to get away from her for a while. Return to being the nonemotional bastard who cared about one thing and one thing only.

Vengeance.

"I'll be back when it's dark," he told her, pushing away from the door.

"Maybe I should go shopping alone," she said. "Or another night. Maybe you need to find blood—"

He cut her off. Couldn't hear anymore. Not about blood. Not right now.

"Just be ready, love," he said, then left the room and closed the door behind him.

The Order was not gathered at their long table in the reality of sand when Dillon found them. Instead, all nine were in a remote mountain *credenti* in Colorado. Teaching and preaching, Dillon called it. It was something the Order of old liked to do to keep track of the Pures and Impures inside the *credenti* walls. Some *credenti*s really dug the visits, especially if they were Impure heavy. Sebastian, the Impure *credenti* member with the movie-star looks who'd been chosen after all three of Gray's Impure Resistance buddies refused the position, was an interesting guy. He had a great backstory and worked well as a go-between with the Order, and Dillon was pretty sure Feeyan and the rest of them liked him a whole helluva lot better than they liked her.

And with what she was about to reveal, that moderate amount of dislike was about to get upgraded to full-blown loathing.

Seated in a large chair between two massive pine trees, Feeyan turned away from the ten or so *credenti* members and their discussion on cold-weather agriculture and looked up expectantly at Dillon.

"So," she began imperiously, "do you have our Purebloods or is a war between the vampires and the shifters imminent?"

The *veana* was ridiculously dramatic sometimes. "I don't have them."

Feeyan's brows lifted. "So a war then?"

"No. No war." Dillon sighed. "They're no longer in the Rain Forest."

The leader of the Order looked surprised. Clearly, she hadn't expected this development at all. She leaned back in her chair, which was a little too much like a throne for Dillon's taste. "Where are they?"

"New York City."

"Why should I believe you?"

"What?" Dillon stepped back.

"Let's not pretend you don't have friends and family involved here." Her white eyes narrowed. "It wouldn't be beyond your scope to lie to me to protect them."

"Oh, brother," Dillon muttered. She really hated this job.

"Bring them before me," Feeyan commanded.

"Are you kidding me?"

"Do I look like a *veana* who uses humor to convey her wishes?"

Dillon had to bite her tongue against saying what the *veana* did look like to her. And it rhymed with "witch"! "I'll try, okay, but they're free Purebloods living outside the Rain Forest. If they don't want to come I can't make them."

"Oh, dear me. Why can't you be more like Sebastian?" Feeyan said, turning her gaze from Dillon and eyeing the handsome Impure male, who was speaking to a group of Impures near a large campground. "Why do I have to pull everything from you? Remind you what you are now? What you signed on for? It's annoying."

Dillon's lip curled. *You want to talk annoying, lady?*

"Just find a way and bring them," Feeyan said. "Now, if there's nothing else . . ."

Dillon didn't move. She wanted to. More than anything. But she was bound by their stupid Order code, and she had to report the newest problem in the shifter world.

"Cruen's still there," she said. "Somewhere. In the Rain Forest. He took off, and we can't find him."

That bit of news brought the white-haired *veana*'s attention right back. "We?"

"The Romans, the shifters, the *mutore*. You know, the whole lot. We all looked for him."

Feeyan didn't say anything for a moment. She seemed to be thinking, processing. Maybe even wondering how important Cruen's life was to her. Finally she released a heavy breath and said, "Twelve hours. Tell your band of fools to find him or I will be going to the Rain Forest myself."

F.U.C.K.

"You know, it's funny, Order Member Nine," Feeyan said evenly. "I would say that Cruen's more committed to preserving the lives of vampires than you will ever be. But we know why that is, don't we?"

Burn, Feeyan, Dillon thought with a mental eye roll. "Look, I know you wish you could have the great and powerful bastard of the Eternal Breed back on the Order, but you're stuck with me." *And I'm stuck with you.* Dillon gave Feeyan a big old grin. "I suggest you get used to it."

She flashed from the pine forest before Feeyan even had a chance to respond.

* * *

When Syn had come to her room to pick her up for their evening shopping trip, Petra hadn't had a clue what to expect. Cab ride to a few places. Maybe a walk to the nearest department store. The last thing in the world she envisioned was a freshly showered, smartly dressed male at her door and a limousine waiting downstairs at the curb.

Still dressed in her wrinkled Rain Forest clothes, Petra sat in the back of the black stretch limo and glared at the male across from her. He was sitting casually on the black leather, legs bent and spread, like he owned the world.

"Really?" she said.

He raised one dark eyebrow. It was a good look for him. "What?"

She pointed to herself. "Look at me." Then she pointed to him. "Now look at you."

He did, then shrugged his powerful shoulders. Again, a really good look for him.

"I don't see the problem," he said.

You're gorgeous. That's the problem, Bub.

Utterly and completely and ridiculously gorgeous.

Again, she pointed to herself. "I'm in a grungy old outfit and you look like a freaking Calvin Klein model."

His lip curled. "Calvin Klein? Really. That's almost as insulting as Abercrombie and Fitch."

"Who?"

"Exactly."

She rolled her eyes.

He chuckled. "Come on now, love. I understand

you're feeling uncomfortable in your clothing. We're about to remedy that."

As if to emphasize the point, the car came to a stop before a series of storefronts. When the door opened, Synjon got out, then offered her his hand.

"Come along, darling."

She took his hand, let him help her out of the limo, but once they were on the sidewalk, she eased her fingers from his grasp and said, "Don't call me that."

"What? 'Darling'?" He gave her a blank stare. "I'm British."

"That's no excuse."

He chuckled, pointed to where they were headed. As they walked, he leaned over and whispered in her ear. "After the day we've had, lovely Petra, our nearly dual climaxes separated by only a thin slab of wood, my referring to you as 'darling' shouldn't seem all that strange."

She continued to walk, but her eyes had gone wide and her face hot. She'd really been hoping they weren't going to talk about the bathroom incident, that maybe they'd even pretend it hadn't happened. After all, nothing had been said about it since.

Clearly, she wasn't that lucky.

"Where are we?" she asked as he held the door of a very beautiful store open for her.

"Rosie Pope," he said. "She's going to take care of you."

"Make me look a little less like something that crawled out from under a rock?"

"You need to stop."

"Fine. Something that would be acceptable standing next to Synjon Wise, International Male Model."

"That does it." He took her shoulders and turned her to face him. "You, my dear, are the most exquisite creature on this godforsaken planet. I drool every time I look at you. My cock is stiff as we speak. And yet, unfortunately for me, I've made a vow to keep my twitching hands off of you." He grinned. "For tonight."

Petra just stared at him, her mouth open. She was pretty sure everyone in the very beautiful store had heard him. Stiff cocks to twitching hands. She just wanted to burrow into the floor.

"Good evening, Mr. Wise."

Perfect.

Syn greeted the pretty saleswoman with a polite but cool nod. "Take care of her. Give her whatever she needs and fancies."

The woman fairly beamed. "Of course, Mr. Wise."

"I'll be back in, say, an hour and a half?"

Petra turned to him. "You're going?"

"I have something to take care of." His voice suddenly took on a rough, sexy timbre. "You don't want a male hanging around here helping you pick out knickers and the like, do you?"

Petra heard a few feminine giggles behind her. "Well, not a male who says 'knickers' with a straight face."

His mouth twitched. "Cheers, love."

Along with every other set of female eyes in the place, Petra's watched him walk out the door and head for the limousine. She wondered where he was going. If he was going to meet someone. A female someone.

Oh, gods.

There was no end to her ridiculousness. She needed some clothes. That was it. End of story.

"What shall we start with, Mrs. Wise? Undergarments? Casual day wear?" The saleswoman grinned. "Or should we go straight to the fun stuff? Evening gowns?"

Petra was going to correct the woman. Tell her she wasn't a Mrs. Anything, but before she could utter a word, three women came forward with three of the most beautiful dresses she'd ever seen.

She sighed at the wondrous sight. "I'm thinking we start with the fun stuff."

12

"**D**o we have a new plan, sir?"

Cruen didn't answer, didn't even acknowledge the guard beside him as they moved through the forest by way of the river. His strength was waning, and he had to fight to keep hold of his mental state. It had taken all his reserves to keep himself hidden from the Romans, particularly Lucian Roman, as they searched the river cabin.

But one thing was certain, confirmed by the brothers as they worked out their next move. Synjon had taken Petra from the Rain Forest and brought her home to Manhattan.

Back to New York City.

Cruen felt the frustration all the way inside his bones. This had been a pointless, fruitless trip. A waste of everything. And now the *paven* was on his home turf. Cruen knew he didn't have the strength to deal with Synjon there. Not with just the one guard. And the more vampire flesh he brought into this problem, the higher the body count would be later.

But what choice did he have? The Order would be of no help to him now. He must flash home, gather his small army, and attack. If he didn't, he wasn't going to survive. Not in body or in mind. He could feel it. And he had to survive. For his work, his never-ending goal of bringing about the ultimate vampire. He had been so close. The power of the Devil, Abbadon, within his grasp. Now the male was dead by his daughter's hand, and Cruen had been stripped of the mediocre amount of magic he'd had left.

No. He had no choice but to take on Synjon Wise anywhere he could get to him.

He heard a splash to his left, and then something darted out in front of him. His reaction time was slow, but his guard had already rounded the creature and had a blade to the young male's neck in under a second.

Pale brown hair was pulled back in a tie, and dark green eyes found and held Cruen's. The young male didn't appear frightened by what he saw. On the contrary. He seemed quite eager.

"What do you want, shifter?" Cruen asked. "Why do you jump upon us as though you wish to attack?"

"I can't believe it's you," the male rasped, his tone high and excited. "I thought I recognized you when you traveled the river earlier."

A small thread of unease moved through Cruen's already tired body.

The young male grinned. "Don't you remember me?"

Cruen inspected the male. "No. What is this? What game do you play?"

"You took samples from my mother a long time

ago." The male waited for that to sink in, then continued. "I helped you, remember? I was very young. No more than three. You gave me a small dagger to play with."

"Water shifter," Cruen uttered, his mind darting backward, all the way to the first set of shifter samples he'd taken.

"That's right," said the young male happily. "What are you doing here?"

Cruen motioned for his guard to drop the blade and step back. "Looking for one of my kind."

The male nodded sagely. "The vampire male. Petra's."

"You know about that?"

The male shrugged. "Everyone knows. But they've left."

"Yes," Cruen ground out. Clearly, it was time to go. There was no reason to remain here. Not to hike around aimlessly, or catch up on the past.

"But you don't have to," the male said as if hearing his thoughts. He stepped forward. "My family, my faction, would love to see you."

"Would they?" Cruen said with disinterest.

The male nodded. "My faction is also interested in science. In fact"—he lowered his voice—"we believe we may have found a way to slow aging."

"Interesting," Cruen said without much enthusiasm. "But unless you've developed something that infuses the body with power, magic, or strength, I'm afraid I'm going to have to take a rain check."

Cruen motioned the guard to leave. The male had claimed he couldn't flash inside the shifters' forest, so they needed to return to the gathering stones. He started to walk away, but the young male called after him.

"We have something! Something like what you describe!"

Cruen stopped, turned around, his skin suddenly prickling with keen curiosity. "Go on."

"It's very new, and has a short shelf life, so to speak. But it has intense power." The male lifted his dark brows. "Interested now?"

"I believe I am," Cruen said. "Take me to see your family, shifter. A reunion is definitely in order."

Synjon stepped out of the limousine, glanced around, and righted his cuffs.

The plans he'd made had taken only an hour, and though he didn't want to barrel in and interrupt the party, he had this unstoppable need to see Petra.

No. That wasn't right.

What he had was an unstoppable urge to know she and the *balas* were all right. He blamed it on instinct. Protecting his young and all that. Instinct was the best excuse he could come up with lately for the way he was acting, reacting. The alternative was simply inconceivable. Something about emotional attachment, falling in love, seeing a future.

The door made a quiet trilling sound as it opened. He hadn't noticed that before. He moved inside the store, looking for life. Looking for her. When he found neither, he felt a sudden punch of concern compress his gut. What would he do if she'd been taken somehow? If her brothers or the Romans had come, to return her and the *balas* to the Rain Forest?

He moved deeper into the shop, heading toward the back, and was about to shout Petra's name when he saw her emerge from a dressing room. Someone followed her, but Syn took absolutely no notice of the other being. His breath had left his body, and inside his chest something squeezed. Something he'd thought would never stir again.

Standing in the center of a veritable swimming pool of tissue-paper-lined bags was Petra. Her long, thick, straight dark hair framed her exquisite face, but it was her eyes that made his chest constrict once again. Lined with a thin smudge of coal, her ice-blue orbs popped with color and life, and when she looked up and caught him staring at her, she smiled.

Instinct, you ruddy bastard, he warned himself. *Nothing more. Can't be anything more. You don't have it to give. You already gave it away to her father on that cold stone floor.*

"You like?" she said, her voice uneven, as if she were a little nervous.

His gaze traveled the length of her. The dress she had on was nearly the same color as her eyes and hugged every inch of her extraordinary body, including her *swell*. She looked like a fucking princess. He'd never seen anything so beautiful, or so sexy, in his life.

"You're a stunner, love," he said, walking toward her.

Her smile widened. "Well, thank you."

He'd spent an hour on their evening plans, and yet all he wanted to do now was take her home and remove that dress. Slowly. Kissing every inch of skin that was revealed to his hungry gaze.

"They said I needed to wear a cocktail dress for to-night?" She narrowed her eyes at him, but in a playful, sensual way that make his cock twitch.

Yes. Home, bed, naked, kisses, sounds good. And in that order, if you please.

"They even had shoes brought over from Barneys," she continued. "What's going on, Mr. Wise?"

Synjon first turned to the saleswoman, thanked her for her help, then addressed his driver, who had followed him in. "Take care of the bill, then put the bags in the car, please, Tom."

"Very good, sir."

Petra also thanked the saleswoman, who made a beeline for the register, and then she continued her quest for information. "Come on now," she urged, meeting Syn halfway. "Tell me what you're up to."

"I suppose one could call it a gesture of goodwill."

"And what would you call it?"

A date.

He took her hand, laced his fingers through hers. "You look fucking incredible," he said, his eyes locking with hers. "Breathtaking."

Her cheeks went pink at his compliment, but her expression grew uneasy. "Syn . . . I don't know if this—"

"Come on," he said before she had a chance to continue thinking. "I have a surprise for you."

For most of her life, Petra had existed on flora and fauna, animals and sunsets, fresh, moist air and the entertainment of nights around a roaring fire, filled with laughter and tales of shifters gone long ago.

Tonight was a revelation.

A first.

And as she sat next to Synjon once again in the back of the limousine, she silently prayed it wouldn't be her last. She loved her life in the forest, never wanted to give it up completely, but this—tonight . . . She was blown away. She was addicted. She had to have more.

"You're quiet," Syn remarked. "Everything all right?"

All right? She grinned and shook her head. "I've never seen anything like it."

"There's no dancing in the Rain Forest?" he asked.

She turned to look at him. "Not this kind. Not costumes and leaps and women dancing on their toes to the most beautiful music in the world."

Clearly pleased with her assessment, Syn smiled. "I'm glad you enjoyed it."

"I didn't enjoy it, Mr. Wise." She was pretty sure her eyes were two limpid pools of dreamy female. "I'm transformed."

He laughed. "Then we must do it again." He reached down and removed her shoes.

"What are you doing?" she asked.

"Ease back on the seat, love." He brought her feet to his lap and began to rub the soles. "Just a little massage."

She sighed at the instant relief she felt and let her head fall to the side against the leather before she uttered a breathy "Why?"

"I heard that females in *swell* appreciate it."

"Who did you hear that from?"

He glanced up, though his fingers continued to work the bottoms of her feet. "Alexander."

She smiled. "Well, I guess he would know." It was so

odd to think that both she and her half sister were pregnant at the same time. And yet they hadn't spent a moment alone together. She wondered if that would change anytime soon.

"If you enjoyed the ballet"—he raked his hand up her calf, massaging deep into her muscle, making her feel so good she wanted to groan—"there's so much more I can show you, introduce you to. There's the opera, Broadway. I believe Eels is playing at Webster Hall, and Swedish House Mafia's over at Barclays. There's also comedy, a few irritating Christmas shows I'd force myself to watch if it pleased you, and if you appreciate art, I know a Pureblood *veana* and her twin brother who have a show opening this Friday in Brooklyn."

Between the massage and all the suggestions of what they could do together in the coming nights on the island of Manhattan, Petra felt her rational brain slipping away. "I've never been to an art gallery."

His hand slid behind her knee, then slowly worked its way back down. Her sex clenched, wishing he would move that hand up between her legs instead.

"You'd like their work, I think. Whimsical but dark. Fairy tales gone wrong."

She stared at him in the glow from the red taillights of cars up ahead and internally swooned. He was so gorgeous. Dark hair and eyes, heavy lips and sharp cheekbones, all wrapped up in a perfectly cut charcoal gray suit.

"I was thinking about buying a few pieces for the house. I have all those empty walls. I could use an opinion."

"Syn."

He looked over at her, his dark brows lowered over those magnetic, impossible-to-read eyes.

She wanted to stay in the bubble of tonight. The clothes, the compliments, the tutus, and how his hand had reached out and taken hers when the lights in the theater dimmed, then hadn't released it until they went back on again. After all, she'd spent months, as she searched for her father, fantasizing about just this kind of attention from this exact person.

But it was all just that. Wasn't it?

A fantasy?

"I don't understand," she said, her tone gentle as she eased her feet and legs from his grasp. "This—you and me—it was supposed to be all about blood and the *balas*."

"Are you saying you're not enjoying it?"

"I *am* enjoying it. That's kind of the problem."

His expression was utterly impassive as he said, "I don't see a problem if you're enjoying it."

"That's because these experiences, dates and . . . et cetera . . . well, they don't mean anything to you." The words felt like jagged glass in her mouth. "Except maybe as a precursor to sex."

His jaw tightened.

She sighed. "Look, I don't want to argue or make things uncomfortable, because frankly I've come to terms with the fact that I'm staying here, with you— that the baby needs you. But I'm concerned."

"About?"

Yes, Petra. About? Can you say it? Actually get the words out without your head exploding from embarrassment?

He was staring at her expectantly.

"Okay. Here's what." She put a hand to her belly. "We've already established that there's a bond that's been formed between you and Little Fangs here. I don't think it's a good idea to form one between you and me."

His expression remained impervious. "Because of the bear shifter?"

"No." She shook her head. "Because you have no feelings for me besides physical ones. That might've been okay in the past. A fun night and nothing more. But I'm about to become a mother. I'm trying to build a family."

"With the bear shifter."

"Jeez. Does it matter?"

He didn't answer. Instead, he reached down and retrieved her shoes, then slowly, sensually, placed them back on her feet like she was freaking Cinderella.

"Petra?"

She shivered at the sound of his voice. "Yes?"

His gaze lifted, dark eyes under dark, imposing brows. "You're not going to name the *balas* Little Fangs, are you?" he asked as they pulled up in front of his building. "It's bloody awful."

13

The bear shifter.
  Syn stood on the terrace in the bitter cold and
tried to reason with himself. As the wind smacked him
in the face, he tried not to think about Petra, about the
night they'd just shared, about Little Fangs, and about
how right now she was probably in her room removing
the goddamn dress he'd fantasized about removing
himself.

The bear shifter.

She'd been in a real bloody hurry to get away from
him after that speech in the car. He turned and leaned
back against the stone balustrade. Seconds after entering the apartment, she'd thanked him for a lovely evening and for the clothing, then left him standing like a
complete knobhead in the hall.

The fucking bear shifter.

He was only interested in the *balas*? How could she
think that after tonight? Was she truly going to make
him say it out loud? Admit that something deep and
disturbingly wonderful was happening between them?

He stared through the glass doors and into the apartment. The apartment he'd purchased for only one reason. What the bloody hell was he doing? Out on the terrace pining for the daughter of his enemy? He should be preparing for Cruen, his arrival and his slow progression into pain-filled madness. Here . . . where Petra and the *balas* were staying . . .

Ahhhh . . . *Bollocks!* His mind swam. He was so ruddy conflicted. It had all been so clear before he'd given Petra his blood. With every lick, every suck, every pint, he grew more and more weak with regard to the true goal of his existence.

He couldn't let that happen.

Not even for the *balas*.

The buzzer at the front door drew his attention.

Who the hell could that be at this hour? he wondered, heading inside and across the living area. Better not be the Romans, come to talk him out of keeping Petra here. Of course, those three *paven*s wouldn't be bothering with the door—a flash to the terrace was more their style.

"That's right!" came the loudest female voice Syn had ever heard. "Time to party!"

Standing outside in the hallway, some of them still exiting the elevator, were twenty or so of his most dedicated revelers from the past week. His gaze moved over them, males and females, all sharp and sexy and ready to take down another case of whatever he'd purchased for tonight.

Problem was, he hadn't purchased a bloody thing. Not for them, at any rate. In fact, he'd completely forgotten they existed.

He leaned against the doorjamb and shook his head. "Not tonight."

A male who Synjon knew had just come directly from his Broadway show moved to the front of the group. "Not tonight? I thought it was every night, man."

"Just for a few hours." The woman beside him whined in an irritating baby voice. "I came all the way in from Queens."

Synjon stared at the lot of them. Were these the same gits who had practically taken up residence in his apartment every night this week? How had he not noticed how bloody awful they were?

Another woman, dressed in some kind of leopard print costume, glanced past Syn. "Well, look here. Someone gets to party with you. Who is she?"

Something moved inside Syn at that moment. Clearly, Petra stood behind him, and he didn't want anyone's eyes on her. Especially not those of the males in the crowd. He crossed his arms over his chest and stood directly in the doorway. "Good night."

The male snorted. "He's having a private party, y'all. Let's blow."

"Not at all," Petra called out. "I'm only a friend. Come in. Please."

Syn turned to look at her. "What?"

Which in turn freed up a good amount of space for the group to push their way into his entry hall.

Letting the fools move past him, Syn just stared at Petra, who was wearing a set of black loungewear. Her breasts were pushed up, and she looked sexy as hell.

"What did you just do?" he asked her.

She shrugged. "You don't need to curb the partying for me."

"Wasn't for you, love," he lied.

"Fine. For the *balas*, then."

"Perhaps I just don't feel like dealing with company tonight."

Her eyes raked his body. "Doesn't sound like you."

No, it didn't.

The elevator opened again behind him and more people poured into the penthouse.

"Listen," she said, "one of these very lovely one-night stands could be your blood donor. Have you thought of that?"

"No." In fact, the thought repelled him.

"Well, you should." She gave him a very tight-lipped smile before turning and walking away.

"Where are you going?" he called after her.

"To my room."

He wanted to go with her. Or take her to his room. They could lock the door and remain lost there for days. If he could just get rid of these tossers.

Someone turned on his stereo, and music blared from the speakers. He heard the pop of champagne corks. Female voices called to him. But he didn't even spare the lively living room a glance. It was as though that world, that existence, didn't include him anymore. He followed Petra. Caught up with her just outside her bedroom.

Before he could say a word, she turned and leaned against the doorframe. She looked so beautiful. Long dark hair, lush pink lips. And how the fuck was he ever going to get over those eyes? The color and the sharpness and the heat.

"Just because I'm staying here," she said softly, "doesn't mean you should stop your life."

"Why? Because once you leave, you won't be stopping yours? Is that what you're saying, Petra?"

She released a breath and stepped inside her room. "Good night, Syn."

"This isn't my life," he said just as she closed the door in his face.

Fucking bear shifter.

He turned back and headed down the hall again, completely uninterested in the thirsty crowd that awaited him.

Dillon had never been so thankful to have her *mutore* brothers near. Helo and Phane bracketed her as she sat at the dining table in Wen's home and faced the heads of each shifter faction. The ones who governed, counseled, and had divided up the Rain Forest lands long ago to accommodate each species of shifter. The Order's words—no, Feeyan's commands—lay heavily on her mind, and she was still pretty clueless as to how to keep the vampire world out of this one.

She'd sent the Romans and Dani to take care of Syn and Petra, see if the pair would agree to a simple "hi and bye" before the other nine. She prayed they would. It would be one less thing for her to deal with.

"Why would your Order want a war with us?" said the Avian leader, a small, aged female with bark brown eyes and a pouf of gray hair on top of her head. "We've done nothing."

"There was a mix-up," Dillon explained. "Two vampires were here, and it was believed they were being held against their will."

The leader of the Mountain Beasts, which claimed as its members anything from bear to gorilla to fox, leaned forward on the table. The male looked very young—Dillon would guess not even twenty—but his emerald green eyes held intelligence beyond their years. "You speak of Petra. And the father of her cub."

Dillon nodded.

"But they're gone now," said the leader of the Plains, his golden cat eyes bright against his deep chocolate skin.

"Yes, but there's another who remains." Dillon glanced around the table. "This vampire was once here a long time ago. He was granted samples of your DNA. I think he's still here. Maybe he's hiding among your people, trying to get more samples out of them." She rolled her eyes. "I wouldn't put it past him."

Both the Avian leader and the young Mountain leader looked over at Helo, then Phane, then back to Dillon. "You are all part shifter, aren't you?" the male said.

Helo was the first to speak. "Water. So, Mountain faction, I suppose."

Phane glanced at the Avian leader. "Hawk."

The leader of the Plains continued to stare at Dillon. "And you?"

"Jaguar," she said simply. "Listen, back in our world we're not prized, not respected. In fact, we're pretty much thought of as trash."

All three leaders recoiled in shock.

"Trash?" said the Avian female, her bird eyes narrowing.

"This vampire who remains here is responsible for creating us." Dillon took a deep breath. "He took your DNA and mixed it with vampire DNA. He's kind of a monster."

"Why would he do such a thing?" said the Plains leader.

"And why did we know nothing about it?" asked the Avian female. "We must go to our shifters and talk."

"Fine," Dillon said. "But first we need your help."

"What do you suggest?" asked the young Mountain leader male, his interest in her and her jaguar clearly visible in his amazing eyes.

"We need to find him and bring him back to our leaders." Dillon looked at each faction leader in turn. "Unharmed."

"But if all you are saying is true," said the Plains leader, "he should be exterminated."

Oh, Dillon sighed internally. *I really hated my job.* "Yes, he should," she agreed. "But if Cruen isn't returned alive, the Order will come." She took a deep breath. "And they'll bring war."

Damn right she was going to sleep through a party.

Petra finished brushing her teeth, then turned off the bathroom light and got into bed. She didn't pull up her covers right away, but instead began rubbing her belly in slow, gentle circles as outside her door the steady, almost rhythmic sounds of conversation were punctuated with the jarring shock of laughter and the heavy beat of a bass line. The baby was really active tonight, moving and pushing against certain internal organs. Petra grinned. Maybe this wasn't going to be as easy as she thought.

She was about to reach for the television remote, see what late-night programs were on, when the bass line ceased abruptly, and she heard the most beautiful sound rise above the din. She stilled, drew back against her pillow, and closed her eyes.

Someone was playing the piano out there, and whoever it was had some serious talent.

Petra took a deep breath and just focused on the music. As if the *balas* heard it too, the kicking inside her womb gentled, and a lovely calm moved over the entire room.

It had been a long time since she'd felt like this. Calm, steady breaths in and out of her lungs as she relaxed, without a worry about the *balas*, where she was going to get blood she could actually keep down, or her emotional state.

Granted, this feeling of complete peace couldn't last. But that didn't mean she wasn't going to enjoy it while it was here.

Though the music eased her body, it unfortunately couldn't eradicate all thoughts from her mind. She wondered if Syn had spotted something he liked out there, something that would satiate his hunger, some-*one* who could take the pinch of his fangs while granting him several pints of her blood.

A low growl broke from her throat, interrupting the Zen vibe she'd had going on in her bedroom. Shit, if he was drinking from someone right now, it shouldn't bother her. The idea of his fangs penetrating another female's skin? Shouldn't bother her. The image of her blood flowing down his throat, feeding him, sustaining him? Or the sounds, the almost sexual groans of satisfaction when he was finished? Shouldn't—

This time she groaned and rolled onto her side.

Goddamn it, no, it shouldn't bother her. After all, feeding would keep him healthy and stable for her and the baby. But . . . it did. It just did.

In that moment the piano music ended. Strangely and abruptly. Petra stilled, waiting for it to come back. What had happened? She missed the slow, emotional rhythms already. A scream jarred her and sent her gaze to the door. Was that a woman? Close by, loud chatter and the sounds of several pairs of shoes clicking across hardwood could be heard.

Without a thought, her mouth dry with concern, Petra got out of bed and grabbed her robe. She was just slipping her arm in the fuzzy sleeve, when the door burst open. The earsplitting sounds of about forty retreating partygoers spilled into the room, along with one very pissed-off female shifter.

"You have got to be shitting me."

Petra stared at her best friend. "Dani?"

"Glad you remember my name," she said, glancing around the room. "Thought the evil vampire douche bag might've erased your memory along with your rational thought."

"What are you doing here?" Petra asked, slipping her other arm into the remaining sleeve of her robe.

The hawk shifter walked into the bedroom and slammed the door. "Oh, you know, saving you from making mistake number freaking two, Pets."

14

Lucian tossed him a cue, lifting one pale blond eyebrow. "We do this over pool, Brit Boy."

Synjon caught the stick easily, then rounded the table, which was positioned on the far side of his living area. "Do what exactly, Frosty?"

Lucian's eyes widened. "What the fuck did you just call me?"

Synjon grabbed the chalk and said nothing. He was thinking about Petra, and all that was being discussed in that spare bedroom. He didn't like leaving her alone with the hawk shifter. That female hated him. With good reason, but still . . .

"Frosty?" Lucian repeated. He turned to Nicholas and Alexander, who were standing around the large billiard table with sticks of their own, waiting their turn. "Hey, boys. Did Brit Boy here just insult me?"

Nicholas grinned. "Don't get emotional, Luca."

"Please," Alex agreed. "That would be embarrassing for all of us."

Leaning over, Syn adjusted the shaft of his cue stick,

aimed, and with an audible crack knocked the cue ball into the stripes and solids.

"You're changing," Lucian said, leaning over directly across from him, setting up his shot while inspecting Syn. "How?"

Syn's eyes flipped up. "There's no change. I'm an emotionless bastard. My desires and plans are the same as they always were." *Just waiting for Cruen to come to me, beg me to put him out of his misery.* Except maybe that wasn't his first thought anymore. His gaze shifted toward the spare bedroom. They were taking forever.

"You want Cruen," Lucian said, then sent his cue into the ball, dropping a solid in the right side pocket. "We want Cruen."

"What?" Syn glanced at the other two *paven*s. "What are you talking about?"

"That stupid piece-of-shit *paven*," Alexander said. "As usual, he's made a mess of things. This time in the shifter community."

"He's still there?" Syn said before leaning down and sending a striped ball into the far left corner pocket.

"Still?" Nicholas said, his sharp eyes locking with Syn's. "How did you know he was there at all?"

Bloody brilliant, Mr. Wise. Get your head out of your arse and think before you speak. "Petra made a phone call home, remember? Now. Is he being hunted or made a guest?"

Though his gaze remained curious, Nicholas shrugged. "Not sure. Helo, Phane, and Dillon are speaking with the leaders of the factions now, trying to persuade them to go on a little search and capture."

Syn didn't mind the search. It was the capture he

was worried about. If the shifters, the Romans, the pussy brothers, or whoever caught Cruen, that would mean a different plan. One that utilized his past skills as a spy.

"And what?" Synjon began. "You're here to ask for my help in tracking him."

"No," Alex said, his cue aloft, his focus no longer on the game. "We need you and Petra to go before the Order—"

"Petra's not going anywhere." The words were far too quick exiting his mouth. He'd have to watch that.

All three Roman brothers stared at him, studied him.

"We need you to tell them you were never held against your will," Nicholas said.

"You want me to lie?"

"Fuck, yeah," Lucian snorted, leaning over the table to try a difficult shot. He was the only one still in the game. "Unless you want a war brought to the Rain Forest."

Synjon once again ventured a glance at the hallway leading to the spare bedroom. "Why would you think I'd care about the Rain Forest and its occupants?"

Alexander eyed him, the corners of his mouth kicking up. "I don't know. Maybe because that's the home of the pregnant *veana* you stole and brought here because you're feeling . . . ?"

A curl of annoyance went through Syn, but he kept it in check, kept it hidden. For all the things they thought they knew or had noticed about him, they didn't know shit about what was going on inside him, or with him and Petra, or with him and the *balas*. Or how he couldn't stop thinking about her, wanting her, wanting the *balas*, and how with each passing minute he grew more and more protective of them both.

"So?" Lucian said, after sending two balls into the left side pocket. "You gonna be a help? Or are you gonna be a total dickhead with no conscience?"

Without even looking at the table, Synjon smacked his cue into the ball. But instead of hitting one of his own, he sent the eight ball into the far right pocket. "That's a *knobhead* with no conscience, Frosty."

Luca grinned, broad and excited. "I've missed you, Brit Boy."

Cruen stared at the pale gray flesh and sneered. "What do you call this exactly?"

"Cacuba," said the young water shifter. "It's a type of eel."

They sat in the low rock caves near a waterfall spring. Several water shifters swam or sunbathed on the rocks like mermaids, while Robes, the young water shifter, and his older sister, Nore, cut up pieces of what they claimed to be magic-infused flesh.

"And why do you believe this gives one power?" Cruen asked, wondering if he'd made a grave mistake in remaining in the Rain Forest, expending his last shreds of mental and physical strength on a hope.

"We have used it," Nore said, her dark eyes wide with excitement. "In hunting. In our rituals."

Cruen took stock of his surroundings. He'd been to this very spot many moons ago, had taken samples from this same species, and yet, as he turned back to the plate of rotting gray flesh that was to make him powerful again, he felt no delight in being here once again. If this was a mistake, if nothing came of it, how could he return to the gathering rocks? Have the strength to return? His guard hadn't been allowed to follow, and was waiting for him there. To flash him home, or to the table of the Order.

Flash *him*.

Oh, gods, the humiliation at his loss of power grew worse with every breath.

"Go ahead," urged Robes, pushing the plate closer to Cruen. "You will see."

He had fallen. Far and painfully. He grabbed the slimy eel flesh and stuffed it in his mouth. The taste was one of the most vile he'd ever experienced, and instead of chewing, he swallowed it whole.

"Now you will see," Nore said, clasping her hands together.

Yes, Cruen thought, *but will I feel? Will I feel power racing through my veins, my blood? Will I be able to flash to the balcony of one Synjon Wise and force him to remove his emotions from my mind?*

Or will I be walking back to the gathering stones, searching, praying to all who will listen that I don't lose my mind or my breath before I get there?

Petra sat cross-legged on the bed, picking at the imaginary lint on the new sage green comforter Synjon had insisted on buying her. Across from her, a plush striped green pillow separating them, was Dani.

It was like old times.

Except for the digs.

"There's only one answer," Petra said in what she hoped was a firm voice, because Dani rarely responded to anything less.

"So." Dani cocked her head to the side. "You're saying this is really about the baby?"

"Of course it's about the baby."

The hawk shifter shook her head, disbelieving. "You need to do your repeats."

"Dani—"

"Here, let me go over them with you."

"No, thanks."

"Synjon Wise is a complete ass-cake."

"Hey, wait." Petra pointed at her and scowled. "That's a new one."

Dani shrugged. "Well, you know, they're all along the same lines."

"Listen," Petra said, eyeing her closest friend in the world. "I don't need to do any of that shit. I'm a grown female with a *balas* on the way."

"Right. And the father of that *balas* just happens to be the guy you've always had a huge thing for. The guy who has whisked you off to his cocksure penthouse on top of the world, *Pretty Woman*'d your ass, and once again tried to get up your skirt. Did I leave anything out?"

Petra leaned back against her pillows—her very pretty, very green pillows—and grinned. "Yes."

Dani's eyes widened. "Oh, that motherfucker! What more did he do?"

"The part you left out is me saying no to the up-your-skirt."

She sniffed. "For now."

Petra shook her head. "Don't. Don't do that. I'm not an idiot."

"Of course you're not. But you're into that bastard. You may even be in love with him."

Petra's chest tightened, and the air inside her lungs released in a rush, but she still managed to push out a pretty convincing response. "Come on."

"I'm eye-rolling right now in case you can't tell."

"My plan is to come home after I have the baby and start a life and a family with Brodan."

Silence claimed the bedroom for a good ten seconds, and then Dani said, "Brodan, huh?"

"Yes." That tightening in Petra's chest upgraded to a rusty, painful vise.

"He's a good male."

Petra nodded. "He totally is."

"The best."

"Definitely."

Again Dani paused. Then, "Yeah, that'll never happen."

Petra broke out laughing. "You asshole, Dani."

Dani started laughing too.

"I love you—you know that?" Petra said, climbing off the bed.

The hawk shifter followed suit. "I love you too."

Petra linked arms with her as they walked out the door and down the hall. "Come on. I'll take you to your launchpad."

"Fine." Dani gave her a warning look. "But you've got my number."

"Damn right I do." Petra gave her best friend a wry grin as they entered the living room.

First thing Petra noticed was that all three Roman brothers were gathered around the pool table talking. The second thing she noticed was that Synjon wasn't among them.

She pushed past Dani and eyed the brothers. "Where is he?"

"Gone," Alex said, placing his stick on the table.

Dani came to stand at her side. "No freaking way."

Petra's gut twisted, and she looked from Alex back to Dani. "What? What's wrong? What did you do?"

Dani turned and gave her a mixture of a smirk and a sneer. "Yeah. You don't dig his ass at all." Shaking her head, she left Petra's side and walked toward the sliding glass door. "That selfish *paven* has done something unselfish, that's all."

Confused and growing slightly concerned, Petra turned to Alex, Nicholas, and Lucian. "Where is he?"

Nicholas put his pool cue down next to Alex's. "He's going before the Order."

Petra gasped. It was as if her unbeating heart had suddenly dropped to her feet. "What? Oh, my gods. Why?"

"To tell them the shifters are harmless," Lucian answered. "And that he wasn't taken or held there against his will."

He was going to lie to the Order? "Why would he do that?"

Nicholas stared at her strangely. Lucian shook his head and placed his cue on the table with the rest of them.

"Perhaps he has some feeling after all, *veana*," he said, his Merlot eyes soft as they swept over her belly.

"But that's not possible," she said. "Is it?"

Alex smiled. "Who's to say what's possible when it comes to matters of the heart? My mate is an Impure. We're about to welcome a *balas* I was once terrified to even contemplate." He raised one dark eyebrow. "Is it all that hard to believe that even if our old emotions are stripped away, we can't grow new ones in their place?"

Petra felt tears behind her eyes. Tears that had nothing to do with her *swell* or hunger or the strange, over-whelming, and debilitating problem she'd been suffering from all week.

"We should get out of here," Lucian said to Nicholas. "Grab Mr. Hallmark Card over there and let's motor. I want to see my *veanas*. Lucy's first fang is growing in."

"You don't know if that's fang," Nicholas retorted, heading for the sliding glass door.

Outside, Dani snorted again. "Don't fall for it, Pets. Not for Alex's pretty words or Wise's pretty face." Then she turned to the Roman brothers. "I'm assuming the three of you don't need a ride."

"Nope," Lucian said. "We're all good, shifter."

Dani gave Petra one last grin before stripping down, shifting to her hawk, and taking off into the cold night air.

15

With the exception of the Impure, they were all as bloody arrogant and insufferable as they ever were.

Syn stood front and center at their table, feet in the sand. It was so predictable. Couldn't they mix it up a bit? Change the climate, ditch the table?

"Synjon Wise." It was Feeyan who addressed him first, because clearly she was now the leader in Cruen's stead. He wondered if the *veana* admired or despised the ex-leader. He imagined a little of both. "What an unexpected pleasure."

"It's no pleasure of mine," he said coolly. "And how unexpected could it be? You demanded I come before you."

Her lip curled just a fraction. "So Dillon found you."

"I was never lost."

She swept her arm down the table, indicating the others. "After we heard news of your abduction and imprisonment we were quite concerned."

"Never happened."

"Which one?" she asked. "The abduction or the imprisonment?"

"Both."

Her flour white eyebrows lifted. "That is not the information I received."

Syn's gaze moved down the row of other Order members. They had to be getting tired of this act, this routine. The Impure male sure looked bored.

"And who gave you this information, then?" Syn asked, returning his attention to Feeyan.

She inclined her head. "That is confidential."

He sniffed, laughed softly. "You're dealing with Cruen again, aren't you? After all he's done. All he's guilty of. The lies and the manipulations."

"Your personal history colors your—"

"He murdered my *veana*." He cut her off, but the words were no longer impassioned on his tongue. It was simply a fact. There was good in having his emotions bled, even if it kept him from the ability to love and care for others. "He stole her, kept her in a cage like an animal. Lucian Roman, too. These were Pureblood vampires. The ones you claim to care about, wish to fight an innocent group of shifters over."

Feeyan didn't like this line of conversation, and down the row of Order members there was a stirring, questions and chatter. Feeyan hissed at them, then tried to steer Syn in another direction. "You were instructed to bring the *veana*, Petra."

Where there had been little emotion before, there was a small tidal wave now. "The mother of my *balas* is resting, as she should be."

"Then you may tell me," Feeyan said far too graciously. "Were you or were you not held by the shifters?"

"Not."

"Do you consider them a threat?"

"Far from it. They seem a right peaceful lot. The opposite of us."

She tossed him a death stare. "That's enough. You may go, Mr. Wise."

He grinned coldly. "Lovely. So you'll leave the Rain Forest and its inhabitants alone."

"Not yet."

Synjon drew closer to the table, his eyes pinned on her frigid white orbs. The Order members around them started whispering. "I just told you—"

"You may be out, you may have been freed, but there is another there who has not."

Shite. That bloody prat.

Syn eyed every member at that table, his tone ultra-serious now. "If you allow Cruen to force you into a war with a peaceful tribe, you'll regret it. The Breed will regret it."

"No one forces me, Mr. Wise," she practically snarled. "I am the leader of the Order. I make the decisions."

"You sound as though you're trying to convince yourself of that fact." He cocked his head to one side. "Having a little trouble living up to the title?"

As the whispering intensified, Feeyan pushed to her feet, her eyes boring a hole in his head, and waved a hand at him, sending him back to the Hollow. She wanted him gone. She wanted his words, ideas, concerns, and truths cut off and buried before the other

Order members started developing minds of their own.

And before they realized their leader was not as secure in her position as she wanted them to believe.

Petra paced back and forth before the glass doors, feeling like an asinine teenager. The Order was purported to be cruel, vindictive, and unpredictable. Which would they be with Synjon?

She heard Dani's voice in her head. Her best friend's warning was a completely legitimate one. Worrying about, caring about, maybe even falling for Synjon Wise might be the greatest mistake of her life. But she couldn't help herself.

"Tearing up my rug, are you, love?"

She gasped and whirled around to see Synjon standing in the frame of the sliding glass door, snow dusting his clothes. "What did they say? What did you say?"

He stepped inside and closed the door. "Everything's fine."

" 'Fine,' " she repeated with mild irritation. "That's all you're giving me?"

He brushed the already melting flakes from his jacket. "You look worried."

"I am."

"About the shifters?"

"Of course. And the Rain Forest. Is the Order still threatening to go there and make trouble, or are they satisfied that you're no longer being held prisoner?"

"They are." He walked past her over to the couch. "They have a new issue."

She followed him. "What now?"

"Seems there's a Pureblood *paven* still in the forest. His whereabouts are unaccounted for since he left the party he came there with."

Her gut twisted. "Cruen."

He nodded.

"Maybe he went there for me, to make sure I was okay. Maybe he heard about how I was feeling this past week and . . ." She stopped talking. Even as she said the words she didn't believe them. She wondered why he was really there. Whether he was once again trying to get something from the shifter community—something more than their DNA this time.

She hung her head. Her father just continued to be a disappointment.

"And for a moment I thought some of that manic pacing might be for me."

Her eyes came up, swept over the gorgeous male vampire sitting with cool casualness on the leather sofa. "You can handle yourself, Mr. Wise." She itched to join him. Maybe snuggle up against his side while he whispered things in her ear. Dirty things. She mentally rolled her eyes. "You don't need any help or worry from anyone."

His gaze locked with her own. "I told the Order I went and stayed in the Rain Forest of my own free will."

"Thank you." She bit her tongue against asking him why. Who was that act of kindness for? What did he have to gain by helping the shifters?

"And if Cruen doesn't fuck things up royally, you and the bear shifter can set up house without any fear of intrusion by the vicious and calculating vampires."

"Vicious and calculating." She grinned at him. "Are we talking about the Order or yourself, Mr. Wise?"

"The Order, of course. Why would I interfere in that budding romance?"

A sudden pain shot through her abdomen and she gasped. She reached out for a nearby chair, curling in on herself.

Syn was off the couch and at her side in seconds. "What is it?" He eased an arm around her waist. "Petra?"

She licked her lips, stared straight ahead and waited. When no other pain surfaced, she gingerly straightened. "Nothing. It's gone."

Syn heaved a great sigh. "Bloody hell, *veana*. How long have you been on your feet tonight, wearing down my rug?"

"I'm fine. It was just a little twinge."

But he wasn't listening. He scooped her up in his arms and carried her out of the living room.

"Seriously, I'm fine," she assured him.

He didn't say anything, just kept going. Jaw tight, eyes trained forward, he took her into her bedroom and placed her gently on the bed. When she lay back against the pillows, he sat beside her.

"Where's the pain?"

"There is no more pain," she said. "It's gone."

"Then where was it?"

What was he doing? Why was he acting so concerned when he didn't have the capacity or the ability to feel that emotion? Then she realized with a deep sense of melancholy that he did have ability, or the instinct. Not to care for her, but to care for the *balas*.

She pointed to the underside of her belly near her hipbones. "Here. But it's gone now."

Before she could even get that last part out, he had

the edge of her black lace pajama top between his fingers. His dark eyes met hers. "May I?"

She nodded. "All right."

He lifted the material just a few inches, to the very
top of her belly, then placed his warm hand on the spot
where her pain had been and began to rub in slow, gentle circles. Mesmerized, entranced, confused, Petra
watched his large, strong hand massaging her swollen
belly. Would her child's hand look like this someday?

Oh, gods.

She lifted her gaze to his face. His stunningly handsome face. If she had a male *balas*, would he look like
Syn? Would he have carved cheekbones and a full
mouth? Deep, soulful eyes that pinned a female where
she stood, then made her melt?

Her chest went tight and she bit at her lower lip.
Would she really go through her life seeing Synjon
Wise in every expression or movement her child made?

"What's wrong?" he asked, his hand stalled, his eyes
burning a hole through her. "Is the pain back?"

"No." *Not that kind of pain.*

He looked relieved, then started again with the circles on her belly. "This all right?"

"It feels good." Too good. What was she supposed
to do here? Stop him? Tell him that every time his
hands were on her, she wanted them inside her as well?

"Look, Petra."

The sudden youthful tone in his voice had her looking up. "What?"

"It follows me." The smile on his face stunned her. It
was completely real, almost innocent.

"What follows you?"

"The *balas*. It follows my hand."

She looked down, watched as he moved his palm slowly across the top of her belly and down. A soft moan escaped her lips as she felt the deep and intense movement within her womb.

"Look," he said.

And there it was. Her child's head or elbow or foot following along behind Synjon's hand.

She pulled away from him, from his touch, from the idea that he might somehow have control of her little *balas*, and rolled to her side. "I'm really tired."

Syn didn't say anything, but his hand flexed.

"You know, from all that pacing." She didn't look at him. She couldn't. What had just happened here was the most intimate thing that she'd ever experienced in her life, and she didn't know what to make of it.

"Good night, Syn," she said almost breathlessly.

He stood, hesitated for a moment, then walked to the door. "I want to know if that pain comes back."

She curled into her pillow.

"Promise me, Petra."

His tone, almost dark, worried her. "I promise."

This time, when he left, he didn't close the door all the way.

He felt.

Not just the keys beneath his fingers as he worked the Bösendorfer with Debussy, but something deeper, something that had nothing to do with instinct, when he got close to the *balas*.

How could that be possible? Instinct he was willing to accept, but an emotional connection?

Cruen had drained him absolutely. Syn had made sure of it—then made sure all those emotions were permanently embedded in the asshole *paven*.

He played on. He played until he felt nothing at all. He played until the room grew cold and the snow outside accumulated against the glass doors leading to the terrace.

He played until he felt someone watching him.

His hands stilled over the keys and he glanced up. To his right, halfway between the hall to her bedroom and his piano, was the most beautiful swollen-bellied angel. Her hair loose and falling about the high white mounds of her breasts, barely encased by the black lace of her tank.

His mouth started to water. "Is the pain back?"

"That was you?"

"Is the pain back, love?" he said again.

"No. No, I'm fine."

He took a deep breath and blew it out, then began to play once again. "You shouldn't be out of bed."

She came to stand beside the piano bench, bringing her scent with her. It made his gut clench with hunger and thirst. "You were the one playing at the party."

He looked up at her. "You heard me over that crowd?"

"It was the only thing I wanted to hear," she said. "It was beautiful. It *is* beautiful. I had no idea you could play."

"The secret life of Synjon Wise," he muttered, then switched gears, his fingers dancing over the keys as he played the very same song he'd played earlier that night. When he'd wanted to block out the party, his hunger, and his ever-growing desire for the *veana* who stood just inches away.

When he stopped, Petra sighed. "Incredible. I wish I could play like that."

"You can," he said.

She laughed. "Come on now."

"I don't mean right away. But you can learn, start from the beginning." Then he added impetuously, foolishly, "I could teach you."

"I'd like that, but I'm not sure I can fit on a piano bench in my condition. Where's the belly going to go?" She laughed. "On top of the keys?"

"We could give it a try, and if it's not comfortable, maybe after the *balas* is born . . ."

"Right," she said quickly. She was quiet for a moment, no doubt thinking about returning to the Rain Forest after the birth of Little Fangs. Or not returning.

It was a thought he refused to entertain.

"How long have you been playing?" She came around to stand behind him.

"Since I was a *balas* of six years." He started playing something soft and a little sad. Seemed to suit the mood. "Took to it right away."

"No lessons?"

He shook his head. "Not a one."

"That's amazing. I wonder if Little Fangs will have—" She stopped abruptly. "Sorry. I know you hate the name."

"I don't mind it, really." He looked over his shoulder, found her gaze. "And I hope so."

She swallowed tightly and her eyes shuttered.

Syn took his hands off the piano and turned around

to face her. His hands went to her waist, his thumbs on her stomach. "I hope the *balas* has something of me. Though it may seem impossible to see at this moment, with what I have become, there are traces of good within my blood."

She gazed down at him. "I remember."

"Oh, Petra." He leaned in and placed his head on her belly. It was so warm. *She* was so warm.

Her hands found his hair and tangled in the dark strands, the pads of her fingers massaging his scalp. Syn turned and nuzzled her belly. He gently lifted her tank and pressed a kiss to her skin, then dropped his head and kissed down the side of her *swell*, over her hipbone.

He growled, his nostrils flaring. "I scent your heat, Petra," he whispered against her skin. "I want it."

She shifted in his hands, her body and her breathing unsteady.

He lapped at her hipbone with his tongue, then started pulling down her pajama bottoms.

She moaned, her fingers digging deeper into his scalp as he eased the black silk down to her knees.

"I'm so thirsty, love." He gazed at the beautiful wet pussy that was nearly at eye level as he sat on his piano bench.

"Syn . . ."

The whisper of his name made his cock stir. "I can't drink your blood, love. But I can lick your cream."

"Oh, gods," she cried softly.

"Tell me yes, Petra."

"Yes. Yes. Yes."

As his head bent, his hands went around to cup her

ass. With his first lick, his first taste, blood surged into his cock. He'd never had anything on his tongue that compared to this, to her, and he realized in that moment that no matter how long he feasted at her spectacular cunt, he'd never be satiated.

He wanted her for life.

Growling away the thought, he slipped one hand down the curve of her ass and up again, finding her wet sheath. Flicking his tongue lightly over her clit, he eased two fingers up inside her.

Her deep-throated groan matched his own.

Ruddy hell, she was so tight, so drenched in cream.

His dick begged to be let out, released, so it could find and capture and bury itself in the hot, fist-tight cage it desired so intensely. His emotions were gone, or so he'd thought, but this . . . fuck, this connection he had with her—this connection he'd had since she'd saved his sorry ass—was never going to recede.

And he didn't think he wanted it to.

Her hips were moving now, swinging, bucking against his mouth. It was all Syn could do to keep his face planted in her sex, his tongue swirling on her clit and his fingers fucking her deep. The room no longer felt cold. In fact, it was blistering with heat and sweat, groans and heavy breathing, and Syn wanted to rip his clothes off and feel her skin to skin again.

His eyes closed as he pressed his tongue against her clit, moving his head up and down. On the backs of his eyelids he saw them, the two of them, in the strange, beautiful, tree house bathroom, his body over hers, her eyes on him, his cock thrust so deep he'd nearly lost his mind.

She ripped her fingers from his hair then and gripped his shoulders for support. He could feel the heat gathering within her, her slick, honey walls clamping around his fingers as he pumped. She was going to climax. And when she did, he was going to drink her down.

Not her blood.

But her sweet come.

With a growl of hunger, he consumed her, his tongue moving through her wet slit, then circling. He eased a third finger inside her and started fucking her fast and deep. Her head fell back and she began to shake.

"Oh, gods, yes!" she cried, her nails digging into the skin of his shoulders.

Syn left her ass and looped his arm around her waist to hold her in place. Then his lips covered her clit and while he suckled, while he coaxed the hot bud to swell against his tongue, his fingers thrust up into her cunt and remained.

Petra gasped for air, her knees buckling.

Inside her sex, Syn flicked the pads of his fingers, hard and quick, back and forth, until he heard her cry out, felt the walls around him shudder and go slick. Then he pulled out of her and thrust his tongue inside.

She came hard, bucking and writhing, cream pouring out of her cunt and down Synjon's greedy throat.

16

Petra felt boneless and worked over, and when Synjon picked her up in his arms for the second time that night and carried her off, she didn't argue or question. She just curled into his chest and breathed deeply of his amazing scent.

She wanted to chastise herself for allowing him to touch her, but she felt too weak, both in body and in spirit. Dani was a hundred percent right about her. She was falling in love with this *paven*, and if he wanted to touch her, kiss her, or rub her belly and watch their *balas* move against his palm, she would let him.

She wasn't sure if that made her weak or honest, but right then she didn't care.

The air inside her room felt cold, and when he placed her back in bed, she thought very seriously about asking him to stay. Maybe curl up behind her, drape his arm over her belly, and fall asleep against the back of her neck.

But his expression stopped her.

Or his lack of expression. Once again he looked utterly impassive, from his mouth to his eyes.

Had this meant nothing to him? she wondered. Was it physical desire only?

And then he did the strangest thing. He gathered the blanket at her feet and pulled it over her, all the way to her chin. The gesture was so odd for someone who had no emotion.

"The pain?" he asked.

"Gone," she whispered.

His eyes softened with relief, and he leaned down and kissed her, a kiss so soft and gentle and sweet it nearly broke Petra's heart.

"Sleep," he said, walking out of the room. "I'll see you in the morning."

Again, he left the door ajar, and for the second time that night, Petra curled up with her pillow. This time she fell asleep within seconds.

Phane climbed the steps of the small mountain house he and Helo were going to stay in while they were in the Rain Forest. It had been chosen for them. Phane wasn't sure who had selected it, but it looked pretty damn good from the outside. It was centrally located and had a river for Helo to swim in, as well as easy access to the sky and a perch for Phane.

He pushed the door open and went inside. The place was a total pit, but he hardly cared. He was beat and hungry. They'd been flying for hours, combing every inch of the Rain Forest looking for Cruen. Coming up with a whole lot of nothing. That bastard *paven* was slicker than a rattlesnake dipped in oil.

"Don't get too comfortable."

He glanced over his shoulder at Dani, who had done the escorting-him-home bit, and who Phane was pretty sure wanted to be elsewhere. "I'll try, but this place makes it hard, you know?" He grinned. "It's paradise."

Her eyes widened innocently. "It was the only free house we had available."

"I'm sure."

Her mouth twitched with amusement. He bet she liked making males squirm. It was one of the many reasons he found her so freaking hot.

"So, bird-slash–blood boy," she said, moving past him and into the wreck of a living room, "how long do you and your brother plan on staying?"

"That's undetermined."

"What fun for us."

"With Syn's information about the Order's potential threat, we don't want to leave the Rain Forest unprotected."

She looked up from the couch, which was missing two of its cushions and the one that remained had several gaping holes in it. "Unprotected." She snorted. "So arrogant for one so pretty."

Pretty, eh? He wasn't sure if he liked that or not. He headed into one of the bedrooms. Dani followed him. If it was possible, the room was even worse than the living room. The floors were wrecked and damaged from water, and it looked as though at some point in time the entire contents of the Rain Forest had been blown through the broken window.

"So, you know where I'm bunking down," he said, turning to face her. "Where do you live?"

"Oh, here and there."

"Never heard of it. Is it as nice as this?"

"Not even close." She grinned and checked out the adjoining bathroom. "You have running water. 'Course, it's probably running brown this time of year, but who do you really have to shower for anyway?"

How pissed would she be if he grabbed her, kissed her, and asked her how bad he smelled? He imagined pretty pissed, but the thought made him grin.

"So you don't live with the Avians, then?" he asked, checking out the dirty broken window.

"I'm a nonconformist. I sorta do my own thing."

Shocker, Phane thought with a chuckle. "Do you have a male?"

"Uh . . . exactly how is that any of your business, vampire hawk?"

He turned, his back to the window, and crossed his arms over his chest. "I'm interested in you."

His honesty must've stunned her. But only for a few seconds. "Really?"

He nodded. "So? Do you?"

"Do I what?"

"Have a male?"

She grinned wide and wicked, and Phane's chest tightened with desire. That is, until she said, "I have many males."

The front door opened and soon Helo appeared in the doorway. "You've got to be kidding."

Phane laughed. "Thank Dani. It's all her doing."

Helo turned to the female and glared. "Thanks, Dani."

"Sure thing," she answered. "Try not to stay too long."

"Hospitable, ain't she?" Phane muttered to Helo, then followed Dani out of the bedroom and over to the front door. "Come again soon," he said, leaning against the doorjamb.

She grinned wickedly at him as she passed. "I always do, bloodsucker. I always do."

"You know, I'm not just a vampire," he called to her back.

She turned around. "Oh, I know. Feathers and talons and—"

"Fangs."

"Oh, my!"

He laughed.

Her grin widened. "And what does that make you exactly?"

He lifted his eyebrows and lowered his voice. "Intriguing."

"Vampire. Hawk. Hmmm . . . What else is in there I should know about? Human, maybe?" She widened her eyes dramatically. "Gargoyle?"

His mouth twitched. He would have this female. Nothing and no one would get in his way. And if they tried, he'd make sure to schedule a little blood taste test.

"Maybe I could show you sometime," he said casually.

"Maybe. But right now I have plans." She started walking away, down to a patch of flat ground.

"Hot date?" he called.

She stripped down, tossed her clothes into a tree, and shouted back, "Is there any other kind?" before she shifted into her hawk and spread her wings wide.

Phane watched her take off and sail into the air, his dick hardening with every beat of her incredible wings.

The alley stank of human food and human sex.

Two things that held absolutely no interest to Synjon.

"He still in the Rain Forest?"

Adrian nodded, his fangs a quarter inch lower than they should be in primarily human territory, even in the late hours of the night.

"Does he know I'm no longer there?"

Again Adrian nodded.

"Then why does he remain?" Synjon asked the male who had his sister's eyes and burnt auburn hair. "Why isn't he coming after me? And more important, as his very trusted guard, why aren't you assisting him?"

Juliet's brother, the only other male on earth who wanted Cruen to suffer more than Synjon, glanced down the alley and sighed. "He was on his way out, on his way to you, when some water shifters stopped him."

"Water shifters?" Synjon narrowed his eyes. "What did they want?"

"They remembered him. From when he was there collecting samples." Adrian laughed bitterly, his breath smoky in the frigid air. "They told him they had a power source of some kind."

"Fuck me."

"Yes, exactly."

"What is it?" Synjon demanded.

"No idea. They wouldn't let me go with him."

"Go back, Adrian. Find out what it is, if it works,

how it works. I need him as weak and defenseless as possible."

The male nodded. "Is the plan still the same? His next flash is to you."

A week ago, Syn would've given the *paven* before him, the *paven* who had the same eyes as the female Cruen had stolen, then killed, a rapid-fire affirmative, but tonight he hesitated. And bloody hell, he despised that hesitation. He wanted Cruen. He wanted to torture and maim and make that bastard beg, but right now Petra was asleep in his house, the *balas* sleeping with her. Was he truly bringing Cruen into the new, almost blissful world he'd just created?

"Syn."

He looked up. "The room's ready to go."

Adrian reached out and the two clasped hands. "Juliet will finally be avenged," he said with deep feeling.

A feeling that no longer existed within Synjon. "You'd better get back."

The male nodded. "Later, brother."

Adrian flashed from the alley, and Syn walked out, down a few side streets and onto Broadway, which was still sporting moderately heavy foot traffic, even at this hour. Christmas swag and lights shocked his senses at every turn as he moved through the crowds at a brisk pace. He could've flashed home when Adrian flashed back to the Rain Forest, but he needed some air, some time to get his head together. His emotions about Juliet and her death were gone, but not his commitment to bringing the male who killed her to justice.

Why couldn't he stay the course on this?

He was just rounding the corner of Forty-fourth

Street when something caught his eye in a brightly lit window of one of the shops. He slowed and went to check it out. The toy store was closed, but the front window was lit and dressed for the holidays. A large toddler-size bear sat on a small leather bench in front of a child-size Steinway, its fuzzy paws placed on the keyboard to look as though it was playing.

Petra's incomplete query rolled through his mind. What would the *balas* inherit from him? His face? His sharpness? His hatred of his grandfather?

His gaze moved over the well-made instrument.

Would the *balas* have his abilities at the piano?

That unwelcome, though now strikingly familiar something pinged inside him. His desires had expanded beyond the simple two of physical release and unemotionally executed vengeance. Now they included a female he should never touch again, and the growing life inside her, which might very well sport his eyes.

He pulled out his cell phone, barked a quick order to the male on the other end of the line, then leaned back against the shop door and waited.

17

Petra woke to the scent of blood and instantly curled around it, her fangs descending. No doubt she was still dreaming, but it was the kind of dream she appreciated. Syn's blood, Syn's thick, masculine wrist. Her fingers pressed into the skin of his arm just as her fangs rested on top of the pinprick holes that had already been prepared for her. She made a keening sound, then thrust herself deep into his vein.

The moment the blood entered her mouth, she came awake. With a gulp and a sputter, she opened her eyes and pulled her fangs from Syn's wrist.

"Oh, my gods, I'm so sorry." She looked up, dazed and confused. Syn was propped up on a pillow beside her. She looked down at his wrist, then back up at him. "What are you doing here?"

"You were calling out in your sleep."

"Calling out for what?" *Or for whom?* she thought with a groggy sense of embarrassment.

"Me, love."

Her chest deflated. *Great. Fabulous. Humiliating.* It

wasn't enough that she made her desire, her need for him known in the waking hours. Now she was begging for it while she slept.

"And my wrist. And my neck." His mouth twitched as he watched her cheeks grow hot. "And my blood."

She made a groaning sound that was meant to convey how completely mortifying this was. But Syn just chuckled.

"Drink, *veana*."

"I think I'm becoming an addict," she muttered.

"Just as long as you keep coming to me for your fix."

His dark eyes moved over her face. *Why does he have to say shit like that?* Petra wondered. It made her want him more than she already did. It made her want things, *hope* for things that were impossible when it came to this male.

Gods, this is going to end badly.

"I'm bloodying your sheets, *veana*," he said.

With a slight growl, she dropped her head and sank her fangs in him again. Instantly the blood flowed. Hot and sweet and plentiful, into her mouth. Each drop she consumed was better than the last. As she sucked like the greedy wench she was, took his life force into her own, she wondered how she would survive without this when she left.

How she would survive without *him*.

Above her, she heard him groan, hiss, and she realized she'd gone a little deeper into his vein than she normally did. But that was how she was when she fed from him. Every millimeter tasted better, sweeter. Like liquid gold.

Finally, after several minutes of intense feeding, her

belly was full, and she lifted her head and stared at the twin bite marks. With a quick inhale, she blew on them, slowly back and forth until they closed. Then she looked up. In the milky shadows of the moonlight streaming in behind her, she saw the strain on Synjon Wise's gorgeous face.

Her brows knit together as her gaze moved over him, assessing. His eyes were narrowed and dilated to black. His skin looked paler than usual, his cheekbones were more pronounced, and his lips held a bluish tinge.

"Are you eating?" Her eyes rose to meet his.

"I ate the meal of a lifetime." A quick fire lit his black eyes. "Just a few hours ago."

Her cheeks flushed, and her skin tightened over her bones. *At the piano.* Yes, she remembered too. So did her body. Especially the muscles between her legs.

"Don't concern yourself with me, *veana*," he said. "I can take care of myself, remember?"

"Yes, but you're not."

His eyes dropped to her mouth.

"Why?"

"Why what, love?"

She sighed. "Don't be obtuse. Why aren't you feeding from someone like you said you would?"

"Haven't had the chance." He eased his wrist from her grip and shifted to sit on the edge of the bed.

She spoke to his broad back. "You had a party here. Plenty of veins to choose from."

"None that were available."

"Bullshit. Hey." She touched his shoulder. "What's going on?"

"Why does it matter? Eh? *Love*." His tone was back

to being unaffected, and she shivered. "All you need to be concerned about is feeding the *balas*."

She snatched her hand away. Cursed softly. "I wish that was the case. Gods. I want to not care about you or your health or your eating habits, because frankly, you didn't give a shit about me when—"

"Don't."

"And I would love to put your ridiculously handsome, yet overly pale face out of my head, because you put mine out of yours."

"Stop it, Petra. I mean it."

Fuck him. Really. She moved around him, crawled onto his lap, grabbed his face. "And I really want to pretend that the reason you won't take blood from another female has everything to do with me because, *love*, I want you to want only me. Desperately and forever. Until I leave you for another guy. No. Even after that. I want you to want me even when I'm in his arms, moving under his body—"

"Fuck." Syn crushed his mouth against hers, then ripped back. "I told you to shut your bloody mouth, *veana*."

"Even when he's rocking our *balas* in his arms at night."

Syn stared at her, his nostrils flared, his fangs fully extended. "Fuck you, Petra."

"I thought you'd never ask, Syn."

"I'm not asking." His arms went around her and he took her mouth so hard she was pretty sure she was going to have a bruise in the morning.

Petra moaned into his kiss, following him as he

changed the angle, the suction, and uttered words and threats at her she couldn't make out. She didn't care. Let him be pissed. It was something. It was emotion. And if he didn't care, if the things she'd just said to him meant nothing, he wouldn't be reacting this fiercely.

His hands raked up and down her back, gripping her one moment, releasing her the next. Her breasts were swelling, her nipples pressed hard against the lace fabric of her tank, and below her waist, between her legs, she was soaking wet.

Then suddenly he pulled away. His gaze searched her face like he wanted something from her, something out of her. Words, action . . . she didn't know what. But he was breathing heavy, too heavy. And behind his eyes, she saw something impossible break.

"You're crying," she whispered.

His eyes widened and his lip curled. "Never."

She reached up and brushed her index finger over his lashes. It was a lone tear, and it quivered on the tip of her finger. She showed it to him. "What's this, then?"

He stared at it and his brows slammed together. "Impossible."

"Syn . . ."

He lifted her and put her back on the bed. Every inch of him was tense as he walked toward the door.

"Syn!" she called again.

But he didn't answer her. He left the room. Left her feeling turned on, cold, and like a complete and total bitch for shoving his new and unexplained emotions in his face.

*   *   *

Power felt so good inside him. It belonged there. Running through his veins, making his blood expand. The only problem was it didn't last long enough.

Cruen eyed the small group of water shifters. "Tell me what you want for this." He held up the gray flesh. "What is your currency?"

"We want your help," said the young shifter who'd brought him to the secret waterfall in the first place.

"What kind of help?" Cruen asked imperiously. Truthfully, he would pay almost anything for the magic surge in power, but he didn't want the shifters to know that. He didn't want them to know just how desperate he was.

"What you took from us," said the male. "The DNA?"

"Yes," Cruen said warily.

"You mixed it with your own blood, right?"

Where were these water beasts going with their questions? "I conducted many experiments. Some were successful. Some were not."

"We want your DNA. Vampire DNA."

Cruen couldn't quell the immediate expression of disgust. "Why?"

"We'd like to experiment too." The boy glanced around at the small party gathered. "We'd like to see what kind of creatures we can grow from our DNA and yours. There are so many of us who lack power and strength. Our animals are weak by nature, which in turn makes us weak as shifters. We want what the lions have, the bears. We want that strength and the ability to fight our enemies and protect our own."

The boy, who may not have been a boy at all but a small, weak shifter adult, eyed him seriously. "This would be our secret, of course. The faction leaders would not approve."

Cruen stared long and hard at the male. He understood the shifters' desire to be more than what they were, but he wasn't sure he approved. They were the equivalent of an Impure in his mind, and he would not hand over pure blood or anything to make them stronger and more powerful. And yet these creatures had the magic flesh—

"We've heard about a hybrid who's here in the Rain Forest," said an older female to the boy's left. "A water shifter like us—"

"Helo," Cruen supplied readily.

"Is that his name?"

"He isn't exactly like you." No. He wasn't. Cruen hesitated. Perhaps . . . yes, perhaps that would satisfy. Giving up Pureblood vampire DNA went against everything he stood for. But *mutore* . . . "I could get you the water beast's DNA. In fact, I might be able to bring him to you."

As all the other water shifters started talking at once, the young male's eyes widened. "Yes, that would do well. He is part vampire. But would he come? Would he keep what we're trying to do a secret?"

"I'm not sure." Cruen waited for their faces to fall from disappointment and then added, "But with the right amount of flesh paid to me, I can make sure that after you're done with him, he doesn't have the ability to reveal anything to anyone ever again."

The desire to feel nothing had been viciously stolen by the overpowering desire to feel everything.

With her.

His hands spread wide on the glass, Syn stood at the doors leading to the terrace and stared out at the New York City skyline. It was ungodly late and snow was falling on the terrace floor in heavy flakes. What had he done? Stealing her away from the Rain Forest and her family? Thinking he could take care of her and the *balas*? Didn't he get it that existing was the only thing available to him? He hadn't been saved from the sun, from following Juliet, to have another chance at life and happiness.

He swiped at the condensation building on the glass. All he deserved was the chance to make things right, pay his toll for failing Juliet. And that toll was the complete and total destruction of Cruen.

"I'm sorry."

His hand stilled on the glass. He hadn't heard Petra come up behind him. Shite, he was really losing it.

"Syn." She paused. Then, "Look at me."

Looking at her seemed to be the bloody problem. Why couldn't he just stand here and admire the snow and the view?

"Please," she said, her tone softly impassioned.

Releasing a heavy breath, he turned, leaned back against the cold glass, and then, when he got a good look at her, wished he hadn't. *Bollocks!* Did she have to glow in the goddamn light of the snowflakes behind him? Did her eyes have to be so fucking blue and beautiful and haunting? Did her skin have to scream for his touch, his mouth?

"Okay." She looked everywhere but in his eyes. "I'm going to be real honest here. And I hope you will be too."

Honest? Did she really want that from him? Did she even know what that meant when it came to the two of them?

His gaze moved all over her. Black silk and lace against ripe white skin and breasts that insisted on overflowing their confines every chance they got. His hands twitched at his sides. They wanted to be on her, inside her. Along with his cock, which was filling with blood this very second.

Fuck. What was happening to him? And how could he stop it? Curb it? Destroy it?

Or was that impossible now? Was it truly his destiny to want what he could never have?

Never have unless he gave up the very thing that kept him breathing.

"I'm angry at you."

His eyes snapped up, and this time her eyes met his.

"I'm angry at you for not caring. Because . . . well"— she shook her head—"because I care. About you. I haven't stopped, you know. And no matter how this rolls along, how insanely attracted we are to each other, it can't end well. Right? I mean, your need to kill my father is kind of a deal breaker for me. He's clearly not a good father or even a decent male. And maybe he should be contained in that vampire jail situation." Her eyes implored him. "But I can't sit by and watch or accept his death by your hand. You've got to understand that."

"I do." It was why he'd allowed his emotions to be stripped in the first place.

She chewed her lip. "But you don't care?"

Gods, she just didn't get this, get *him*. "Of course I don't care." He growled slightly. "Petra. He murdered my female. Do you understand that? Right in front of my fucking eyes." He pushed away from the glass. "He destroyed a being. It's what he does. Hurts and kills and destroys to get what he wants. Now, that doesn't take away from the fact that he fathered you. I'm grateful." His gaze moved over her, over her belly, back to her eyes. "Shit, I'm grateful to him for that. But it doesn't cancel out what he is—what he continues to do."

She just stared at him, shaking slightly. "I know."

He looked at her, hard. "He killed my life," he said again. "What would you have me do?"

It took her a moment to answer. "Start a new one?"

"I don't know if I can."

Her eyes widened. Tears filled them. She turned and started toward her room. His chest tightened and he called after her.

"But I do know I want you! Only you!"

She stopped, her hand reaching out for the wall.

Fuck, this is misery. "And I know I can't bear to take another female's blood."

She stayed where she was, still giving him her back.

"The idea makes me feel bloody sick to my gut. Yes, Petra. Yes, love. I said 'feel.'" He scrubbed a hand over his face. "I don't know what the bloody hell is going on. I should feel nothing. But with you, with the *balas*, I am something impossible." He pulled in a deep breath. Released it. "Turn around, love."

She didn't move.

"Please. Remember that word? You used it on me not more than five minutes ago."

Her head hung forward for a second. Then she sighed and turned back to face him.

He shook his head when he saw her expression. It was sadness, the sweetest, sexiest thing he'd ever seen, and he wanted to flash to her and cover her mouth, pull moans from her sighs of frustration.

"I never stopped wanting you," he said, knowing that the words coming out of his mouth were surely damning him. But who the bloody hell cared now? Either way, he didn't stand much of a chance in the happy-endings department. "Never stopped thinking about you. Cursing you. You tell me what we're supposed to do now. I did my very best to keep this from happening."

Her hands went to her belly.

"There's a war raging inside me, love. Wanting you, wanting to destroy him. I can't let go of either one and survive."

Silence filled the space between them as they just stared at each other. Syn was sure she was going to turn around at any moment and go back to her room. She should. She really should. But then her gaze flickered past him and narrowed.

"What's that?" she asked.

He glanced over his shoulder, saw what she was talking about, and laughed softly. "Further proof that I'm losing the battle."

Completely captivated, she left the safety of the far wall and walked past him into the living room. He followed her with his eyes, watched as she ran her hand over the top of the small piano.

"Where did you get it?" Her head came up and her eyes locked with his.

"I saw it in a shop window."

"You put it next to yours."

"Of course I did."

Tears filled her eyes and she ran at him, threw herself into his arms. "You're killing me."

He pulled her against him. "Right back at you, love."

Her hands were on his chest, her belly was tucked into him the way he liked it, and her eyes were searching his own. "Take me to bed."

He grinned. "Fuck you?"

She grinned back. "Please."

His nostrils flared, and he shook his head ever so slightly. "I don't know if I have the strength to keep my fangs to myself, love."

She sighed with what sounded impossibly like relief. "Good." Then she grabbed his hand and pulled him toward the bedroom.

18

Syn's bedroom.

That's where she'd led them.

The last time she was in here, he was wearing only a towel. Now she wanted him in nothing at all.

The room was relatively dark when they entered. Except for one thing. One amazing thing. A round five-by-five skylight cut into the ceiling directly above the bed, the moon fairly overshadowed by the clouds that were raining down snowflakes, the tiny bits of erratic light scattering on the plush gray quilt. How had she not noticed that skylight before? Had it been daylight? Had it been closed, sealed up to keep the sun at bay?

Syn came up behind her and kissed her neck. She smiled, realizing he'd already removed his shirt, and turned in his arms. Gods, he was beautiful. And terrifying. And breath-stealingly sexy. She ran her hands up his hard stomach to his chest, her fingers vibrating with the sensation of warm male skin. They were going to do this. Again. Syn inside her. Taking her, again.

Syn reached for the edges of her tank and slowly

lifted the silk and lace over her head. At first, he just stared. His eyes flashing hunger as they roamed over her belly and breasts.

"So beautiful," he said. "Bloody hell, *veana*."

And then he filled his hands with her, feeling the weight of her heavy breasts, squeezing, then releasing her to tug gently on her nipples.

Instantly heat and moisture pooled in Petra's sex. She drew air through her teeth, and her face became a mask of erotic desire. In her mind she imagined Syn leading her to the bed, pulling down her pajama bottoms, and sinking into the already soaking-wet heat of her cunt.

But instead, he made her nearly come where she stood.

His head dropped and, squeezing one sensitive mound, he took her hard pink nipple into his mouth. Petra cried out as he suckled. Never in her life had she felt anything so delicious. Cream leaked from her pussy and dripped down her thighs. His tongue continued to lap at her, but he brought his thumb up to meet it, and the two took turns. Tongue. Lash. Thumb. Flick.

Groaning, mumbling incoherently, Petra brought her hand to the waistband of her pajama bottoms and was all set to send it down and through her slit. Gods, he was making her insane. She had to. Had to touch herself. She couldn't wait.

But Synjon growled against her wet nipple. "No."

She whimpered. "Syn . . ."

"No," he said again, more firmly. "You will wait, love."

Fine, she muttered to herself. But if she couldn't touch herself, she was going to fill her hand with him.

As he continued to drive her to madness with his

tongue and fingers, she fumbled with the metal that kept his jeans resting on his sexy hipbones. It didn't take her long to get in, get down, find him. After all, he had already busted out of his boxers and was so rock hard that he pressed against the skin of his belly.

Petra wrapped her hand around his thick length and squeezed. Syn's teeth came down on her nipple, and they both sucked in air.

"Oh, bloody hell, yes," he muttered, switching to her other breast and nuzzling her nipple with his nose.

Petra loved the feeling of him in her hand as she stroked him. So hard, so smooth except for the pulsing veins beneath his skin. Her mouth watered, but not for his blood this time, and she released his cock and tried to maneuver him onto the bed. It was like trying to move a brick wall. He was completely absorbed by her top half.

That is, until she whispered, "I want you in my mouth, Syn. I want to taste you."

His head came up, and his eyes went hooded and dark. "Crikey, *veana*. I may just come from your words alone."

She grinned. "Lie down."

"Fuck me. Anything you say, love." He tore off his jeans and rocketed onto the bed before she even made it to the edge of the mattress.

Her gaze moved over him. Feet, to powerful thighs, to thick, blood-heavy cock, to waves of muscle, to a chest that begged for a female's sweaty cheek. Petra licked her lips. He was lying on his back, his hands behind his head. He looked like the ultimate bad boy. He looked exactly like what she wanted.

She eased her silk pajama bottoms down to her ankles, then stepped out of them. She knew he was watching her and she liked it that he was. She felt no shame in her body, in the swell of her belly. They'd created this, together, and it felt so right to be with him.

The glow from the skylight above, the dancing snowflakes, was a beautiful, moving spotlight on his body, and as Petra climbed onto the bed and cat-crawled toward him, she saw the glistening wetness of precome on the hard planes of his abdomen. Her mouth watered in anticipation. Just the thought of him inside her mouth, pumping, filling her, made her insides pulse and hum.

She was at his side in seconds, her hand wrapping around the base of his cock, her head lowered to take him into her mouth.

But first she had to taste him. Lick the wetness, the sensual tears, off the head. They were for her, after all.

With a moan of excitement, she swiped her tongue across him. Syn cursed blackly, and his hips jacked up. Salty. Creamy. Perfect. She growled and took him in her mouth, slowly, letting him slide himself in. He was thick and so hard, she wasn't sure she could accommodate him. But, gods, she wanted to try. She loved his taste, loved the way his hand now moved up and down her back, mimicking her rhythm as she sucked him.

"You feel so bloody good, *veana*," he muttered, his free hand fisting the sheets. "Too good. Your mouth is like liquid fire, and your tongue . . . fuck, the way it's pressing against my shaft, I want to come right now. But fucking Christ, it's got to be in your pussy."

The insides of Petra's thighs were soaking wet as she

worked him, as she moaned and squeezed and suck-led.

Synjon cursed again, his back arching. "I've been dreaming about your tight, hot pussy for months."

Her sex clenched with his erotic words, and she squeezed him tighter, took him deeper, wanted him at the back of her throat when he came.

But Syn had other plans. He thrust into her; then when he pulled his ass back into the mattress, he managed to free his cock from her mouth. And once he was free, he moved so fast she didn't know where he'd gone at first.

Suddenly his mouth was by her ear, his wet cock was on her back, and she was on her hands and knees. "I want you to be comfortable, *veana*," he whispered, lapping at her sensitive lobe.

He spread the cheeks of her ass, and she gasped.

He made a sound of approval, and she felt his fingers at the opening to her sex. "Because I'm going to take you so deep, you won't know where I begin and you end."

Oh, gods. "Syn—"

It was all she managed to squeak out before he drove into her cunt and lightning flickered on the backs of her eyelids. For one moment he just held there, and Petra panted and groaned and smiled and thought that she'd never been so happy in her entire life. He was claiming her. Maybe not with words, but with actions, and for now—for right that minute—it was all she needed to let go and come.

The climax rippled through her and she heard Syn curse. He gripped her hips tightly and remained deep inside her as she trembled and saw stars and creamed against his steely cock.

"Move," she whispered, her head shifting from side to side as she tried to get her bearings. "Fuck me, Syn. Hard. Deep. Fast. It feels so good. *You* feel so good."

The sound their bodies made, the slap of his sex thrusting in and out of her wet core, was the ultimate music to Petra. The only thing she wanted to hear. For hours, days, months. Even after the *balas* . . . She gasped, her mind falling apart as her body took over. She cried out and swung her hips to meet him.

It was carnal.

There was no other word for it.

Hunger drove them, over and over and to the edge of madness and perfection, and when Syn coiled over her, resting his cheek on her back as he took both her breasts in his hands, Petra felt tears behind her eyes. They were one. Maybe it was a strange and immoral thought to have in the middle of a deep, mind-bending fuck, but she and Syn and *balas* were completely and totally one.

Tears rained down her cheeks, and as Syn pummeled her with deep thrusts and light tugs to her nipples, she came again. Heat and electric currents battered her cunt, and she turned wild, bucking and crying out as Synjon's thrusts turned manic. Hot seed surged into her sex, making them both so wet her pussy couldn't contain the onslaught. Seed and cream flooded her legs, and Synjon cursed and pulled out of her.

For a moment Petra wasn't sure what was happening, where he was going. If he was leaving her. Then he flipped her gently to her back, spread her thighs, and settled between them.

Her blurry gaze widened.

But Syn only grinned and lowered his head. When he touched her, when his hot, thick tongue made contact with her sensitive flesh, a moan of absolute ecstasy tore from her throat, and she fell back on the pillows. He was licking her. Not just her sex, but her lips and her thighs. Cleaning her, tasting her—eating her. Gods, she was going to die from it.

"Drink from me, Syn," she called out, her head thrashing from side to side against the pillow.

"I am, love," he whispered, his breath tickling her skin. "Your pussy just keeps quenching my unending thirst."

Her legs shook. "No. Not that," she muttered as she felt his teeth nibble at the lips of her sex.

"How about this, then, m'dear, m'darling?" He plunged his tongue deep inside her cunt, then retreated.

"Oh, fuck," she gasped. "No, Syn. Gods, I love it, but no. My blood. Christ. Drink my blood."

He stilled, his body, his mouth, and his breath, coming quick against the entrance to her sex. "Petra . . ."

"It's okay," she said. "I promise you. I swear. I know it." She came up on her elbows, locked eyes with him. "I think this is how it's supposed to be, Syn. With . . . a couple."

His eyes darkened, and though he kept his gaze on her, he ran his tongue up her slit.

She cried out.

"Mates, Petra?"

Yes. Yes. "Bite me," she commanded. "Drink from me."

He growled, his fangs dropping.

"Do you want to feed from anyone else?" she said with almost sexual menace.

"Fuck, no, love. You know that."

"Then do it."

She saw the struggle in his eyes, but the hunger was there too, and thank the gods it was the stronger of the two. He pulled back from her sex but remained between her legs. His hands rested on her hot core, while his head turned and his tongue flicked out to lap at the skin of her inner thigh. Petra watched him, her breath tightly caught in her lungs. She remembered how it felt to be bitten by him, but this time was so different—this time hunger was caged in a haze of erotic compulsion.

She felt his fingers part her sex, felt the pad of his thumb move impossibly lightly down her lips.

"Please, Syn," she begged.

He nuzzled her skin, then scraped his fangs over the spot he wanted to bite.

Best. Feeling. Ever.

Her eyes slammed shut.

Except for maybe this feeling.

She fell back on the pillows, her mouth forming a small O as Syn's fangs pressed deeper and deeper into her flesh. And then he was drinking. Her blood. Taking it in big gulps as he followed the seam of her pussy with his thumb, all the way to the opening of her sex, clearly determined to make her come again. The most perfect shared ecstasy.

Alex watched his mate very closely as Dillon paced the floor of the library in his house in SoHo. The entire family was gathered: Romans, *mutore*, Impure Resistance, Celestine, and Wen. And Alex was worried that Sara's concern about Petra and the shifters was wearing on her. She was growing so close to her time, which made Alex all the more protective.

"Are you all right, my love?" he whispered in her ear while Dillon went on about the heavy search of the Rain Forest and how there had been absolutely no sign of Cruen.

Sara turned to him, her blue eyes beautiful as always, but tired. "I'm fine." She touched his face. "You worry too much."

He growled lovingly at her. "It's never too much when it comes to you and our *balas*."

She leaned in and kissed him. "Wait until after it's born. There'll be plenty to worry about then."

"What does that mean? Do you foresee a problem?" His gaze moved over her. "Shall I call for Leza?"

She laughed softly. "You're losing it, honey."

Then she kissed him again, and Alex forgot all about his fears. Hell, he forgot his name. He reveled in the feel of her warm, soft mouth, and played with her tongue. He was about to wrap his arms around her and really start the tasting, when Dillon interrupted with a curse.

"Hey!" she shouted. "Lovebirds! Trying to stop a war over here."

Alex eased back, but he didn't take his eyes off his mate's mouth. How was it possible that she tasted sweeter with every day that passed?

She grinned up at him. "We'd better listen to Dillon. You can ravish me later."

"Oh, my god," Dillon groaned. "Getting nauseated over here."

Laughing, Sara turned back. "Sorry, D."

"I'm not," Alex said, curling his lip at the *veana* who was working his rug down to the fibers. "Okay, D. If Cruen's so deeply hidden in the forest that even the shifters who live there can't find him, what can we do?"

Dillon glanced around the room. "The Order will come and find him if we don't."

"That's not the answer to the question I asked," Alex said, dropping his arm around his mate's shoulders.

"Fine. We have two options at this point. We can let the shifters deal with it on their own, and by 'it' I mean the Order coming into the forest, finding Cruen, and taking out anyone who gets in their way . . ."

"And what's the other option?" Nicholas asked.

Phane sat forward and Helo too, but it was Lycos, who'd just shown up in the doorway after basically being a ghost for the past few days, who spoke.

"She wants us to stand with them and fight," he said. His eyes cut to Dillon. "Right, sis? Protect and serve a race that's not our own? Well, you can count me out."

"Already had, brother dear. Already had." Dillon barely spared him a glance. She was looking at the Romans, Helo and Phane, even Celestine. "I won't pretend, unlike others, that I'm not connected to the shifters. That they're not a part of my blood. Maybe even more so than the vampire in me. And if they need my help, I'm going to give it. You'll all have to make that decision too. But make it quick." She inhaled deeply. "Because I fear it's only a matter of time before Feeyan feels the pressure to carry out her rash threat, and lands at the gathering stones, her power ratcheted up to high."

*   *   *

He could worship at her temple forever.

His fangs pulled from her thigh, Syn licked and kissed the two pinprick holes until they started to close; then he rose above her. He felt like a new *paven*, impossibly strong, deeply possessive, achingly satisfied and ... Bollocks, dare he say it? Happy?

He gazed down at her, black hair against the white pillow, cheeks and lips stained a deep pink, and those eyes ... they killed him, stole his unbeating heart, reached inside his mind and emptied it of all thoughts but the ones that involved the two of them, naked.

"You sure you're all right?" he asked.

She grinned and stretched around him. "Never felt better in my life."

"Oh, *veana*, you know I can't resist a challenge. Not when it comes to you ..." He grinned. "Coming."

"Then don't." She wrapped her legs around his waist and locked her ankles just above his ass.

He went hard instantly.

She glanced down and grinned. "Wow. My blood's everywhere in you, it seems."

"It's bloody magic, love," he growled. "Truly."

"Then I must be a witch."

He grinned. "A sorceress."

"Able to cast spells on her enemies—"

"And her lovers."

She laughed. "Of which she will have too many to count. One for each day of the week—"

Petra stopped talking when she felt Syn go rigid around her. His gaze dropped.

"Syn. What is it?"

His eyes on her belly, he eased back, then thrust inside her hot, ready pussy. Petra gasped. Clung to him. Worried about him.

As her sex stretched to accommodate him, Syn's eyes locked on hers. "No other male will play father to my *balas*."

Petra swallowed tightly. "Syn . . ."

He eased out of her, then thrust back in possessively, making her gasp.

"No other male will linger above you. Waiting . . . just waiting for the chance . . ."

He started moving inside her.

His eyes, their black heat, bored a hole straight through to her soul. "No other male will lick you, drink from you, fuck you, or make you scream."

She cried out as he pulled out of her, then slid all the way down to her sex and plunged his tongue into her cunt. For several mind-altering seconds he fucked her, speared her. Then just as quickly, he left, replaced his tongue with his cock again, and covered her mouth with his own.

Petra nearly climaxed right there.

She kissed him fiercely, tasting herself on his tongue. The combination of the two of them was shockingly heady, and she wanted more. She wanted everything. And Syn was determined to give it to her.

He tunneled under her body and lifted her hips. The harsh cry that escaped her lungs when he drew back and thrust into her rent the air around them. Slightly weak from a long night of lovemaking and Synjon's intense blood drain, Petra could only hold on and take whatever he had to give her.

Syn gripped her ass cheeks and pummeled her with stroke after honeyed stroke until she was breathing heavy, moaning his name, and ratcheting up her hips for one last thrust as she came. One loud, raspy scream tore from her throat, and Syn followed her, draining his hot, creamy seed inside her sex.

Coated in a very sexy layer of sweat, Synjon eased out of her and collapsed to the side. Before she could even release the breath hovering inside her lungs, he caught her up in his arms and pulled her ass to his groin. Petra sighed and melted into his chest. And just when she thought it couldn't get any better, any sweeter, he covered her—her and their *balas*—with the softest, thickest blanket in the world.

19

Petra woke to near blackness, and it took her a moment, and a good glance around, to realize where she was.

Syn's room.

Syn's bed.

And it had to be morning because the skylight overhead was sealed.

She glanced over her shoulder. She was alone, though the impression of Syn's body on the mattress remained. And, of course, his scent. It was everywhere. On the sheets, in the air, all over her naked body.

Swinging her legs over the side of the bed, she spotted the robe she'd gotten on her shopping trip. It was laid out over the arms of an almond-colored leather chair against the wall. She smiled, knowing Syn had placed it there for her. In any other situation, at any other time, she would've let her mind run wild with that gesture. The implications, the potential outcomes. The hopes. But she wasn't going to do that this time.

She got out of bed and scooped up the robe. She refused to ruin herself and the wonderful memories of the night before by overanalyzing. When reality settled in, whatever happened, happened. But right now she was going to live in bliss for however long that lasted.

After slipping the black silk robe on and tying the sash above her belly, she ventured out of the room. Clearly, it was full-on morning now, because every window was sealed and the house was lit by all things electric. As she walked down the hallway, past the teardrops of metal art on the wall, she wondered if Syn was even at home. It was so quiet. She also wondered what she was going to do today. She knew she needed to check in with her family and with Dani. The last thing she wanted was for them to worry about her and once again come to Manhattan to investigate.

Especially Dani. That female would force her to recite a virtual laundry list of affirmations about never sleeping with vampires named Synjon Wise and listening to genius best friends who were always right.

Petra laughed to herself at the thought, and didn't see Synjon until she was nearly on top of him.

Well, Synjon and a . . . pine tree?

"Morning, darling," he said, plugging something into the outlet behind him. "How did you sleep?"

"Good." Lights erupted inside the pine tree. "Oh!" She looked from the tree to Synjon and back again. "What's this?"

She stepped over a small pile of boxes, wrapped in beautiful silver-and-gold paper.

Synjon was looking at her like she had two heads. "Christmas. Don't you know about that?"

Oh, right. She'd seen trees lit up when they were in

the city. "We don't celebrate it in the Rain Forest, but I've heard of it. Seen pictures. But"—she looked at him with a confused expression—"why are you doing it?"

He gave her an almost boyish shrug. "You had a chance to shop for yourself."

"I know. It was great. I loved it." She still didn't understand.

He stood up, went over to her and ran his hands up her black-silk-covered arms. "Sexy. Crikey, I don't think I'll ever get enough of you, love."

"Back atcha," she said, smiling. "Now, tell me what this is, please."

"All right. I thought you should have the same chance for the *balas*." He gestured to the gifts. "Go through them, see if there's anything you like."

She stared at the boxes. "You got things for the baby?"

"It's nothing. Just a few bits and bobbles."

Petra felt a huge lump form in her throat. "You picked out gifts for the baby." It wasn't a question. Gods, it wasn't even directed at him really. She was just unloading her surprise. This wasn't the Synjon Wise who'd had his emotions drained and who had seemed completely impassive with regard to her and the *balas* growing inside her just a few days ago. And frankly, this wasn't the Synjon Wise from the Rain Forest tree house so many months ago either.

She turned to look at him. This was a Synjon Wise she'd never met before, but had fantasized about in the wee hours of the night when she'd been on her own, looking for Cruen, scared, lonely. The real and open Synjon. The nurturer, the gentle, thoughtful, sensual, playful caretaker.

"They'll come to pick up whatever you don't like," he continued, his eyes on her, studying her expression.

She heard him, knew what he was saying, and yet she found herself asking, "When did you do this?"

"While you were sleeping."

Overcome with the moment, the gesture, the happiness inside her, she rose on her toes and wrapped her arms around his neck. Her eyes searched his. "Santa, right?"

He laughed. "No, *veana*. Just a father."

She gasped, stilled, her gaze locked with his. *Oh, gods. His words. This was bad. Or it could be bad.* Even she hadn't gone there in her mind. She'd wanted to. So badly. But she knew where it led. That impossible road. Damn it, why did he have to say that? Something so completely committed? When neither of them knew what the future held. When he was still determined to destroy her father.

"Petra?" His eyes searched her own. She wondered what he saw there. The truth, or a *veana* so in love that she was overcome by his thoughtfulness?

"I don't know what to say," she said.

"You like it?"

She nodded. "I bloody love it."

His face broke into a ridiculously gorgeous smile. "I told you. No one claims this *balas* but me."

Right. The balas.

And what about her?

Don't ruin it. Don't. For yourself. For him. For Little Fangs. Just don't. Because odds are you'll hear something in there you don't want to deal with right now.

Her gaze traveled the length of the beautiful pine

tree. It smelled amazing. It smelled like family and memories, and a new couple sharing their first Christmas.

She wondered if it would be the same next year. Or if this was it, all she would get.

He broke from her grasp, leaned down, grabbed one of the presents, and held it out to her. "Ready?"

If this was all she got, she was going to enjoy it without regrets.

She ripped off the paper, flung open the box, and squealed like a young female when she saw a tiny T-shirt with the words "Little Fangs" printed on it.

He was nearly ready to return what should never have belonged to him in the first place. What had been forced on him. What had tried to take him down, make him so ineffectual and weak he might've truly gone through with what the bloodletter had said.

Begged Synjon Wise to remove his emotions.

But that was no longer the only option. The water shifter's flesh, though beyond vile to force down, was slowly rebuilding his power grid. Granted, each burst was short-lived, so he'd been experimenting with stacking his feedings. Once every few hours, then once per hour, then every thirty minutes.

The water shifters had watched him carefully. Taking notes, asking questions, making sure that Cruen had the best and most aged flesh. He'd even been experimenting with his flash. Short trips, and only at night because he knew the Romans and the *mutores* were searching for him. It took consuming flesh at nearly fifteen-minute intervals, but he could finally travel and return without feeling weakened by the effort.

Tonight, he was going to see his guard. Make sure the male had remained near the gathering stones. If he had, it would tell Cruen everything he needed to know about the guard's loyalty.

Perhaps he wouldn't have to die after all.

Stuffing a good-size chunk of flesh into his mouth and another in his pocket, Cruen left the water shifters' haven and flashed to a stand of trees just a few yards from the gathering stones. Looking around, sniffing the air, he didn't see or sense the guard, and his anger flared to life, bringing forth visions of quick justice. But then he realized that the male would not remain out in the open. Not with the search for his master going on.

He hated to use his new power for anything other than taking down Wise, but he needed to meet with his guard first.

Checking for movement in the surrounding forest, and finding it quiet, he flashed to a wooded area at the back of the stones and waved his hand in a deep arc.

The guard's position, his hiding spot, was instantly revealed. And though Cruen felt a twinge of the old weakness stir within him, he moved steadily toward the male.

"Good. You remain."

The male, who was just emptying his bladder, turned and nodded at Cruen. "Of course, sir."

"I have nearly completed my business with the shifters and will soon be returning to the States."

The male eyed him a little too closely. "And when will that be, sir?"

Cruen sniffed. "You don't question me, male."

He lowered his head, but his eyes remained fixed on Cruen. "Of course, sir."

"But I will tell you this, since you have been a loyal servant to me thus far. My strength has nearly returned, and I won't need your flash."

"Yet you want me to remain, sir?"

"I will be using your abilities for something far more satisfying than a mere flash." His mouth curved upward, and his hand reached into his pocket and palmed the slimy flesh. "Be ready, male. We will be traveling soon."

Syn had amassed his fortune by blowing up shit, protecting shit, rescuing shit, and keeping his nose out of shit that didn't concern him. He'd been a ghost and an assassin. A lover and a bastard. A good Samaritan and a decent friend. But he believed that in all that time, all those years, he'd never experienced a moment that was perfectly and utterly fun.

Until now.

He leaned back against the club chair and watched Petra go through all the toys and books, baubles and clothing again, her face glowing like a bloody candle. Who would've thought that a soon-to-be-stack-of-firewood, some lights, and a few baby gifts would make a *veana* so happy?

He grinned.

He'd done this. And he was right bloody proud of himself, he was.

"Anything you don't like, love?"

"Are you kidding? It's all perfect. I don't know how you managed it."

"Could be because I myself am perfect."

She glanced up, gave him a crooked smile. "Yeah, that must be it."

He chuckled. "Well, it's not over yet."

"Oh, jeez," She glanced around, "You don't have a pony or something stashed somewhere, do you?"

Pony. Yes, all children liked to ride those small animals. He'd have to buy a house upstate. Somewhere with a lot of land, stables.

"Synjon."

He looked up. "Yes, love?"

"I was kidding. No one needs anything else here."

"Except you." Grinning like a bloody fool, he reached behind himself, under the chair and took out a final gift. "Happy Christmas, Petra."

She took the small box from him, then found his gaze and shook her head. "What is this?"

"Just a little something for you."

"You've already done way too much." Her shoulders slumped and she looked embarrassed. "And I don't have anything for you."

He leaned toward her, put a hand on her belly. "Yes, you do."

He watched her eyes turn color. From the palest of blue to a rich, brilliant sapphire. And within those beautiful orbs, Syn saw something that equally pleased and terrified him. Love. Petra was in love with him.

Something gripped his heart muscle and squeezed the ruddy shite out of it. He thought it was probably his conscience, but he'd been under the impression it wasn't working. Petra loved him. They had a *balas* on the way. And he was still intent on Cruen's destruction. In this very fucking house, no less.

His mind hummed. Maybe Petra didn't have to know anything. Maybe he could keep the fact that Cruen resided and suffered and died under this roof to himself.

His lip curled.

Was he truly that cold?

Christ, he used to be. Now things were different. So different. Because of her and the *balas*. They'd changed him somehow. They'd forced new and compelling emotions out of him. He didn't know how that could be possible, but it was true.

She was still staring at him with unabashed affection.

He nodded at the box, commanded gently, "Open it."

That seemed to pull her out of the trance she was in, and she shook her head and tugged the red ribbon off the box. Her hands shook slightly as she pried off the top.

"Oh . . . ," she breathed, her fingers running over the small diamond key necklace. "It's beautiful."

"I want you to stay, Petra."

She looked up. "What?"

"That key. It's not a real key to the door, of course, but it means the same." Christ, he sounded like a rambling idiot. Which made him realize how desperately he wanted her to say yes. "Will you think about it?"

She shook her head, her eyes filling with tears.

Synjon felt the first of many waves of excruciating pain wash over him. He started to get up, but Petra's hand on his arm stopped him.

"I'm shaking my head, Mr. Wise," she said, her mouth curving up into a brilliant smile, "not because

I'm declining your offer, but because I don't have to think about it."

"Oh, bloody hell, *veana*. I nearly lost my mind there for a moment."

She reached up and touched his cheek. "I'm willing to give up the Rain Forest, my family, all I've known for you."

He grinned broadly.

Her eyes remained serious. "What will you give up for me?"

"Anything. Everything," he said without hesitation.

"Will you give up my father?"

Synjon's smile died a quick, disastrous death, and his gut tightened painfully. What she was saying . . . Christ, what she was asking . . . She didn't know . . .

"Can you do that?" She swallowed, watching him carefully. "If you can't, please tell me now. I promise there'll be no hard feelings, no anger, no bitterness. I know how important the *balas* is to you, and I wouldn't keep him or her from you. But I need to know for me." She closed her eyes and took a quick breath, then opened them again. "I want to be with you more than anything. But if this is something you truly can't let go of, you're going to have to let go of me."

Synjon stared into her eyes and searched for an answer. Within her, within himself. His chest was so bloody tight, he wondered if he'd be able to take another breath.

"Can you let this go?" she repeated, her voice completely resolute.

He didn't know. Fuck, he didn't know if he could. But the one thing he did know for certain was that there was no way he was letting this *veana* walk out of his life. And, bloody hell, into the arms of another male.

"Yes, *veana*," he said without a blink, a breath, or a "but." "I will give up my revenge."

For several seconds she just stared at him, her eyes searching his. Maybe she was wondering if she'd heard him correctly, or if he was about to change his mind. But then her face broke into a smile so wide, so happy, so relieved, that his gut ached.

He was such a vile prat.

He didn't deserve her.

Almost giggling, Petra took the necklace from the box and handed it to him. "Will you put it on me?"

His gaze dropped to the key. They key that meant a thousand things he couldn't say. The thousand things he wished and wanted for them. He undid the clasp and fastened it around her neck.

It was what he so desperately wanted. She was his. Because she wanted to stay. Because she cared for him. Because she might even love him.

Because she believed the lie he'd just told her.

20

Feeyan didn't glare at Dillon. She didn't snarl or snip, make a rude comment about Beasts or *mutores* or gutter rats. She simply turned to the other Order members at the table and said, "A Pureblood vampire is missing in the Rain Forest. Shall we go and find him?"

Seated behind the table, Dillon stared straight ahead, not listening to the discussion around her. She was pretty sure the Impure would vote her way, but she wasn't about to try to convince anyone else. Feeyan was the leader of this brood, and like it or not—agree with her or not—the majority tended to side with her.

Fear and ancient ways still ruled the Order. A more modern approach to governing a community wasn't about to suddenly take effect just because they now had a *mutore* and an Impure among them.

It would take time.

Feeyan rose from her chair and her voice boomed down the table toward Dillon. "Will you lead the way, Order Member Nine? Or is this a trip we must take without you?"

Dillon's jaw was so tight, she was afraid it might snap. She turned toward the *veana* and said in the steadiest voice she could muster, "If you choose Cruen over common sense, I will stand with the shifters." Then she turned back and faced forward again.

Around her the shocked and appalled prattle began.

As the hot spray pummeled her back, Petra dropped her head and fingered the key around her neck. Even in the dim light of the shower, the diamond charm sparkled brilliantly. She couldn't believe what had happened this morning. The tree, the presents, the promises. It was perfect. And if there was one thing she knew didn't exist, it was perfection.

But when she was around Synjon, when he looked at her with an almost covetous glint in his eyes, she felt reality slip away. She wanted this. Him. Them.

She just prayed he could keep his promise.

Deep in thought, she didn't hear Synjon slip into the shower or feel him curl behind her, until his arms were wrapped around her belly and his lips were pressed to her shoulder blade.

She gasped as he trailed a line of fiery kisses up her shoulder to her neck, pausing when he was close to her ear.

"Playing with your key," he whispered. "Your mind elsewhere. Having second thoughts, love?"

Even in the hot, steam-filled shower, she shivered. "Perhaps."

His hands drifted up, over her belly to cup her breasts. "What about, then?"

She sighed at the feel of his large, slightly rough palms. "Well, this key," she replied. "It's not very practical." Her nostrils flared as he started gently pinching her nipples. "It doesn't unlock anything."

"Bollocks." He rolled his hips. His cock was like steel against her back. "I think the bloody thing unlocks my heart."

She melted at his words. "Isn't your heart as silent as mine, vampire?" Gods, she wanted this, him. And she wanted his cock inside her again.

He chuckled softly, then eased her legs apart with his foot. "Doesn't mean it can't be opened. Allowed a little light and care."

"Oh, Syn," she said breathlessly, her skin tightening, tingling.

His hands moved from her breasts around to her back. As the shower rained down on both of them, he traced the line of her spine. "Do you want me to be open to you, love?"

"Yes," Petra breathed, anticipating the descent of his fingers as she let her hands rest on the wet walls in front of her.

"Because I want you to be open to me. Always." Synjon continued downward, moving through the crease in her bottom, flipping his wrist just in time to ease two fingers inside her.

Petra's groan of lust echoed throughout the stone shower.

He nipped at her shoulder. "A little farther open if you will, love."

She arched her back.

"Mmmmm, there it is."

"Please, Syn." Her insides were tight and trembling. "I need you."

"Brilliant," he growled. "Because I need you, too, Petra, love." He slipped his fingers out, and she felt the head of his cock nudge against her sex. "More than you'll ever know."

He punctuated his words with one perfect thrust into her cunt. Crying out, Petra arched her back and circled her hips, trying to get his iron cock to hit every inch of her creaming walls.

She heard Syn hiss, then felt his arm move over her shoulder. The sudden and intoxicating scent of hot, rich blood encircled her and instantly her fangs dropped. As Syn moved inside her, his strokes slow and shockingly deep, Petra drove her fangs into his waiting vein.

All thoughts drifted out of her mind, never to be analyzed again, and she became one humming, raw thread of feeling. Behind her, Syn growled and hissed and continued to drive up into her with a perfect rhythm that was designed to send her screaming over the edge.

Blood cascaded into her mouth, slid down her throat, fusing with the sensations of impending climax. It was a smoking leaf to a vast forest of dry brush, and Syn's thrusts caught that fire and quickened. The sound of wet bodies slapping against each other filled the air, and Petra's legs started to lose their purchase. She dropped his arm and leaned against the shower wall as inside her trembling pussy, Synjon's cock swelled mercilessly.

Brilliant light burst inside her mind, and she slammed

her hips back and came hard, moaning and whimpering, bucking and cursing, and wishing she could sustain the intensity of her climax for hours, days . . .

Syn gripped her ass and growled, the unearthly sound making the hairs on her arms stand up as he pounded ruthlessly into her.

And then Petra spread her legs even wider and leaned over, giving him full access. She heard him curse, felt him lightly slap her right cheek, and with four deep, driving thrusts, he came inside her.

Hot seed coated her walls, and she whimpered. She loved that feeling, loved having him impaled inside her.

For several long moments, neither of them moved. As the water turned cool, and Syn's fingers lightly brushed the skin of her back and buttocks, the only sound was heavy breathing diminishing into soft pants of satisfaction.

Exhaustion claimed her, and Petra barely noticed when Syn eased out of her, shut off the water, and wrapped her in a warm towel. She curled into him as he lifted her and carried her out of the bathroom.

"Sleepy, love?" he whispered.

"Hmmmm," she answered, nodding her head against his chest, kissing his smooth, hard skin.

He chuckled as he placed her on the cool sheets. When he drew back to get the covers, Petra grabbed his arm.

"Don't leave," she whispered in a bleary tone.

The mattress dipped with his weight, and he moved in close behind her. "Never." He pressed his body right up against hers and dropped a kiss to her shoulder. "Sleep now, m'dear, m'darling."

Smiling to herself, she snuggled into the curve of his body, loving his words, loving his heat, loving his closeness.

Gods.

Loving him.

Synjon strode into the diner and headed for the back booth. Leaving Petra, all warm and wet and soft in his bed, was the hardest thing he'd ever done. And he wasn't even going to think about how he was lying to her in more than a few ways. *Prat.* He was just fecking worthless, truly. But once again, Adrian's text had drawn him out—out of what was so perfect and happy, and toward something dusty and vile-smelling that he just couldn't seem to turn away from.

"I can't be gone long," he said, slipping into the red leather booth across from the badass, ginger-haired *paven.*

"Neither can I," Adrian said, glancing around the diner before turning his eyes on Syn. "Cruen's nearly ready to leave, and he's gaining strength."

A shot of unease moved through Syn's gut. "How?"

"I don't know."

"You need to find out." Syn leaned across the table, his voice low and calculating. "We can't have the old Cruen on our hands. Not until he's in chains and under lock and key—and the heat of the midday sun." He said the words with such fury and conviction, he knew in that moment that letting go of his need for vengeance wouldn't be nearly as simple as a promise made to the *veana* he wanted.

"Problem is," Adrian said, "he won't allow me to

come with him. Whatever it is that's filling him with new strength comes from the water shifters there." He paused, thoughtful. "I say we move now. I'm ready. You're ready. Right?"

Bloody hell, he'd been ready for so long he couldn't remember what it felt like to be unburdened. Synjon stared at the *paven* before him. Juliet's brother wanted this, needed this. Shite, deserved this. It was decision time. If he could just make this happen without Petra finding out . . . But that wasn't possible, and he knew it.

"Syn?"

Syn's eyes rose, locked with Adrian's.

"Tomorrow?" asked the *paven*. "At first dark?"

A flash of Juliet's face moved across Syn's mind, and he winced. Her death, her murder, had to be avenged.

He gave the male a quick nod. His deal with the devil had been made a long time ago, his seat in Hell kept warm by just the idea of being the one who rid the world of that sodding bastard Cruen. It was time to end this—end him—once and for all.

21

"I think I'm set on onesies until the *balas* is in college." Under the cool, crisp light of the midday sun, Sara tossed Petra an overwhelmed expression. "How about you?"

Petra couldn't help but laugh as they walked down the busy street toward Syn's apartment. "Not sure about the onesies, but I have diapers to last until then. Or for a month, depending on how many times I have to change him or her per day."

"How many times *you* have to change . . ." Sara narrowed her eyes, but said playfully, "Come on now. You know that's the dad's job, don't you?"

"Diaper duty?" Petra asked.

"Dealing with all the shit." Sara's face broke out in a wide grin.

Petra laughed again and sidestepped a mom and her stroller. When Sara had called this morning, Petra hadn't been all that sure if the *veana*'s suggestion to do a little baby shopping was a good idea or not. For one thing, Petra had all those baby things that Syn had got-

ten her, but for another—and maybe this was what concerned her the most—she hadn't had any true
interaction with her half sister since she'd found out
the truth about their mutual parent. She had no idea
what to expect. Would the *veana* be outwardly friendly,
but unable to mask a cool distrust behind her eyes? Of
course, that worry couldn't have been further from the
truth. Sara was welcoming and kind and funny, and
cool in a good way. And damn if they didn't have several things in common besides their bellies.

The morning had been a mass of sunshine, but now
gray clouds were starting to move in and it felt like snow
was on the way. As they walked, and as the air grew
colder and the holiday lights and decorations winked at
them in their merry way, Petra felt a deep sense of connection move through her. And yet she didn't want
there to be any confusion about other members of the
family. Particularly Sara's mother.

"I'm really glad you called," Petra said as they came
to Syn's building.

Sara's smile was brilliant. "Me too."

"But I need you to know, I'm just sort of coming to
terms with where I came from and how. Being the off-
spring of blackmail, and all that."

The truth in her words, and no doubt the memory of
learning that her mother, Celestine, had gone to Cruen,
slept with Cruen, only to get her mate released from
imprisonment and impending castration, made Sara's
face fall a little.

"Petra, you don't have to explain any of this to me,"
she said sadly.

"No, I want to. I want to have a relationship with

you. I'm just not ready to call anyone else mom. Don't know if I'll ever be."

Sara nodded. "I totally understand."

"Okay, good." Petra nodded too and smiled. "Thank you."

"But maybe we can bring Gray along next time?" Sara's eyes, so similar to Petra's, widened with hope. "I know he'd love it."

"More baby shopping?"

Sara laughed. "Totally. He's about to be an uncle to two *balas*, after all. We'll make him try out toys and hold our breast pumps and carry stuff."

"You're kind of evil," Petra said with a slow grin. "I love it."

Still laughing, Sara embraced her. It was a nice feeling. All her life, she'd had brothers—and she completely adored them—but this . . . this was something special, female . . . And she wanted it to last.

"Hey," Petra said, "are you getting nervous?"

"You mean, for the birth?"

Petra nodded.

"A little." She shifted her bags to her other hand. "But I have Alexander. He's going to get me through it, deal with my cursing and my death grip on his hands during contractions."

Petra laughed.

"And you have Syn. Right?"

Her laughter softened, then downgraded to a tight-lipped smile. "Yeah. I guess I do."

Above them the sun had been overtaken completely, and the world was suddenly plunged into a cold shade of gunmetal. "What is it?"

She shook her head. "Nothing. I'm happy . . ."

"But you're worried something will screw up that happiness?"

"Pretty much."

Snow started to fall as Sara dropped her packages and took Petra's hand. "Listen, I know this didn't happen right, and I heard all that you said about the past and the present and my mother, but I want you to know I care about you. I'm here for you if you ever want to talk, or bitch." She grinned. "Or just hang out. I really want us to be friends, and maybe someday"— she shrugged—"sisters."

"I'd like that too." Petra gave her a quick hug, then eased back and smiled. "I'll see you later?"

"You got it," Sara said with a smile of her own. She picked up her bags, gave a wave, then headed down the street.

Petra entered the building and seconds after she hit the elevator button realized she'd forgotten to get a key from Synjon before she'd left. Thankfully the concierge remembered her, took one look at her belly and all the packages, and supplied her with one.

The ride up to the penthouse was quick, and after she battled her packages to the door, she entered the apartment with a thankful sigh. It was dark and quiet, and after dropping the bags in the living room, she went to look for Syn. But the rest of the place was just as dark, just as quiet. Strange—he hadn't said anything about going out when she'd left this morning. And it was daytime.

Maybe he was downstairs at the gym, or maybe he knew about the tunnels below the city that Sara had told her about today, and was hanging out with the Roman brothers. He seemed to have a relationship with the very blond, sarcastic one, Lucian.

Gathering up her packages again, she headed into her room. She set them on the desk, glanced at the bed and thought about grabbing a nap. It was good for Syn to have some normal chill time with friends. She couldn't imagine he did that often. She looked for her robe, the soft, black silk one she liked to sleep in when she wasn't sleeping naked with Syn, but it wasn't where she'd left it. Or thought she'd left it.

Tossing her coat over the end of the bed, she left her room and headed for Syn's. No doubt she'd left it in there, and maybe she would just take her nap in his bed instead of her own. She grinned as she entered his room, which still held the scent of their lovemaking from the night before. Yes, definitely in here. And when Syn came home, he could just strip and crawl under the covers with her.

Her body instantly went hot at the thought.

"That's what he does to you, girl," she mumbled as she entered his bathroom. She didn't bother with the light. Her robe wasn't on the hook beside the shower where she'd expected to find it, and she was about to return to her room and just sleep in the buff, when her gaze fell on the walk-in closet. Hanging up there, next to his suits and sexy black shirts, jeans and robe, was her lovely piece of silk.

Had he put it here? With his own clothes?

She went over to it, but didn't pluck it off the hanger right away. Instead she fingered the charcoal gray sweater next to it. The fabric was so soft. She knew what this would look like on him, feel like on him, hard, unyielding muscle through soft cashmere.

She brushed the sleeve against her face and nearly moaned, but at that very moment, she heard a sound. Strange, unnerving, and coming from beyond the closet. Her instant thought was that it was the neighbors, but Syn didn't have any neighbors. Or an animal burrowing in the walls? But the sound wasn't animallike at all. It was more of a metallic whine.

She let go of the sweater and ventured deeper into the closet. The sound was probably coming from outside. Maybe they were erecting another building close by or something. But when the sound came again, louder and stranger, her skin prickled with fear. At this point, she was really hoping it was an animal.

She moved her hand through a row of heavy coats and jackets, feeling for the back of the closet, or gods, an animal's sharp teeth. When her fingers touched wood, she shook her head at her silliness and sighed with relief.

Then the wood moved.

Petra gasped, her gut clenching terribly. Instead of being solid, it gave way. Like a door.

Her breath now coming in quick, shallow pants, she told herself to turn around and walk away. But the rational part of her brain refused the call, and her curiosity and instinct propelled her forward, almost maniacally compelling her to part the jackets and step inside.

Everything happened unbelievably fast after that. One moment she was amid waves of wool and leather, and the next she was being pulled inside a dimly lit room by a shocked and pissed-off Synjon Wise.

"W-what?" she stuttered, looking from him to her surroundings. "What is this?"

He growled, hissed, turned away from her, then turned back with a ferocious glare. She'd never seen him so angry. "Bloody hell, *veana*. What are you doing here? How did you get into the apartment?"

She gasped, her hand jerking up to cover her mouth. At first she thought her eyes were fooling her. Or that maybe she was actually napping and this was a nightmare. The room she stood in had no windows, but the ceiling had the same black covering that was on all the windows during the day, so she suspected the entire thing was glass. But it wasn't the ceiling that disturbed her or made her gut twist and ache. It was the contents of the room. Whips, knives, machines—all things that were designed to torture, kill.

She whimpered against her shaking hand, her eyes moving over the scene again, back and forth. She didn't even have to ask. She knew who this room was meant for.

"I'm the monster now, right, love?"

She didn't look at him. Couldn't look at him.

"How long?" she asked. "How long has this been here?"

He exhaled loudly. "The room was already built when I bought the place. I customized it to my taste."

The shock was starting to wear off, and horrific, nightmarish reality was moving in, quick and painful. "It's perfect."

"Petra . . ."

"You still plan on using this, don't you?" She turned from the living nightmare and finally looked up at him.

He was the most gorgeous male in the world, and the most haunted. She shook her head at him. "With me and the *balas* here. Are you fucking out of your mind?"

He scrubbed a hand over his face. "You don't understand."

"You lied to me!"

"Yes," he ground out.

"Then I understand perfectly."

"Petra—"

"Your emotions are definitely back, Syn. And they're just as sad and dated and misguided as they ever were."

She didn't spare him or the room of torture another glance. She turned and walked through the open doorway, pushed back through the closet. She'd been so right to be wary when all she wanted was to believe in him, believe that he could let this shit with Cruen go so they could build a family together.

"Stop right there!" he called, coming after her. "Where the devil do you think you are going, Petra?"

"Does it matter?" she called back, hurrying out of his bedroom and down the hall.

"Of course it fucking matters!" he shouted after her.

She ignored the grinding pain in her gut, ignored the love she had in her unbeating heart. She would have to ignore it forever now. "I'm going home, Syn. Where I belong."

When she reached the entry hall, he was right beside her, his hand hitting the front door at the very moment hers curled around the knob. "No."

She turned around and pushed at him, but it was like trying to move a slab of ten-feet-thick granite. "You don't get to say no to me."

"We're a bloody family, Petra."

She froze. How dare he . . . How fucking dare he . . .

She whirled on him, poked her finger in his face. "You don't know what that word means. You're an empty shell, Syn. No life. Nothing real. And that's been your choice from the beginning." Her jaw as tight as her resolve, she glared at him. "No matter what you think happened that day near the caves, I didn't save your life. Because you were already dead before I got there."

His eyes went wide and his lips parted, but nothing came out. And the second he took his hand off the door, Petra yanked it open.

"There's no future for those who continue to live in the past. Good-bye, Syn."

A heavy sob threatened to burst from her chest, but she managed to hold back her tears until the elevator door closed and she was racing down to the lobby.

22

Syn stared down at the diamond key, glittering on the hardwood floor. When had she ripped it from her throat? When had she tossed it away so carelessly?

His gut tightened painfully and he groaned.

He was one to talk about careless. It was all he'd been for months.

He leaned down and picked up the key. It fairly burned in his hand. The platinum and diamonds didn't want to belong to him. Not after they had been resting against someone, something so pure.

Fucking hell, what had he done?

His mind and gut screaming in unison now, he left the hall and stalked past the kitchen and the metal artwork on the walls to his bedroom. Her face. Shite, her eyes, when she'd walked through the door into his ready torture chamber. He would never forget it. It was imprinted on his mind.

Utter horror.

Entering the closet, he pushed through the wool and leather and stumbled back into the room. He looked around, trying to take in everything as if for the first time. Witness it as she had witnessed it.

Fucking utter horror.

And it had been exactly what he'd wanted. All he'd wanted. The place where, he'd been convinced, vengeance would finally be his.

He moved into the room and grabbed one of the blades from the wall. Three feet of deadly polished steel. He slashed it through the air, cursing, hating himself more than usual.

Cruen had killed his first love. Now Synjon was allowing the mad vampire to destroy his last.

Sighing with frustration, with confusion, with misery for the life and future he'd just lost, he dropped onto the hard metal bench. He hated to admit it, but his need for revenge had started to wane the day he'd been abducted by the pussy brothers, placed in a cabin by the river, and given the opportunity of a lifetime: to feed his *veana* and his *balas*.

He stared at the blade.

Out there, in his living room, under a sweet-smelling pine, were baby books, a tub shaped like a duck, two stuffed toy rabbits, and a shirt with the words "Little Fangs" printed on it.

Syn's throat went scratchy and tight. Bullocks. He had been about to bring filth and hatred and sickness into this house, into that sweet and innocent perfection. And the very worst, he'd lied to the *veana* he loved. The *veana* who had done nothing but save him. Over and over.

His gaze shifted from one implement of torture to the next. Cruen had no place here anymore. Maybe he never did.

Unfortunately, convincing Petra that he understood now, that he'd changed, that he saw what was real and right, and acknowledging that "desperately sorry" would never make up for what he'd put her through, was going to be a nearly impossible task.

But impossible hadn't seemed to contain him lately. Not his emotions, and definitely not his capacity for love.

"I made ice cream," Dani said in a playful singsong voice that she reserved for very special occasions. Like breakups, and *Battlestar Galactica* marathons. She circled her bowl in front of Petra's nose. "You know you want some."

Sitting in a chair on the tree house porch, overlooking the Rain Forest under a dome of twilight sky, Petra gave the female hawk shifter a tight smile. It was blatantly forced, but Dani knew that was how things were right now.

Broken heart and all.

Dani dropped into the chair beside her and started going at it, her spoon deep in the center of the chocolate scoop. "You sure? It's the best I ever made."

The soft, warm breeze blew Petra's hair off her face. She'd missed it here. She'd been a fool to leave. She'd just been a fool, period. "Sorry, bestie. Blood's my thing now."

Dani made a retching sound. "Well, I ain't offering up that."

"Good," Petra said with a soft laugh. " 'Cause I hear yours is a little sour."

Her mouth dropped open in mock surprise. "Who'd you hear that from?"

"Oh, one of the many males you hang out with."

Dani pointed her spoon at Petra. "Now I know you're lying because I don't let anyone bite me." She pretended to shiver. "That's so weird and gross. How do you do it?"

A shock of memory barreled through Petra. Her fangs in Syn's vein, his fangs inside her. The most perfect meal in the world, and she could never have it again.

"I don't do it," she said softly. "Not anymore."

Dani sighed. "You'll get over it, Pets."

"I don't know." And she really didn't. She'd allowed herself to believe in him, and in them as a family. How did you just get over something like that? Everything you ever wanted, desired, dreamed of, there for the taking. Then ripped from you without even a warning, or some heavy-duty pain-killers.

"You will," Dani assured her, her ice cream momentarily forgotten. "And, girlie, it wasn't meant to be. You know that." She tilted her head to the side, her eyes filled with empathy, anger, love. "His whole deal, his world, his purpose was wrapped up in destroying your father. Now, granted, your father sounds like a big old douche, but seriously, that romance was doomed from the start."

Maybe, Petra thought morosely. *Probably*. But even knowing that, admitting that, she wouldn't wish it away. The beautiful times with him had been the very best times of her life. They may have been wrapped up in something ugly, but they'd been absolutely beautiful.

"Brodan?"

Dani's one-word shock bomb had Petra turning to glare at her. "What?"

Dani laughed at her expression. "Just asking."

"Seriously, Dani? Now? Right now?"

Shrugging, Dani slid a massive spoonful of ice cream into her mouth. "I'm just saying. Don't waste too much time. Brodan's been in love with you forever. All you'd have to do is say the word."

The only words Petra wanted to utter with the bear shifter were friendly, brotherly ones. "Brodan deserves way better than me."

"There is nothing better than you, bestie." Dani granted her a wide grin, complete with chocolate-stained teeth.

Petra laughed in spite of herself. "You're so pretty."

Dani started laughing too. They almost didn't hear a rustle down below, at the base of the tree house. Only when they quieted for a moment, listening, did they hear the sound.

"We have company," Dani said. They both jumped to their feet and raced to the porch railing. Leaning over it, they saw Sasha crawling up the rope ladder.

"Oh, jeez," Petra muttered, releasing a sigh of relief. "It's just my brother."

Dani eyed her. "Who'd you think it was? Or better yet, who'd you hope it was?"

"Your ice cream's melting," Petra said.

"Nice. Very smooth."

"I try to make my evasions quick and sweet-tasting."

Dani glanced down at Sasha, who was nearly at the balcony. "I wondered when they'd hear about this, you returning home and all, and come running. Or climbing." She snorted at her joke, and the moment Sasha swung his large body over the balcony, she attacked.

"What do you want, Whiskers? For fuck's sake, can't a girl and her best friend have some—"

"Stand down, Dani. Christ," Sasha interrupted, his tone and his expression heavy with concern. "They're here."

"Who?" Dani asked, drawing back, instantly serious.

Petra stilled, wondering if her brother was talking about Syn, and maybe . . . Sara or her mate. But that impossible hope was quickly crushed with Sasha's next words.

"The Order," he said, his eyes shuttered. "They're all at the gathering stones."

Petra felt a shock like electricity move through her. Forget her and forget Synjon—the Order was looking for her father now. They believed him to have been abducted by the shifters. Held against his will. Something that Petra knew wasn't possible. Once again Cruen was up to something. What a mess this whole thing was. Synjon had wanted to be the one to abduct Cruen, and yet her father had run off with some underground water shifters and was now becoming a dangerous, threatening problem to Petra's family and friends.

Gods, why did she continue to care about that *paven*'s well-being?

Why did something inside her still hope and wonder if he might love her? Or at the very least, care about her.

"So what?" Dani said, already stripping out of her clothes. "Are they looking for a fight over that geriatric vampire who went looking for trouble in our Rain Forest?"

Sasha nodded, but his eyes remained on Petra. "Something like that."

"Well, then, let's give 'em one."

Shifting into her hawk, wings spread and flapping in the breeze, Dani screeched at the two of them to climb aboard. And when they did, she wasted no time in soaring into the sky, her eyes narrowed on the growing firelight in the distance.

The jaguar, the hawk, and the water beast stood between the shifters and the Order in the center of the gathering stones. The night was very dark, punctuated only by a brilliant full moon in the sky and a bonfire down below.

Dillon didn't know about Phane and Helo—and who the hell knew where Lycos was hanging out these days—but this wasn't about choosing between vampire and shifter. This was about right and wrong. Bully and innocent. And the Order had just crossed that line.

For fucking Cruen.

"We are getting word that Cruen is staying with a group of water shifters," Dillon said, her eyes flickering toward the leader of the Water Faction.

The male knew that a small band of his kind had broken off, were experimenting on themselves with plants and animals, trying to gain power and strength. And it wasn't too far a stretch that Cruen would end up with such a pack.

"Produce him so we may see for ourselves," said Feeyan, her white eyes shockingly bare in the light of the bonfire. She looked almost blind.

"He won't come out for anyone," Dillon told her. "These shifters aren't following the rules of their land."

"So, we're dealing with rogue shifters." Feeyan glanced behind her to the other Order members. "Even worse than I thought."

Shit. Dillon should've known her boss would see things that way, would spin them that way. She should've anticipated. Now there did seem to be an actual threat.

"We ask you to step aside," Feeyan said, her stark gaze running over every faction leader, Petra's mother, and a few other shifter males, including the doctor. "Let us find Cruen and deal with the ones who took him."

Overhead, a hawk was coming in for a landing. Dillon barely gave it a glance. She knew who was arriving, and wondered if it would have any effect on the situation. She guessed not. Feeyan had something to prove. Dillon had noticed it ever since she'd become the leader of the Order. And it had gotten worse as of late. It was evident in her actions, reactions, choices, even the way she continually looked to the other Order members for approval. From what Dillon had heard, Cruen had never given a shit about what the others thought or about gaining their respect. He did what he wanted, what he thought was right, and screw what anyone else said.

It made Dillon wonder if that was why Cruen remained important to Feeyan, and why the *veana* hadn't attempted to investigate the *paven* for any of his many crimes.

"And if we don't step aside?" Wen asked boldly.

Behind Feeyan, two of the more ancient members hissed. Looking pleased, she raised her hand to quell their ire. "We will have to wipe out this entire forest. Clean house, so to speak."

The leader of the Mountain Faction stepped forward, close to the fire, and growled. "How dare you come here and threaten us, our home?"

"There is no threat, only an understanding."

"Bloodsuckers will not dictate our actions or control our world!" cried the leader of the Avians.

"You either give back who you took or we go in and find him ourselves." Feeyan beamed. "You see? Very simple."

Petra came running into the gathering stones, her brother and Dani flanking her. "I'm Cruen's daughter," she said in a loud, clear voice. She looked around, searching, and when she found Feeyan, she addressed her directly. Dillon had to hand it to the pregnant *veana*. She had some serious balls.

"And a full-blood *veana*," she continued. "Long ago, Cruen left me here. I was just an infant. He knows this species, has used them for experiments, and gave his only child to a pride of lions. They raised me beautifully. Clearly he trusts them, feels comfortable among them. If he wanted to leave, all he'd have to do is flash. He's a powerful *paven*, is he not?"

The skin around Feeyan's eyes twitched. "All Purebloods are powerful."

"But Cruen is more so," Petra said, lifting her chin. "Did you ever wonder why?"

Behind Feeyan, the other members stood stock-still, listening intently.

"He dipped into many species," she continued. "Shifter, demon, gods know what else, all in the name of power. He wanted the ultimate vampire, and to do that he added the DNA of other powerful beings." She stepped forward. "Do you really think he's worth a war?"

Feeyan didn't speak at first. She seemed less confident, almost worried, as she stood there and regarded Petra. Dillon stared at her, wondering what she was thinking, how she was going to play this now that Cruen's daughter had proclaimed him able to leave this land anytime he wanted. If Feeyan fought that charge, she was basically saying that Purebloods were weak. If she didn't, she herself looked weak.

Behind her, several of the Order members started whispering. Dillon heard things like, "We look like fools" and "Are we truly negotiating with animals?" and "Cruen would've never let this go on."

Feeyan seemed to make a choice right there. Everything about her changed in an instant. Her demeanor, her stance, even the way she spoke. Clearly, she wasn't about to let the Order members see her as weak. Even if that might be the truth.

"We want access to the Rain Forest," she said finally. "We will find him ourselves. Question him about his activities ourselves."

"Maybe he doesn't want to be found," Dillon said with a tight shrug.

Feeyan's lips twitched with humor. "No matter what his daughter says, no Pureblood vampire wants to live in this jungle. And after this day, none ever will." She turned to address the three Romans brothers and their mates, who had been silent and seething as they sat upon the rocks. "It sets a bad precedent," she continued authoritatively. "The Eternal Breed and . . . whatever these things are will not live together."

With one hand on her belly, Petra glared at the Order. "You can't control where we live."

A false smile on her face, Feeyan raised her hands above her head, then abruptly brought them down. Instantly, snow started to fall.

The shifters gasped and leaped to their feet, touched their heads and shoulders, wondering if they were being burned. Clearly, they had never seen snow before.

Feeyan eyed Petra. "I can control everything, my dear. This—what you see before you—is just a whisper of my power." She turned to Wen and the faction leaders. "I will search this forest, find my Pureblood. And I will do it either with your approval or with your blood on my fangs."

23

Synjon landed at the mouth of the caves, the caves where he'd watched Juliet's body burn, where he'd held and kissed Petra, where he'd realized something had changed within him and that his dead emotions had somehow sprung up from the ashes and were growing once again.

The moon was a spotlight above him, bathing the interior of the cave in ghostly white for a good ten feet. Adrian waited for him inside. They were going to make the trek to the gathering stones, where Cruen was to meet up with his trusted guard. That was the plan anyway.

A whimper from inside the caves drew Syn forward, and he followed the dim light all the way to the back of the cave walls. He'd been here twice in eight months, had witnessed his own mental collapse as well as the confusion and sexual desire and despair of the greatest kind. But never had he come upon something so impossible to resist as Cruen, unconscious and unchained.

He stared at the bloodied and bruised monster just inches away from his feet.

"Forget the stones," Adrian said to him with a dark grin. "We can take him to his final resting place right now."

The male looked bloody feral, Syn thought, a whisper of concern moving through him. *Completely jacked up on adrenaline.* "How did you manage this?"

Adrian shrugged, his fangs hanging low, the points illuminated by the one thread of moonlight that had tracked deep inside the cave. "Drugs. I stole them from the shifter doctor." Adrian grinned. "It's like some kind of animal tranquilizer."

Spreading like cancer through Syn's blood was the satisfaction of knowing that Cruen could be brought down. That he wasn't even close to his full strength. Containment could be so easy. He picked up the *paven*'s legs while Adrian took his shoulders, and they carried him outside the cave.

"I kept him inside," Adrian said, glancing around. "Can't have the Avians flying overhead, seeing something strange that they feel they have to investigate, can we?"

"I'm taking him to the Order, Adrian."

At first the ginger-haired *paven* didn't react. His expression was blank as he stared at Synjon. Then he broke out in something like a low, sinister laugh. "I'm sure I didn't hear you correctly."

"He'll go to Mondrar."

A muted growl rent the warm night air. "Syn."

Yeah, he didn't blame the male for what was coming next. "That's where he belongs, Adrian, the vampire prison. That's where criminals belong."

Adrian released his grip on Cruen and the *paven*

sank to the ground. He stalked toward Syn, his eyes narrowing with every step. "What's happened to you?"

"Changed my mind, mate. That's all."

"More than your mind, I'd say. I thought he belonged with you, tortured until his last breath." His eyes bored into Syn's and he uttered the one word he knew would not only slide the knife home but twist it good and painfully. "Juliet."

"I loved her. So much." He shook his head, feeling the knife slide out again. "But she's gone."

"Yes," Adrian hissed. "And he did that."

"He'll pay for it."

"It's not enough. It's not enough for him to sit in a cell, breathe easy, and get three blood draws a day."

"No. It's not," Syn agreed. "But his death means more now than it ever did. It means my life is over too. I have a mate and a *balas* on the way. They're his blood. He deserves punishment forever if I can manage it. But not by my hand anymore."

"That *veana* has changed you," Adrian said tersely. "Softened you into something you should be ashamed of."

"No shame, mate. Not for loving. When Cruen drained my emotions, I thought I was dead, lost forever. But Petra and the *balas* brought me back. I want to live a different life for them."

Adrian's lip curled. "You pick this female over my sister?"

"Yes," Syn said without hesitation.

He'd never seen such pain in the male's eyes before. And bloody hell if he didn't understand it.

"If you won't make him pay," Adrian began, crouching in a fighting stance, "make him hurt, then I will."

Fighting Juliet's brother to save Cruen was the last thing Synjon would ever have wanted to do. But he did it. One full minute of jabs to the face, throat, and knees, his own fingers crushed on his right hand from being bent back, and one black eye that had made him see stars for a few seconds.

But then Cruen was up and against him, his head flopping forward as Synjon granted one last look at the bloodied *paven* on his knees before flashing away.

The moon was bright above.

The Rain Forest hummed with the sounds of insects, and the night's heat still infused her skin.

But pelting her shoulders and the top of her head were sugar-light flakes of snow.

Petra glared at the leader of the Eternal Order. This *veana* who felt it was her right to flash into a world she knew nothing about and threaten its inhabitants. She hated that she came from such a line of bullies. Feeyan, her father . . . Granted, she knew there was good in the world of bloodsuckers. Her eyes flickered toward the stand of Roman brothers and their mates. They were ready to fight. Alongside the shifters, against their own ruling class. She just hated that they had to. The last thing she wanted was bloodshed.

Feeyan's gaze was now focused on the jaguar *veana*, the *mutore* Dillon, who was hell-bent on protecting the shifters. "If you fight for the wrong side, Order Member Nine, you cannot continue on the Order."

The female shrugged. "Bummer."

"Such insolence," Feeyan hissed.

"And not so fast," Dillon continued, flakes of white coating her long eyelashes. "Even though I'd jump at the chance to escape your old-fashioned rule, you can't kick me off the Order without the approval of the others."

Feeyan looked smug, then slashed at the air with her hands. Instantly the snow was gone and sand was beneath everyone's feet. "I need nothing. You don't seem to understand this, *mutore*." She started toward Dillon. "One who takes the position of leader of the Order, doesn't need anything or anyone to give permission."

"How about when someone is given the position because the real leader got canned?" Dillon's eyes filled with amusement. "The leader everyone respects, maybe even wants back. The leader who truly acted without fear."

Once again, the Order members started to talk. For as much as their leader tried to display her power and bravado, they saw her weaknesses too.

"I think you've spoken enough for tonight," Feeyan said with brutal hatred.

She brought her hand up to Dillon's face and closed it quickly in a tight fist. Dillon's eyes went wide and she gripped her throat. She looked over at Gray, who was on his feet and snarling, and shook her head. She couldn't speak. Up came the Romans, and the shifters. Petra felt panic enter her gut. This was it. The first blow of battle. Once the Romans and the shifters rushed in, there was no going back.

A sudden shock of sound and light stole everyone's

attention, including Feeyan's. Gray rushed in and grabbed Dillon, who touched her throat and gasped as her mute state ceased. But everyone else stood frozen.

Staring at what had just landed.

A battered and bruised Synjon Wise stalked forward with a groggy male in his grasp.

Petra could only gape, her breath caught in her lungs and her gut tight with tension. She didn't know what to think, what to do. The male she loved and the male who'd given her life were headed straight into the center of the gathering stones.

"Here's your lost *paven*," Synjon said, his eyes hard and narrowed on Feeyan. "Battered and bruised and showing off his pure blood."

Gasps and murmurs echoed in the cavernous space as Syn tossed the unconscious *paven* at the Order leader's feet.

Petra didn't know what made her do it. What made her cry out and rush—not at Syn—but at her father. Curled on the ground, he looked so old, so pathetic. This was her flesh and blood. The male who had given her life, given her to the best family in the world.

Her hands ran over his back, his neck. Someone who did all of that couldn't be completely evil. There had to be good somewhere in him, decency in him. She wanted so badly to know it. Not just for herself, but for her *balas*.

A hand crushed hers, and another gripped her shoulders. She managed only a squeak of shock and protest before Cruen jacked to his feet, yanked her up and slammed her back against his chest. Before anyone could move, he curled one hand around her neck.

24

Syn felt every bloody emotion on the planet run through him as he stared at Petra's face. Fury, fear, love, regret. They were all there and all shockingly intense. His hands twitched at his sides. His fangs dropped low and sharp. And a growl he'd never heard before ripped from his throat.

Life was repeating itself. Only this time, he wasn't going to allow Cruen to take his heart and soul from him.

Around the gathering stones, everyone held their breath. Not only was Cruen slowly pressing Petra's windpipe, but his fangs were out and pointed at a spot on her temple that could shut her brain down in an instant.

"Let her go," Syn said in a low, dangerous voice.

Saliva dripped from Cruen's fangs onto Petra's cheek. "Another female for you to mourn, Wise?"

"And for you," Syn replied, trying not to look at Petra. Her fear, her sadness would weaken him. "As this one happens to be your daughter."

"Yes, that is unfortunate. But power comes before all."

"Especially when you've lost yours completely."

Cruen's gaze flickered in Feeyan's direction.

"That's right," Synjon said. "They know. They know you've been hiding out here, eating the flesh of some ancient water beast to try and retrieve your power. Can you flash yet? Or are you still using your Pureblood guard?"

Behind Feeyan, three Order members gasped.

Cruen growled and pressed his fang against Petra's temple.

"Do it and I will rip your flesh from your bones in under a second," Syn promised blackly, inching forward.

"And I'll fucking eat it when he does," Dani said, jumping down from the high rock to stand beside him.

Petra cried out, flinching.

"Enough!" From behind the Romans, an older female stood up. She was tall and lovely, and her eyes, so similar to Petra's, locked with Cruen's and she shook her head at him. "That is our daughter."

"Cellie?" Cruen's grip on Petra eased and his eyes softened as he stared at the female. "Cellie, you're here."

"Let her go, Cruen."

He shook his head. "I can't."

"You won't take her from me again."

"Cellie, I didn't—"

"You took her. From my birthing bed." Her voice broke with emotion. "Not to protect her, but to forge an alliance with the shifters so you could use them."

Though his eyes remained soft upon her, he didn't deny it. "I could've killed her and I didn't. I did that for you."

Petra whimpered, and Synjon's entire body erupted in flame. He acted without thought, but with a lifetime of military combat training to guide him. Flashing from his spot beside Dani, he landed directly behind Cruen and wrapped his own hand around the male's neck.

Cruen gasped, but he didn't let go of Petra.

"What do you want?" Synjon whispered in his ear.

"You. Dead."

"No. That's not what you want. Say it."

Cruen hissed. "Take them back."

"My emotions."

"Yes."

He could scent Petra, her fear, her sadness, and it made him insane. He pulled air into his lungs. "If I do, you will release her immediately following, or you're dead."

"You must love my daughter."

"I love Petra," Syn clarified. No male who treated his young like this could be called a father.

Still gripping the *paven*'s throat, Syn lowered his head, so his temple was flush with Cruen's face and fangs.

"Go back on your word, and every Roman, *mutore*, and shifter in this place will take you down before you have a chance to pull your next breath."

The last word wasn't even out of Syn's mouth before Cruen's fangs thrust deep into his temple. As before, on the floor of Erion's dungeon, the blood drain was executed painfully, quickly, but this time Syn let go and gave in. As he opened his mind wide, to a world of past hurt and sadness and regret, emotions flooded his senses like a massive and unceasing ocean wave.

And then there was nothing. And everything. And Cruen was pulling out of his head, and he was back, standing in the gathering stones, scenting Petra, gripping Cruen, with his entire arsenal of baggage. All the hate and all the love.

And bloody hell, all the newfound strength.

Syn's fingers dug into the *paven*'s throat. "Release. Her. Now."

Cruen stood there for a moment, unmoving, no doubt thinking and plotting and planning. Could he use Petra another way? Could her death be of benefit? Or her life? And then suddenly, he opened his hand and freed her from his grasp.

"Go, Petra," Syn commanded gently. "Go to your family."

As Petra took off, holding her neck, stumbling forward, dizzy, into the arms of her mother, Cruen shouted at all of them, "You'll never contain me, and you know it. None of you are able to. Even with my power waning, I will always be the one to rule this Breed."

Her eyes frosty, yet the most controlled Syn had ever seen them, Feeyan moved forward. She began with an incantation, then slowly circled her arms around Cruen, wrapping him in some kind of invisible magical vise. She sighed, clucked her tongue. "I've always enjoyed our back and forth, Cruen. Our sharing of knowledge and power. Even our battles. But you have shamed not only yourself but the entire Eternal Breed. Your daughter"—her lip curled—"forcing her to live with these creatures. Not knowing her true worth. A Pureblood *veana*." She leaned in, snarled as he struggled against her magical bonds. "Consuming the flesh of . . ." Her nostrils flared. "You have just insulted every Pureblood on the planet. In truth, I have stumbled somewhat in my governing of our kind as of late. Perhaps I was under the impression that I could not measure up to your way. It made me reckless and far too interested in proving myself to others. But I see now that your way wasn't in service of the Eternal Breed. It was in service of you." She glanced up at Syn, who was still holding Cruen by the throat. "I will take him now. Deal with him in my own way."

"Not a chance," Syn said, shaking his head. "I escort him to Mondrar, walk him into the cell, make sure he's contained by the most powerful magic possible."

Feeyan titled her chin. "You do not have a choice in how the Order punishes—"

"After all that's just happened, I bloody well do."

And with that, Syn flashed himself and Cruen from the gathering stones, the Rain Forest, and the strange sadness in his beloved *veana*'s eyes.

Seconds after Synjon flashed from the Rain Forest, the Order followed suit. Well, all but Dillon. She was still holding her throat, standing close to Gray, who looked like he wanted to put his fist through a fucking wall. In seconds, the sand disappeared, and all was back to normal within the gathering stones.

From his perch on the highest rock, Phane watched the shifter leaders attempt to find calm, understanding. But it was crystal clear to all, now that the Order knew about the Rain Forest and its inhabitants, that things would be very different from now on. They were no longer hidden, no longer safe.

His gaze cut to Dani. The hawk shifter female was comforting Petra, her arms wrapped around the *veana* as she shook with great sobs of grief. Below Phane, her mother by blood looked on, watched her daughter, then turned to look at Wen, who was embracing Dillon.

"I can't thank you enough," Wen said to the jaguar female, who looked both shaken up and pissed off by what Feeyan had subjected her to.

The leader of the Mountain Faction approached Dillon as well. "We won't forget what you did for us. How you spoke up for us. Please know that you are all welcome here at any time. For those who have shifter blood, it would be our honor to introduce you to your kind." His eyes warmed. "We have jaguar in my faction. If you ever want to know them . . ."

The *veana* visibly winced as the male's voice trailed off. Like his half sister, Phane felt the strangeness of being in a place with others similar to himself. But truly, there was something here that called to him. To Helo as well. He shook his head. Foolish Lycos. The male was missing it all because he refused to get involved, refused to see this as an opportunity to know his history, know more about himself.

"My love?" Alex called out, his voice suddenly fearful.

A sound, low and filled with pain, brought everyone's attention around to the large boulder where Sara had been sitting, waiting to see what would happen, waiting to be flashed home by Alexander if a fight truly broke out between the shifters and the Order.

Kate and Bronwyn were at her side. "What's wrong?" the former asked, her tone deeply concerned.

"Sara?" Dillon rushed over to her as well, her own concerns completely forgotten.

Alexander's female looked up, her eyes bright, her smile nervous. "My water broke." She turned to Alexander, who was trying to get past the small crows and the worried *veana*s. "Our *balas*, Alex."

It was a miracle of sorts. The mood inside the gathering stones changed in an instant. From dark and dismal to hopeful and excited.

When Alex finally reached his mate's side, he scooped her up in his arms and barked at anyone who would listen, "Leza needs to be contacted immediately."

Sara laughed and leaned in to kiss her mate's neck. "It's not coming this very second, my love."

"We must also inform Evans," Alex continued, undaunted. "He must get the house ready. Get our room ready. Clean sheets, towels . . ."

"Oh, yeah, someone's about to become a father," Nicholas said with a wide grin.

Getting in on the ribbing, Lucian snorted as he jumped down from his rock. "And look at his face. He looks scared to death. You know Sara is the one who has to do all the work, right?"

Alex growled. "Shut it, Luca." Then he turned to his mate and kissed her gently. "Hold on, my love. I'm taking us home. All three of us."

25

Petra sat beside Sara on the bed and melted at the sight of the one-week-old little bundle wrapped in a soft yellow blanket, sleeping peacefully in his mother's arms. His lips kept pressing out into a cute little pout, as if he were dreaming about his first blood. "He's so beautiful."

"I think so too, but I may be partial." Sara looked up and smiled at her. "I'm so glad you came."

"Me too."

"I've been worried about you. I haven't heard from you in a few days, and after everything that went down at the gathering stones . . ."

Ah, yes. The gathering stones, Petra mused. And the apartment, and the River House, the tree house, and the caves. She'd been through much in the past few months. Revelations and disappointments. Hopes and fleeting happiness. But now it was time to take things slow and easy. Stop moving and build a life in one place for herself and her *balas*.

"I'm good," Petra insisted, reaching out to touch the

baby's soft head. She couldn't wait to experience this. Holding her sweet child in her arms. Such perfection. Such intimacy.

"Well," Sara said, her eyes warm. "You'll forgive me if I have to come by and see that for myself."

"You'd better come by. Have Alex flash you and baby over. It's so beautiful in the Rain Forest now. So green and wet. We'd love to have you stay."

Sara raised one dark eyebrow. "We? So, does that mean you and *balas*? Or is Brodan in the picture?"

A sigh escaped Petra's lungs without her consent. "Let's just say Brodan is going to be a kick-ass uncle."

Over the past week, the bear shifter had been around to see her at her parents' house several times. He'd been his usual incredible self. Kind, caring, generous. And the list could go on and on. But the one thing he wasn't was the one thing Petra wanted more than anything.

Synjon.

"I'm going to make a family for myself," she told Sara, but truly the words were also for herself. She had to keep telling herself that, reminding herself that she would get through this, and that everything would be fine.

"You told Brodan how you feel?" Sara asked gently.

Petra nodded. "I would never even try to care for a male when I am not yet remotely over the one who broke my heart."

Sara exhaled heavily and nodded. "Have you heard from him?"

Petra shook her head. After what had happened at the gathering stones, what he'd done, sacrificed—what she'd experienced at the hands of her father—she'd thought she might. Hell, she'd hoped he would try to contact her, come to the Rain Forest to see her. After all, they'd both made mistakes and bad judgments and choices that were unfortunate and filled with regrets. But clearly he was done. Maybe those emotions that Cruen had forced back into his mind had tamped down any feelings he'd had for her and the *balas*. After all, the loss of Juliet had been among them.

"You know he had the chance to kill Cruen and he didn't."

Lost in thought for a moment, Petra startled. "I know."

"He's looking into doing undercover spy stuff again. Maybe a private firm. Maybe his own."

"That's good."

"And I hear there are no more parties going on."

Petra couldn't help but laugh at that. "Mr. Respectability now, huh?"

Sara shrugged. "Well, let's not go overboard." She grinned. "He'll always be a bit of a scoundrel, not unlike my Alexander or the rest of the Romans, but what fun would it be if they weren't?" She leaned down and kissed her *balas*. The little boy stretched his arms over his head and yawned, causing both females to laugh softly.

"Can't believe I got the most perfect present for Christmas," Sara said.

"He is that," Petra agreed.

"My little Santa baby. And you're what . . . ? Valentine's Day Cupid?"

Petra laughed. "I like that."

Sara's smile widened. "So close in age—our kids will grow up together." Then she blushed and amended her words. "Or could. If you wanted that . . ."

"I do," Petra said quickly. "I want that."

Sara's smile broadened, and she reached for Petra's hand and squeezed it lightly.

Just then, Alex stuck his head in the door and called, "Hey, Petra. Dani's here."

"Ah. My ride."

She stood up just as Alex walked in and over to Sara. He touched his *balas* on the cheek, then leaned in to kiss his mate on the mouth. "How's the most beautiful mother in the world?"

"Happy," she whispered before he kissed her again.

Petra just stood there and watched, like an idiot, like a voyeur. Like a *veana* who had no deeper wish than to have what her sister and Alex had. But that couldn't be her goal now. Maybe someday. Someday when she was settled.

" 'Night, all," Petra said as she headed for the door.

"Come again soon, okay?" Sara called after her. "Samuel wants to hang out with his auntie."

"I promise."

As she headed down the stairs and into the foyer, Petra heard the lively sounds of laughter and banter. It was nice. Warm. Homey. The family all together. She'd hung out with them a bit earlier, talked, discussed the holidays. But now it was time to get back to her family. One of whom was waiting in the back garden.

Pacing the grounds in her hawk form, wings spread and ready, Dani cocked her head when she spotted Petra. "Ready to go home, bestie?"

"Always, bestie." She climbed onto the hawk's back and wrapped her arms around Dani's neck. After a quick, affectionate squeeze, the shifter took off and sailed into the night sky.

The cell he occupied was dark, dank, and cut off from everything and everyone.

Synjon Wise had insisted on it, the Romans and several of the Order members had also, and Feeyan had relented.

Cruen sneered.

That *veana*'s weakness was growing more and more apparent.

Standing before the bars of his cage, Cruen waited for his next blood meal to be delivered. It was nearly time. His fangs were descending even now in anticipation. Granted, the guards never came into his cage to give it to him. Strict instructions from the Order. But someday he would manage to get one of them alone. It was all he would need.

That and his unflinching desire to take back what should never have been given away. Given to *her*.

Feeyan spoke of shame on the Eternal Breed. She was the true shame. A poor man's Cruen. A dull, fearful substitute who acted only when she needed to convince others she was powerful. No. A true leader of the Order acted selfishly. Without second-guessing. Without fear or pity.

Cruen sniffed the air. Yes, his blood was on the way. Perhaps this was the guard, this was the night. Or perhaps he would have to wait until tomorrow.

It was no matter. Someday soon he would be flashing free once again. Someday soon—not only would he be back on the Order, but he would be ruling it.

Without Petra and the *balas* in his life, Syn knew misery times ten. No amount of work or money made up for the loss of them, and he couldn't wait another minute to beg for their return. But he knew he couldn't go straight to her, knew she would no doubt reject him outright.

So he had to go to the one being on earth she trusted above all others. Unfortunately, that being believed him to be the biggest knobhead prat in the world.

The shifters inside the cantina followed him as he walked toward the hawk female. She was sitting at a table by herself, having something that looked like a beer, frothy head and all. Her nose came up the second he was within scent range.

She shook her head, grinned wickedly. "You have some serious balls."

He pulled out a chair and sat down across from her. "I need your help."

"Iron balls," she amended.

"Bloody right," he agreed, feeling many sets of eyes at his back. "I love her."

She gave him the death stare. "You don't deserve her, bloodsucker."

"True."

His agreeing with her seemed to irritate her more. "I don't have time for this. I have a date with my drink here." Her head went down and she pretended to ignore him.

No problem, love. I've got all night. Shite, I've got forever, if that's what it takes.

"Have you ever loved someone, Dani?"

She didn't answer him. Instead, she took a gigantic swallow of her beer, or whatever it was.

"Have you ever loved someone so much that the thought of them being gone from your life forever fills you with so much pain you can't even breathe?"

Again, she didn't look at him, but her head tilted to one side like she was trying really hard not to go there with him. "I know what happened to that female of yours who was killed—"

"No. I don't mean Juliet."

This time the hawk shifter's head did come up, and her eyes connected with his. Around them, the sounds of laughter and chatter and glasses being filled seemed to mute.

"I loved her," Syn said, his gut going tight. "Juliet. I loved her very much. And I thought avenging her death would help me get rid of some of the guilt I felt. But I'm talking about Petra now. And the *balas*."

"Ah, shit," Dani muttered softly.

"I wanted to give up, give in to sadness and death over Juliet," he continued. "But I want to *live* for Petra and my *balas*. I want to be a better *paven*. I care for nothing else but them."

Dani's sharp eyes bored into his skull, assessing him, reading him. "Why should I believe anything you say?"

"You shouldn't." He pushed his chair back and stood up, held out his hand. "Come with me."

She sniffed, glared at his waiting hand. "Where?"

"My place."

Her lip curled. "No, thanks. I've been there before, remember?"

"Do you mean, do I remember what a gigantic bastard I was to you? An unfeeling, uncaring bastard who wished he could block out everything and focus on the unending torture of the male who he believed had ended his life?"

Her mouth twisted. "Yeah, that."

He grinned. "I apologize, Dani. I wasn't myself."

She may have grinned back. It was hard to tell with the hawk female. What she did do was stand up.

"You going to flash me?" she asked.

He gestured for her to come with him. "It won't hurt a bit, shifter."

She sighed and followed him to the door. "This had better be good."

"Not good," Syn said. "Just real and honest and true. For the first time in my life."

26

"I can't wait for my transition so I can flash," Petra said as she leaned over Dani's back as best she could.

"My ride taking too long for you, princess?"

"My stomach's growing bigger every day, bestie, and this position is uncomfortable as hell." Petra laughed over the sound of the wind. The moonless night blanketed them in cool darkness, and though Dani's feathers kept her warm, they did not cushion her backside all that well. "But you know, you just sounded like Lucian."

"That whole family of males is weird," Dani called back.

"I think they're great."

"They're arrogant. Especially that hawk-vampire-combo male."

Oh, yes, Petra mused, the crisp shot of air rushing over her face. She'd seen Dani checking out the *mutore* on more than a few occasions. "Phane."

"And that. What kind of name is Phane?"

"Why do you care?" Petra asked, spotting a broad set of lights in the distance.

"He's totally after me."

"That's 'cause you're a hot piece of tail."

"Feathered tail."

Petra laughed into the breeze as the lights grew closer. Dani had said there was a surprise for her and the baby at the end of this trip, and Petra couldn't help but feel excited. She hadn't had much fun or frivolity since she'd found Synjon near the caves all those months ago.

But as they drew closer, and the light patterns became familiar, Petra realized just what city they were headed to. Her mouth went bone-dry and she gripped the hawk's feathers. "What the hell are you doing, Dani?"

"Just hold on, baby girl," she called, racing ahead, her hawk looking around for aircraft as they entered the city's airspace.

"No," Petra yelled over the sudden onslaught of wind and sound as they dove between two buildings. "We'd better be headed for SoHo. Dani, goddamn it. You, of all people."

"Chill out, Pets," the bird called back.

It wasn't SoHo. Not even close. And when they landed easy and gentle, not on the sprawling balcony she'd expected but on the building's roof, Petra was ready to kill her best friend.

She jumped off the hawk's back immediately and stuck her finger in the bird's face. "Unbelievable. Have you lost your goddamn mind or what?"

"Okay, listen," Dani began.

"You hate him. You despise him. In fact, when I

came back and told you about the room of torture, you wanted to fly to his place, pick him up in your talons, and drop him in the East River."

"Too easy," she remarked, glancing toward the brightly lit building next door. "And I think he's a good swimmer."

"Dani!"

The hawk jerked her head back. "Okay, fine. He was an asshole. When his emotions were stripped, he was without a conscience. He was a dog. No. I like dogs. He was a slug who deserved to be crushed—"

"Oh, my gods, Dani!"

"But now," she said quickly, "I'm not so sure."

Petra's chest tightened, and she pulled her coat closer around herself. "Now?"

"Okay, don't be pissed."

Something close to anxiety started in Petra's toes and began to move upward. "Oh, crap. What did you do?"

"He came to me," Dani said, her hawk's eyes softening. "We talked."

Petra turned away in a huff. "I can't believe this."

"He's different."

Petra jerked back. "You didn't just say that."

"Not because of anything that was done to him, getting his emotions back and all that, but because he wants to be different." She was quiet for a moment, then cocked her head. "For you."

Sudden and irritatingly uncontrollable tears pricked Petra's eyes. She shook her head, the winter wind thrashing her hair about her face. "He conned you. With his dreamy eyes and his piano playing and his accent, and that body, and—"

"No, babe. I've never seen any of that. I'm a shifter girl all the way." Her hawk winked. "My male's gotta have hair or feathers or scales. You get the picture."

Petra sighed deeply. Yes. She got the picture. About it all. Synjon had gone to Dani and told her that he wanted Petra and the *balas*. He'd convinced the most impossible to convince creature on earth that he was all in.

Maybe . . .

Oh, goddamn it. "I'm scared," she whispered. "I'm just so fucking scared to believe . . ."

The hawk lowered her head, nuzzled Petra's face with her beak. "I know."

"So what do we do now? What do I do?"

"Get back on."

It was probably the most foolish move in the world, to believe, to hope. But it had come from Dani. The female who never believed in love. Inside Petra's womb, Little Fangs kicked and squirmed, and maybe nudged her forward and onto her friend's back.

In seconds they took off and then, a moment later, landed on the balcony below.

His balcony.

"Go in, Pets," Dani urged. "He's waiting for you."

With shaking limbs, and fear gripping her heart, Petra climbed off Dani's back. Behind her, she heard the glass doors open. She took a deep breath and turned around.

If it was possible, Synjon Wise had grown even more handsome in the week and a half since she'd seen him, and her fearful heart warmed without her consent. He was dressed all in black, his eyes impossibly dark, his mouth full and highly kissable, and his hair had that tousled look, like he'd just gotten out of bed. He was truly the male of her dreams.

He looked up at Dani then, and nodded. "Thank you."

"Sure thing, bloodsucker," she tossed back with a squawk. "Now don't fuck it up again."

It was just like Dani not to wait for an answer. She spread her wings and leaped off the balcony. Leaving the two of them alone. Leaving Petra to a fate she prayed didn't once again lead to tears.

As he led Petra into the house, Syn felt like a nervous young *paven*. He loved this *veana* so bloody much, wanted her so bloody much, he thought he'd lose his mind over it. He needed her to see that, understand his heart and his hope through his actions.

"I'm glad you came," he said.

"Didn't have much of a choice. Dani tricked me." She stopped for a moment and glanced over at the tree. It was fully decorated now, sporting small white lights, and beneath it were all the things he wanted her to have, all the things he'd found for the baby over the past week.

Her eyes cut to his piano, which stood to the left of the tree, then down to the child's piano he had not only tuned himself but polished as he did his own.

He heard her quick intake of breath, saw her shake her head, and reached for her hand. For a moment, he was sure she was going to pull away. But she didn't. Granted, she wasn't cuddling up to his side or anything, but she wasn't flinching at his touch either.

The realization made him breathe easier, made him hope.

"I want to show you something," he said, leading her through the living room, past the kitchen and down the hall.

"You've changed things," she said quietly, her gaze darting from left to right. "New artwork, different colors, furniture. Why?"

His chest tightened.

"You know why, love," he said leading her into his bedroom.

"I don't know if I want to go in here, Syn," she said tightly. "Don't know if I want to revisit the . . ." Her voice petered out as she entered the room. Her lips parted and she stared. "What did you do?"

He turned to look at her, watch her as she took in the complete remodel of his bedroom—what he wanted to be their bedroom. New furniture, softer fabric, colors he knew she loved. "The pillows you bought with Sara. I used them as inspiration." He eyed her. "You like it?"

Her head fell forward. "Oh, Syn, does it matter if I like it? Really?"

"More than you can possibly know, love." He squeezed her hand, then tugged it a little. "But that's not what I really want you to see. Come."

Petra felt as though the unbeating heart inside her chest was expanding, preparing to burst, as Syn led her into the en suite bathroom, and toward the room beyond. It was truly the last place on earth she wanted to go. She hated what she'd found here. How it had ruined everything. Ended what she'd thought was a true hope for love, a family. Why would—

Her thoughts ended abruptly.

Oh, gods.

Oh, gods.

Emotion caught in her throat. Fear and wonder and amazement. Tears blurred her vision, and she blinked to force them away, down her cheeks. She wanted to see clearly, take in what was before her with cool, detached eyes. But that was just an impossible hope.

It was too incredible.

Gone were the closet, the clothes, the leather and the wool. Gone was the room full of metal and hate and anger and vengeance. And in its place was a completely remodeled space. Pale yellow walls, fanciful artwork, bookcases and dressers, rugs and lamps, a rocker and a crib.

The most beautiful crib she'd ever seen.

Petra bit her lip to keep from crying, from blubbering like a fool . . . or maybe just an emotional pregnant chick. But nothing was going to stop the tears from raining down her cheeks.

A baby's room.

Syn had turned a room meant for such darkness into a room of light and softness and innocence.

He released her hand. She'd forgotten she was holding his, gripping it so tightly that she'd probably bruised him. She watched him walk over to the rocker and sit down.

"I'm so sorry, Petra. For everything. For lying to you, lying to myself. For hurting you." His eyes locked with hers and implored her to listen. Really listen. "I'm not asking you to live here. I know I don't deserve that. But I want you to understand that in my mind and in my heart, you and the *balas* have a home here."

Petra leaned against the doorframe and stared at him in that rocker. That sweet, happy rocker. And envisioned him holding Little Fangs in his arms. She couldn't believe it. Any of it. That he'd gone to these lengths. Was it truly possible that one so hell-bent on revenge could find a new and infinitely more beautiful way to live out his life?

She didn't know. Gods, she didn't know. But she wanted to find out. So badly that she ached with it.

"I may not be the male you believed could be your family, be the *balas*'s father," he said, his dark eyes pinning her where she stood. "But in my mind, my heart, I am."

In her mind and heart, he was too. He'd proved that on the night he'd saved her, sacrificed himself and his need to claim vengeance, for her and the *balas*, at the gathering stones. And he'd proved it with this incredible room.

"You fought for me, remember, love?"

She nodded, not even trying to hold back her tears anymore. And truly, what was the point? This was the male she loved, the father of her child. Her one wish had come true. Tears were more than appropriate. They were called for.

"When I was ready to give up," he said, his eyes full of warmth and hope, "you fought for me. Now I'm fighting for us, for you, for Little Fangs there. We're a family. I want us to be together always. I love you, Petra."

The words killed her. Not the part of her that had still believed in a future with this male, but the part that had wanted to give up, run away because she didn't want to be hurt again.

"Syn . . ."

"I'm not rushing you, not asking you to decide anything or change anything. I just wanted you to see where I'm at. What I'm offering. Long term. Forever. And to know if you could possibly forgive me."

Inside her womb, the *balas* moved, pressing against her skin. Maybe it just wanted to stretch its little limbs. Or maybe, like her, it wanted to be closer to that voice. And to the *paven* it loved.

"Cruen—," she began, hating herself for bringing that male's name into this room.

But Syn was quick to answer, and his tone was completely unfettered. "Love, I'm no longer concerned with chasing your father. I want to *be* a father."

That was it. She needed nothing more. Gods, nothing more than him.

Petra pushed away from the door, fairly leaped across the room and jumped into his lap. Instantly Syn's protective arms went around her and he groaned into her hair. Heat infused her. Love too. And then he started to rock. Back and forth. Back and forth.

"Be my mate, love?" he whispered.

She tipped her chin up and stared into those dark, deeply emotional eyes and grinned. "Yes."

"Wed me under the tree house in the Rain Forest?" He leaned in and kissed her mouth.

She sighed. "I'd love that."

"I love *you*." He placed one hand on her belly, waited a moment, then said confidently, "The *balas* is happy."

Oh, gods. "So's his mother."

Synjon's eyes got big, and he said almost breathlessly, "His?"

She shrugged, her grin widening. "Just a guess."

This time, when Synjon dropped his head and kissed her, Petra could feel the emotions within him. They were warm and intense, and they infused her skin like bathwater. There were fear and happiness, concern and craving, but the emotion that spread the furthest, went the deepest, and heated his blood as he growled and groaned against her mouth, was love.

Epilogue

Phane had done his best to make the place livable. Maybe he shouldn't have bothered. After all, he had the house in New York, a perch to kill for, and the whole extended-family thing. But there was just something about the Rain Forest, about the heat and the shifters—and damn, he wanted to pursue Dani.

Sweat pouring off his body, he continued to scrub the exterior of the cabin. After what had gone down at the gathering stones, he wasn't sure what to expect with Dani and the others. They'd offered to show him how the other half lived, so to speak, but was that real? Would they want him and Helo hanging around, reminding them of just how kind and giving the vampires were not?

He was just turning around to grab a bucket of clean water, when he spotted someone—some *thing*—stalking toward him in the brush.

"I don't believe this." He knew that blond-gray coat and don't-fuck-with-me glare. "What the hell are you doing here?"

The wolf shifted the moment he reached the porch of the cabin. Lycos glanced around, first at the cabin, then back at Phane. He looked uncomfortable as shit. "Come to get you. The Romans said you were taking your sweet time getting back."

Yeah, and they know why too, Phane thought. He wondered if Alex, Nicky, and Lucian had mentioned it. "Sorry you made the trip, brother. But I'm staying." He sniffed. "If they let me."

"Here in sweat city?" Ly sneered.

"I'll always take sweat over snow." He wiped the beads on his face with his forearm. "Besides, I want to get to know my other half."

"The Avians."

Phane nodded, tried out some new material. "They have wolves here, you know? In the Mountain Faction."

Ignoring him, Ly looked past him into the house. "Where's Helo? I bet he hasn't lost his fucking mind today."

"I don't know. I haven't seen him since this morning."

"Is he talking this talk?"

"If you mean does he plan on staying, then yes."

Phane tilted his head, looked at the wolf shifter from a different angle. Something told him that Lycos was more than just irritated at the prospect of his remaining two brothers living full-time or part-time away from what he now called home. But Phane was out of sympathy. He loved Ly, and the male was absolutely family, but he'd dropped the ball on this one. He'd walked away from them too, when they'd all needed him—and that didn't come without consequences.

Phane leaned on the porch rail. It threatened to give way. Another goddamn Mr. Fix-it project coming up. "Are you going to tell me just where the hell you've been? What was so important when we could've used your help? Another set of fists?"

The wolf shifter looked past him, but his face was a mask of impassivity. "Like I told you, I just don't want any part of this."

Stubborn bastard. "We needed family and you took off."

"You don't know what family is anymore. You think it's here? You think you fit in with these assholes? It's just like New York or anywhere else, brother. You, me, Helo, we're all mutts."

"Fuck you!"

"No—fuck you!"

Phane heard something crash inside the cabin. Then a female voice shriek, "Hey! Bloodsucking hawk shifter male, where the hell are you?"

What the hell? He turned back to see Dani at his screen door. "Did you just come from inside the house?"

"I flew in from the other direction. Your window was open."

"Didn't sound like it," he said, eyeing her. She looked hot as hell. Nothing new. "What's going on?"

"Your brother. The water beast."

His chest went tight at her expression. "What? What's going on with Helo?"

"Those fucking rogue water shifters. They're losing their minds. I swear to gods, the faction leaders need to—"

He yanked open the screen door. "Dani."

"Right." She stepped out. "He's been taken by the water shifters. That group that helped the geriatric vampire asswipe, gave him the eel flesh. We need to go. Now. The Water Faction leader is calling a . . ." Her voice trailed off as she noticed who stood near the far edge of the cabin.

Phane nodded at his *mutore* brother. "This is my—"

"Lycos?" she said. "What are you doing here?"

Phane turned to face his brother. "You know each other?"

Lycos just shrugged, didn't even glance at Dani.

Phane looked over his shoulder at the hawk shifter. "How do you know my brother?"

"Brother?" Dani looked from male to male, then broke out in laughter. "Well, well, well. This is interesting, and maybe even a little awkward. Lycos is one of the males I'm seeing." Her brows rose. "He didn't tell you?"

A low, feral sound erupted from Phane, and he leaped from the porch, shifting into his hawk just as Lycos grew fur and howled.

ACKNOWLEDGMENTS

Once again and always, I want to thank my incredible editor, Danielle Perez. The sixth is just as sweet as the first, D.

And my amazing and supportive agent, Maria Carvainis. Thank you so very much for having my back.

My wonderful reader friends on Facebook. You make this job rewarding, fun, and oh so fulfilling!

And to my Girl Writer Collective: Jennifer Lyon, Katie Reus and Alexandra Ivy. 1 Hour 1 K? Anyone? Anyone?

Please turn the page for a preview
of the first novel in
the Cavanaugh Brothers series
by Laura Wright,

BRANDED

Available from Signet Eclipse
in June 2014.

JOURNAL OF
CASSANDRA CAVANAUGH

May 12, 1997

Normally we bribed the cowboys five dollars to look the other way when we saddled up one of Daddy's prize cow horses and rode off. But they'd raised their prices lately, and today it took both our monthlies to pay them off. Damn cowboys. Didn't even care if it was my birthday.

"You still coming to the movies with me on Saturday?" Mac called over her shoulder. "It's a PG-13, but I think I know someone who can get us in."

I wrapped my arms even tighter around her waist as she kicked Mrs. Lincoln into a full-on gallop. "Daddy will never let me go and you know it."

"It's just a movie, Cass," she returned as we cut through the tree-dotted pasture land and headed down for the Hidey Hole, the swimming circle we'd found and claimed when we were seven years old.

"Not to him," I said. Mac doesn't understand my family. Never has. It's just her and her Dad at home, and Travis Byrd lets his daughter run wild and free. Sometimes it made me so jealous I could spit. Sometimes I felt bad she didn't have a Mama. "To him it's me sneaking off to meet boys."

"But that's not true."

"Doesn't matter. I'm his baby girl."

"You're ten years old, Cass. That's not a baby."

A breeze kicked up, making the tall grass shiver around Mrs. Lincoln's feet.

"Everett Cavanaugh is living in the dark ages," Mac continued. "What about your mom? Maybe you can ask her."

"She'll do whatever Daddy says."

Mac snorted as she steered the mare down the small incline toward the swimming hole. "I'll never be that kind of wife."

The idea of Mac being anyone's wife was so crazy, I started laughing.

"What's so funny?" Mac asked indignantly. "Whoa, Mrs. Lincoln." She stopped at the water's edge, kicked one leg over the gray mare's neck, and jumped down into the wet grass.

I followed her. I always followed her. "You getting married. That's crazy."

"I didn't mean tomorrow, Cass Cavanaugh." She wrapped the horse's reins around the base of a young pecan tree, then sat down, kicked off her boots, and plunked her bare feet in the water. "But, you know, someday I plan on getting hitched."

I sat down beside her, but kept my boots on. "To who?"

She turned to face me, tossed her blond ponytail over her shoulder and gave me one of those huge smiles that meant she had a secret she was aching to share. "A very lucky guy."

"Barry Miller?" I asked.

Dark blue eyes filled with heat. "That dope?"

"He's cute," I pointed out.

"He doesn't even know the difference between a stallion and a gelding."

Behind us, a familiar male voice boomed down from the ridge. "And neither should you, Mackenzie Byrd."

Both Mac and I jumped, then jerked around. A few feet up, sitting tall on his horse, Friction, his black Stetson dropped low over his forehead—green eyes as fierce as a wildcat's—was my fourteen-year-old brother, Deacon. It was crazy, but in just over a year that boy had gone from being a beanpole with hair to a big, bossy, thought-he-knew-everything man.

"You two should be home," he said. "Weather's getting testy."

"We like testy weather," Mac piped up beside me, then tossed me a grin. Nothing Mac liked better than to make my brothers bristle.

Deacon's mouth thinned and he turned Friction in a circle. "Your party's been moved indoors, Cass, and while I'm sure Mackenzie here'll be just fine in ripped jeans and dusty boots, Mom's expecting you to clean up."

"I'm fine, too," I said, raising my chin like I'd seen Mac do a hundred times.

"No. You smell like manure."

"How would you know? You can't smell me from there."

His eyes narrowed. "Because you and Mac always smell like manure."

"They say shit's good for the soul," Mac called out, kicking up one foot and splashing me with cold water. "And for the skin."

He eyed Mac sternly. "That's enough out of you, Mackenzie Byrd."

Mac just chuckled and continued to splash. "It'll never be enough, Deacon Cavanaugh."

Once again, he circled his horse at the top of the ridge. "I don't like you hanging around my little sister. Cussing and stealing horses. You're a bad influence."

"And you're a mama's boy, riding all the way out here to fetch us," she called back.

His face went red and he slid his aggravated gaze back to me. "I want you back at the house in twenty minutes, Cass."

"Takes that long to ride," I whined.

"Exactly."

He turned, then gave Friction a hearty "Yup," and took off at a gallop. Grumbling, I scrambled to my feet and made my way over to Mrs. Lincoln.

"Being the only girl sucks," I mumbled, slipping the bridle from the tree.

Mac came up beside me, boots on over her wet feet, and gave me a leg up onto the mare's back. "Good thing you have me," she said, leaping up to sit in front of me.

I laughed, "You know it," and wrapped my arms around her waist. "Deacon's so damn bossy."

Mac shrugged as we climbed the gentle incline. "He's the oldest. Comes with the territory, I guess."

"I know. I just wish he'd ease up a little. Maybe I should find him a girlfriend."

Deacon had been right about the weather changing. Gray clouds sailed across the sky and the wind was kicking up good.

"Does he go out with anyone?" Mac asked as she gave the mare a gentle kick, setting her into a slow canter.

"Shoot if I know. He doesn't tell me nothing. But we sure get a lot of calls after six o'clock at night."

"Well, they can have him for now, I suppose," Mac said, leaning into the wind. "But come my eighteenth birthday, that boy's mine."

"What?" The word fairly croaked out of my mouth. I was sure I hadn't heard her right. "What are you talking about, Mac?"

"The guy I plan to marry someday?" Mac said with a grin in her voice. "It's bossy, overbearing, know-it-all Deacon Cavanaugh."

Shock barreled through me as I turned her words, her declaration, over in mind. But by the time my tongue felt brave enough to work, the gunmetal clouds overhead opened up and cried something vicious, and Mac urged Mrs. Lincoln into a run.

1

2014

The glass doors slid open and Deacon Cavanaugh walked out onto the roof of his thirty-story office building. Sunlight blazed down, mingling with the saunalike air to form a potent cocktail of sweat and irritation. The heat of a Texas summer seemed to hit the moment the sky faded from black to gray, and by seven a.m., it was a living thing. A perfect irony for the day ahead.

"I've rescheduled your meetings for the rest of the week, sir."

Falling into step beside him, his executive assistant, Sheridan O'Neil, handed off his briefcase, iPad, and business smartphone to the helicopter pilot.

"Good," Deacon told her, heading for the blue chopper, the platinum *Cavanaugh Enterprises* painted on the side winking in the shocking light of the sun. "And Magnus Breyer?"

"I have no confirmation at this time," she said.

Which was code for *there was a potential problem*, Deacon mused. His assistant was nothing if not meticulously thorough.

Deacon stopped and turned to regard her. Petite, dressed impeccably, sleek black hair pulled back in a perfect bun to reveal a stunningly pretty face, Sheridan O'Neil made many of the males in his office forget their names when she walked by. But it was her brains, her guts, her instincts, and her refusal to take any shit that made Deacon respect her. In fact, it had made him hire her right out of graduate school. When he'd interviewed her, the ink on her diploma had barely dried. But despite her inexperience, her unabashed confidence in proclaiming that she wanted to be him in ten years hit his gut with a *Hell, yes, this is the one he should hire*. Forget ten years. Deacon was betting she'd achieve her goal in seven.

"What's the problem, Sheridan?" he asked her.

She released a breath. "I attempted to move Mr. Breyer to next week, but he refused. As you requested, I told no one where you're going or why." Her steely gray gaze grew thoughtful. "Sir, if you would just let me explain to the clients—"

"No."

"Sir."

Deacon's voice turned to ice. "I'll be back on Friday by five, Sheridan."

She nodded. "Of course, sir."

She followed him toward the waiting chopper. "Should I ask Miss Monroe if she's free to accompany you on Friday?"

Only the mildest strain of interest moved through

him at the mention of Pamela Monroe. Dallas's hottest fashion designer had been his go-to for functions lately. She was beautiful, cultured, and uncomplicated. But lately, he'd been starting to question her loyalty as certain members of the press had begun showing up whenever they went out.

"Not yet," he said.

"Mr. Breyer is bringing his . . . date—" Sheridan stumbled. "And he's more comfortable when you bring one as well."

A slash of a grin hit Deacon's mouth. "What did you wish to call the woman, Sheridan?"

"His daughter, sir."

Deacon chuckled. His assistant could always be counted on for the truth. "I'll let you know in the next few days if I require Pamela."

He stepped into the chopper and nodded at the company's pilot. "I'm taking her, Rush. Bell's been instructed to deliver another if you need it."

The pilot gave him a quick salute. "Very good, sir."

"Mr. Cavanaugh?"

Deacon turned and lifted an eyebrow at his assistant, who was now just outside the chopper's door. "What is it, Sheridan?"

Her normally severe gaze softened imperceptibly. "I'm sorry about your father."

"Thank you."

After a quick nod, she turned and headed for the glass doors, and Deacon put his headset on, then stabbed at the starter. He hadn't stepped foot in River Black in fifteen years, but he'd planned for his return every day since. While he built an empire, bought companies and ripped them apart only to rebuild and sell, he contemplated the steps he would need to see his ultimate goal realized.

Now the time had come to put that plan into action.

As the blades turned and the engine hummed beneath him, Deacon pulled up on the collective. Once he was at a proper height, he gripped the stick and sent the chopper forward, leaving the glass-and-metal world of the Cavanaugh Towers for the dangerous, rural beauty of the home he planned to destroy.

Mac thundered across the earth on Gypsy, the black Overo gelding who didn't much enjoy working cows, but lived for speed. Especially when there was a mare on his heels.

"Is the tractor already there?" Mac called over her shoulder to Blue.

Her second in command, and the one cowboy on the ranch who seemed to share her brain in how things should be run, brought his Red Roan, Barbarella, up beside her.

"Should be," he said, his dusty white Stetson casting a shadow over half his Hollywood-handsome face.

"Any idea how long she's been stuck?" Mac asked as the hot wind lashed over her skin.

"Overnight, most like."

"How deep?"

"With the amount of rain we got last night, I can't imagine it's more than a couple feet."

In all the years she'd been doing this ride and rescue, she'd prayed the cow would still be breathing by the time she got there. But never had she prayed for a speedy excavation.

"Of all the days for this to happen," she called over the wind.

Blue turned and flashed her a broad grin, his striking eyes matching the perfect summer blue sky. "Ranch life don't stop for a funeral, Mac. Not even for Everett's."

The mention of Everett Cavanaugh, her mentor, and her best friend's father, made Mac's gut twist. He was gone. The ranch was without a patriarch now, its future in the hands of lawyers. God only knew what that would mean, for her, for Blue. For everyone in River Black who counted on the Triple C for their livelihood.

"Giddyup, Gyps!" she called, giving her horse a kick as she spotted the watering hole in the distance.

She had two hours to get the cow freed before showing up spit polished at the church. And she refused to be late.

With Blue just a hair behind her, Mac raced toward the hole and the groaning cow, reining in her horse right next to the promised tractor. Tipping her hat back, she eyed the freshly dug trench lined with a wood ramp. Frank had done a damn fine job, she thought. Maybe the cowboy was thinking the same way she was. They needed this done right quick.

She nodded her approval to the muddy eighteen-year-old cowboy as Blue's horse snorted and jerked her head from the abrupt change of pace. "Leaving us the best part, eh, Frank?" she said, slipping from the saddle with a grin.

The cowboy lifted his head and grinned. "I know you appreciate working the hind end, foreman."

"Better than actually being the hind end, Frank," Mac shot back before slipping on her gloves and walking into the thick black muck.

"She got you there, cowboy." Blue chuckled as he grabbed the strap from the cab of the tractor and tossed it to Mac.

"Get up on the Kioti, Frank," Mac called to the cowboy. "This poor girl's looking panicky, and we got a funeral to go to. I'd at least like to shower before I head to the church."

As Frank climbed up onto the tractor, Blue and Mac worked with the cargo strap, sliding it down the cow's back to her rump. While Mac held it in place, whispering encouragement to the cow, Blue attached both sides of the strap to the tractor.

"All right," Mac called. "Go slow and gentle, Frank. She's not all that deep, but even so, the suction's going to put a lot of pressure on her legs."

As Blue moved around the cow's rear, Mac joined him, and as Frank started the tractor forward, the two of them pushed. A deep wail sounded from the cow, followed by a sucking sound as she tried to pull her feet out of the muck.

"Come on, girl," Mac uttered, using her shoulder to push the cow's hind end, leaning in, digging her boots in further.

Blue grunted beside her. "Give it a little more gas, Frank!" he called out. "On three, Mac, okay? One. Two. Push fucking hard."

With every ounce of strength, Mac pushed. It seemed like minutes, hours, but it was only seconds before the sucking sounds of hooves pulling from mud rent the air, and the cow found her purchase. Groaning, she clambered onto the wood boards. Maybe she was too fast and Mac wasn't expecting it. Maybe Mac's boots were just too deeply embedded in the mud. Whatever the reason, when the cow lurched forward, so did Mac. Knees and palms hitting the wet black earth in a resounding splat.

"She's out!" Frank called.

"No shit," Mac said, laughing, grabbing Blue's extended and muddy hand, and pulling herself up.

"Good thing you have time for that shower." Blue barely got that out before breaking into laughter.

She lifted a brow at his clothes caked in mud, sticking to his tall, lean-muscled frame. "Not you. You're all set. Why don't you head over to the church right now?"

"I can't go like this, Mac," he said, starting out of the mud hole, wiping his hands on his jeans.

Mac followed him. "What do you mean? You look perfect to me."

Blue took off his Stetson, revealing his short black hair. "I need a different hat. This one's dirty."

Mac broke out into another bout of laughter.

Overhead, the sound of a helicopter stole both their laughter and their attention.

Frank looked up from tending to the exhausted cow, and shaded his eyes. "What the hell's that?"

Mac lifted her face to the gleaming helicopter, with a last name she recognized painted on the side in expensive platinum lettering. Damn, doesn't it figure? Covered in cow shit, smelling like a sewer, and he picks now to make his grand entrance.

Turning away, she refused to care.

"That'd be trouble," Blue said in a quiet, stern voice.

"You don't say," Frank answered.

"Deacon Cavanaugh's come home to bury his daddy," Mac reminded them.

"And maybe bury us right along with it." Blue's tone carried a heavy warning.

Mac refused to go there. Unlike Blue, she knew the history with Deacon, his father, and the Triple C. Shoot, she knew that all the Cavanaugh brothers had endured their share of misery before they'd left home for good. Come to that, so had she.

With every rotation of the chopper blades, memories assaulted her: The day Cass had been taken, the night law enforcement had told them all they believed she was murdered, and the morning they all sat in the very same church Everett Cavanaugh would be eulogized in today, their lives changed for good.

But while the boys had wanted out, Mac hadn't been able to leave, couldn't abandon the ghost of her friend. And no matter what Deacon Cavanaugh was coming armed with, no matter how many millions he tossed their way, she wasn't leaving the Cavanaugh Cattle Company.

Snapping out of her troubling thoughts, she got back to work. "Let's get this cow home," she called to the cowboys. "Let's do the jobs we're being paid to do, then go pay our last respects to our boss and friend, Everett Cavanaugh."

Also available from
USA Today bestselling author

LAURA WRIGHT

Eternal Beast
Mark of the Vampire

Gray Donohue will stop at nothing to bring his fellow
Impure vampires the freedom they deserve. Now, if he could
just release his primal need for the beautiful woman who
saved his life—and who rules his thoughts and desires…

Dillon is in mortal danger. She can no longer control the
jaguar within her. Gray is the only man who can make
her surrender to a passion strong enough to overpower her
inner beast. But she doesn't want to surrender—she wants
her life back.

Because she is determined never to belong to anyone,
especially not Gray, the male who destiny claims is
her mate…

"Absorbing and edgy, darkly seductive…
***Eternal Beast* is an enthralling read."**
—*New York Times* bestselling author Lara Adrian

Available wherever books are sold or at
penguin.com

facebook.com/ProjectParanormalBooks

Also available from
USA Today bestselling author

LAURA WRIGHT

Eternal Demon
Mark of the Vampire

When Erion's son is kidnapped by the evil vampire
Cruen, Erion vows to stop at nothing to find his
hideaway—including intercepting the traveling part of
Cruen's beautiful bride-to-be. But instead of a vulnerable
caravan, Erion is met by a feral band of female demons
including Hellen, the bride—a creature of dark magic
and darker passion.

Though the safety of his son is his foremost concern,
Erion can't deny his unexpected attraction to Hellen.
As their bond intensifies, they move toward an inevitable
and terrifying battle. With time running out, Erion
realizes he must not only find and rescue his son but
protect Hellen from Cruen and the underworld forces
waiting to destroy her for her betrayal.

"Dark, delicious and sinfully good."
—*New York Times* bestselling author Nalini Singh

Available wherever books are sold or at
penguin.com

facebook.com/ProjectParanormalBooks